the End is the Beginning

JENNIFER N. LLOYD

Copyright © 2024 by Jennifer N. Lloyd

All rights reserved.

No part of this book may be reproduced in any form or by any electronic or mechanical means, including information storage and retrieval systems, without written permission from the author, except for the use of brief quotations in a book review.

This book is a work of fiction. Names, characters, places, and incidents are the product of the author's imagination or are used fictitiously. Any resemblance to actual events, locales, or persons, living or dead, is coincidental.

This book may not be re-sold or given away to other people. If you would like to share this book with another person, please purchase an additional copy for each person you wish to share it with. If you are reading this book and did not purchase it, or it was not purchased for your use only, then you should return it to the seller and purchase your own copy. Thank you for respecting the author's work.

Cover Art: Kate Farlow
Edited by Virginia Tesi Carey
Interior Formatted by N. E. Henderson

I dedicate this novel to two very special people.

To my beloved daughter, Norah,
At the time of writing this, you are at the tender age of just 3, and you have taught me more about myself than I could have ever imagined. This book is my testament to show you that regardless of age, pursuing dreams is always within your reach. In life, we can wear multiple 'hats' and find happiness and success in each role. If you feel called to pursue a new path, embrace it fearlessly and seize today, my dear, for you're destined for greatness. I hope you always know that my admiration for you is boundless. Your beauty, inside and out, illuminates every step you take and any room you enter. I promise to champion each dream you chase, no matter the twists and turns life may bring. And as you keep telling me lately, "I don't just love you, I love you MORE."

And to my cherished late grandmother, Colleen,
Your unwavering presence and support in my childhood shaped who I am today. The dedication you showed me is a devotion I aspire to mirror for Norah. Your commitment to listening to my stories and guiding me through schoolwork remains etched in my heart. I can remember spending hours

*on the sofa in your living room writing papers. After I wrote a
paragraph, I'd read it back to you, and we would revise it,
adding adjectives and different verbiage until we thought it
'grew' the sentence and painted the picture that I was trying to
convey. That is where my love of creative writing came from—
a memory I hold very near and dear to my heart. So here I am,
grandma. This book is my tribute to you, showing that your
investment in me went beyond mere high scores on my papers;
it laid the foundation for something far more meaningful.
Until we reunite in heaven, I carry your love and precious
memories with me, striving to make you proud every day.*

*With all of the love and gratitude,
Jennifer*

Trigger Warning

Please be aware that this book includes graphic descriptions of violence, explicit sexual content, and discussions of abuse and cheating, which may be distressing for some readers. Additionally, it addresses sensitive topics related to mental health, such as depression and anxiety, and delves into themes of trauma. The narrative also contains graphic content that could be unsettling. Reader discretion is strongly recommended, and consider your own comfort and triggers before reading.

CHAPTER 1
Sandy

June 1975 Age: 35

The screen door creaked open as he stumbled heavy-footed back home. I could hear him groan through slurred words as the door slammed shut behind him.

"San, what have ya fixed up for yo' old man tonight? It had better be something I like, or else I'll be coming after you until you make me something I approve of."

Anxiety courses through me as I begin to rise, springing up from the living room sofa, jolted out of a dead sleep. I had fallen asleep so quickly that evening since Johnny wasn't home when I laid down to watch one of *my* favorite shows for a change, *Mary Kay and Johnny*.

I found solace in it, using it as my mental escape from the traumatic stress I faced daily.

It allowed me to imagine that I was Mary Kay, married to Johnny, and that our life was blissfully happy. It felt good to imagine myself being her despite the irony of *my* Johnny's name being the same as the character, Johnny.

Unfortunately, though, that is where their similarities began and ended. *My* Johnny is nothing like the Johnny on the show. The TV character Johnny is always happy and doing anything to continue wooing his wife. He seems like the ideal husband, always protecting and showing his affection.

The life Mary Kay and Johnny have is the kind of life we all want, I suppose.

A life without any concern over putting food on the table, providing a roof over children's heads, and helping them to survive. Not just surviving by having their physical and mental needs met like food, water, and rest, but actually surviving the continual, unceasing physical and verbal abuse from their father, Johnny.

I know I can't prevent my children from hearing the shouting and screaming when our fights break out, most often due to his alcohol addiction, but I do want to protect them from ever experiencing the physical abuse he subjects me to. I never want them to be on the receiving end of his unruly hands.

I arose quickly from the sofa and scurried to the kitchen to begin fixing Johnny a dinner to help sober him up.

Hopefully, he likes this meal so that I won't suffer another black eye or have the wind knocked out of me like I did two nights ago. I don't want my kids to wake up again tonight and witness it. I know if he hollers too loud, the neighbors will call the police... again.

Having the police come is never an enjoyable experience, but what I hate most is when my kids see the wrath he has unleashed onto me through their young and inno- cent eyes. All the while, the cherry and berry police car lights flicker through the house as we're being questioned over another domestic abuse case, and I worry the authorities will take my children away from me.

Not to mention, it terrifies me to the core to contem- plate what Johnny could turn to David and Lisa and do if he's willing to bring me to death's doorstep every time he loses his temper.

Will he finally succeed one of these times? What will happen to my children? Will they become the unat- tended-to children of our small, less than 300-person town in Lemard? Will they end up in foster care because of the nosy Connors next door?

Even though the Connors seem to always be in our business and I often find it rather unnerving, whenever the police have been called in the past, I almost always have known it was Alice who had called. I also knew Alice Connor kept her eyes out for my children, which I have appreciated even though it makes me extra fearful of them being taken from me.

I can't even fathom the thought of them being raised by anyone besides myself.

Maybe that is where my strength comes from to pull myself back up every time Johnny's backhand slaps across my cheek, and I watch it seemingly in slow motion as blood droplets splatter across the room. Or when his fist makes contact with my stomach and inevitably, I land on the floor crouched over as if I'm crawling, just trying to catch a breath and inch away from him while praying he doesn't stumble after me and strike again.

My usual routine most nights is to get the kids from the bus after school, help them with their homework, make dinner for the night, eat dinner with the two kids, clean it all up, and set aside a plate for Johnny in the refrigerator for me to reheat when he shuffles in from the local bar or from one of his drinking buddy's houses, usually Jimmy's, who lives three houses up the street.

I reach into the refrigerator to pull out the plate that I prepared for him nearly six hours ago when the kids and I ate dinner.

It is 11:55 pm, I note on the microwave clock as I open the door to place his plate inside. I set the cook time to 1 minute 30 seconds, but my shaky finger slips from the 1, and instead punch 4 minutes 30 seconds, but I don't notice it.

I am so groggy from just waking up that my hands begin to sweat. This physical reaction I'm experiencing, I recognize only happens when I'm in the presence of him, coupled with his drunkenness.

I hate that I seem to be so out of control physiologically, and what this means is happening inside of me due to him. I hate that he holds this control over me despite my inability to control it.

I feel that I've gotten pretty good at estimating microwave reheat times for the different meals I prepare so that the food doesn't come out too hot or too cold.

As I hear the beep of the microwave timer, I take the plate of reheated meatloaf and mashed potatoes to Johnny, and I set the plate in front of him with his glass of milk to the left of his plate and the silverware to the right set on top of a napkin, just as they do at the restaurants. "The plate is quite warm, it might be best to wait a few minutes before you eat it so that you don't burn your mouth."

After setting the plate down, I walk to the sink to finish up the dishes from dinner with the kids earlier that I didn't get to.

Reaching into the sink to begin washing, I hear through his drunken stupor, "Listen here, you bitch, I'll eat the damned old meatloaf when I damn-well please. No stupid-ass housewife is gonna tell me how or when I can eat my dinner."

As I turn my head to look at him in disgust, I am abruptly and forcefully met with the plate of meatloaf directly in my face. It falls, landing on my feet first, then onto the floor and shattering, cutting open the skin on the tops of my feet. The warm blood seeps from my feet onto the floor beneath me.

I guess I screwed up that reheat time. How could I have done that? I must have hit the 4 instead of 1. I'm such an idiot.

As I start to remove the remaining pieces of food off of my face, I realize it's been a few seconds or maybe it's minutes at this point, it's hard to grasp how much time has elapsed from the plate hitting my face with such force. I start to see stars, and the skin on my face and chest feels as if it has been lit up by a torch. My head is pounding, my feet are burning as the shards of glass continue to slice deeper into the tops of my feet.

David and Lisa awaken from all of the noise in the kitchen.

The house is just over 1,000 square feet, and the kids' bedrooms are directly off of the living room. Their bedrooms are the first rooms on opposing sides of the hall.

David is 16 and Lisa is 14. They come rushing into the kitchen, wide-eyed and full of panic, knowing full-well what waking up to loud noises in the night in our household means.

Lisa, always being so empathetic and wanting to help, runs over to me. Seeing the pain I am in from the multitude of angles I have been struck, but knowing that when Johnny is angry, it is best to keep quiet, keep your head down, clean up the mess, and avoid eye contact. She immediately assesses the situation and reads the dynamic very quickly, so she begins cleaning up the floor almost too quickly for a young girl. This worries me. I do not want my daughter to grow up in such an abusive and unhealthy home.

Johnny mutters under his breath, "Had you made the meal right the first time, it wouldn't have been sent back to you for a repeat, you dumb whore."

David, who has two more years of life experience than Lisa, is beginning to show more disconnect from our family, especially when these kinds of stunts play out. It is as if he is planning his escape or, worse, planning his revenge. I can't quite make out his stance, and that, in and of itself, alarms me.

How could a young 16-year-old boy, my first baby, who used to be so concerned and quick to come to my rescue, be 'checking out' at a time when he should be 'checking in'? Is he using a coping mechanism that I am unaware even exists? Maybe I need to spend more time with him to learn this skill set from him. Learning how to cope with an abusive husband from a 16-year-old, how pathetic.

Perhaps David sees me as the culprit of our fights instead of the victim? I am not sure of that, but one thing I am sure of, I hate this life, and every day, I try to come up with a way out of it. I deserve a better life, and more importantly, I know for certain my children do too.

A life without the fear of abuse and the anxiety of having to construct creative stories and then recreate those stories of how I get the bruises or why I am a last minute no-show when, on a rare occasion, I'm actually invited to something because he hit me just before I am to leave the house and now my eye is swollen shut so I can't see out of it.

I know deep down that I deserve to have real love with someone. But more importantly, Lisa needs a more stable home life too. I can see that this life is having an effect on both of my children, but Lisa seems to be taking it the hardest, and she cries often. Seeing the reaction that these fight-fests are eliciting in Lisa and apparently having the opposite effect on David too, worries me.

This is my motivation... Tomorrow will be the day. The day I make my plot out of this mess of a life—just me... me and my two kids.

CHAPTER 2
Sandy

June 1975 Age: 35

That night, after the kitchen was cleaned up and Johnny staggered his way to the bedroom, I snuck my way into the bed on my side taking extra caution to not move or ruffle the bed and wake him. I know that when he has drunk this much and hasn't eaten enough to sober him up, he will want *something* from me. That *something* isn't *something* that I want to give to him tonight.

I am exhausted. My face is beginning to stretch and 'bubble up' to form blisters from the meatloaf. My feet have a sensation like they have their own pulse which is beating to the same rhythm of the thump I can hear in my head. It is like I am the one having had too much to drink with how I feel, the room is even beginning to spin.

I hear the bed sheets being pulled over his way, so I

THE END IS THE BEGINNING   9

lay as still as I can amidst all of my injuries in hopes that he won't reach over and pull me on top of him.

I try holding my breath, but the pulsation of my head is too much. After what feels like 30 seconds, I let out a small breath.

"Shit," I whisper.

It came out much louder than I had anticipated.

Even though Johnny has drank as much as he did, it never seems to have affected his ability to hear, which I despise. He moves his arm slowly, searching the blank, cold space of the bed for me. I try to squeeze myself all the way to the edge of my side of the mattress in hopes that I can avoid him noticing me here.

Again, I hold my breath, not wanting to make even an ounce of a movement or sound. He moves his arm again, this time reaching over with his torso.

"San, ya in here? You know what I like, it's the least you could do for me since you burned my mouth with ya hot-as-hell meatloaf."

Johnny rolls over so that he is in the middle of our queen-sized bed. His hands are just inches from my back.

I beg and plead a prayer in my head: *Please God, I can't do this with this man tonight. I just simply can't. I'm in too much pain, I can't bear it. But I also can't stand him beating me if I refuse him. Please help me. I know I am no match for him, and I can never turn him down.*

I tried that just under 16 years ago because I thought I was in the middle of my cycle, and I remembered hearing that if I didn't want the risk of pregnancy, to avoid sex in the middle of the cycle. I heard this from the wives of the husbands that Johnny would party with on one of the very rare occasions I could attend a party with him because Johnny's mother could keep an eye on David for us to go together instead of just him going alone, which was the usual.

I had told him that night that I was tired and also had an upset stomach. I explained that I thought it was a stomach bug coming on and didn't want him to get it too should it turn into that.

I did not actually have a stomachache nor did I believe I was going to be getting a stomach bug.

I simply didn't want to have sex and take any risk of having another child. I did not want to bring another child into this family, knowing full well what this man was capable of doing. Although the only positive about me being pregnant with David, I recall, is he was the least physically abusive to me, but that just meant that the verbal abuse ticked up 10 notches.

Sure enough, that night, he slapped me across the face and said, "San, you married me for a reason. Now be a good wife and give me what I deserve. If you don't, I'll beat you unconscious, and then you won't even feel it when I insert myself into you."

He forced into me with such strength I felt like I was being torn apart from the inside out. There was no lubrication to soften the friction of his erection. I tried to coerce myself to get into the mood to lessen the pain. I imagined I liked rough sex, I liked it when he pulled my hair or tried strangling me, but I simply couldn't pretend.

I grew to hate this man every day and with every experience that was like this one.

When he was finished, I ran to the bathroom to try to wash it away.

I remembered my mother telling me when I was young, "Now Sandra, you remember when you're grown and married, you have got to be careful. In our family, we are what they call 'fertile-gertiles' and we get pregnant quickly even if we don't want to. The Lord always finds His way to make His plan happen in our bodies."

I thought, *Oh God, don't let me become pregnant. You know how bad my situation is with Johnny, and we already have David. I can't possibly imagine raising another child under this kind of tension.*

Just two weeks later, I never got my period. Sure enough, that single night of what was.... marital rape turned into a pregnancy. That pregnancy...was Lisa.

I snapped my thoughts back to this moment. By now, it had to be at least 2:30 am, and I'd need to be up to get the kids ready for school by 6. This made me want to have sex with Johnny even less. My sleep time was dwindling, and I was in such unbearable pain as it was, but I knew there was no excuse that Johnny would see as a reason for me to get out of it.

It is always easier to just go ahead with what he wants, to get it over with as quickly and with as little pain as possible. It is never without pain though. Johnny never cares about what I want in the bedroom or in any aspect of our lives together, for that matter.

There is never any foreplay, kissing, gentle touching, or caressing. It is him with a hard-on ready to insert himself into whatever orifice of me he wants in that moment, and if I am at all disobliging, then he unleashes his beast.

I hear him lowering his underwear and drawing nearer to me. I smell the whiskey on his breath and the smell of his body from the day. His smell repulses me, and all I want to do is jump out of bed, run out of the house with my children, and never look back.

He grabs me by the arm and orders me.

"Get on your hands and knees, bitch."

When I don't move as quickly as he wants me to, he lifts his hands to the sides of my head, pressing his thumbs into my cheeks and digging into my newly formed blisters. He raises his voice louder as he moves his face closer to me and firmly speaks through his whiskey-spitting breath in my face, "If I have to tell you again how I want to take you, I'll fuck you all night while I strangle you and this time, you won't make it out alive."

I don't say a word, I just assume the doggy-style position he demands of me while he grunts as he forces into me.

My arms are fatiguing from holding myself up, and I am sure my feet are bleeding on the bed sheets beneath them. I can hardly feel my toes due to the swelling and the pain in my face and head. It feels like my head just might completely decapitate from my body from the pulsating and pounding sensation.

When he finishes, I collapse onto the bed and begin a prayer to God.

Please, Dear Lord, help me to have a fast recovery from my injuries from tonight's abusive episode, and PLEASE help me not become pregnant. I also ask for you, God, to make Johnny die in his sleep via a severe suffering form of natural death like suffocation. Amen.

What a horrific thing to wish for my husband, I know, but he doesn't deserve to have the life he does.

I loathe him, and if I don't have to see his red-bearded face another day, I will be eternally grateful. I will then know and have proof that there is a God looking out for me after all...

The next morning came quickly, just as I knew it would with going to sleep after 3 am. I thought I felt a little woozy, like when you have a hangover. The dizziness, fatigued with low blood sugar sort of feeling.

It made sense since I hadn't eaten much at dinner with the kids because I knew how much they loved the meatloaf and there was only a pound of meat for this meal, and I needed it to last two days, I let them eat as much as they wanted after I had already set a plate aside for Johnny because heaven forbid, he didn't get a dinner plate one night... Otherwise, I may really not live that down at the mercy of his unforgiving and cruel hands.

I knew why I had a massive headache too. I had undergone another beating last night, but this time from a hot plate of food instead of his hands. I wasn't sure which was worse: when he hit me across the face with the back of his hand, splitting my mouth open from a few nights before, or having what I was sure were second-degree burns on my cheeks.

While making breakfast for the kids, I shook my head, trying to clear my mind for the day. It was very hard to do with only a few hours of good sleep, the hours before

Johnny was even home seemed to be the only sound sleep I seemed to get anymore.

I found it difficult to sleep much from 3 am onward due to the immense physical and emotional pain I was in.

As I finished packing the kids two paper lunch bags for school that day, I heard soft footsteps coming down the hallway. I knew from the sound of the feet, such soft and delicate steps almost scared to round the corner for fear that it wouldn't be her mother in the next room.

Lisa whispered but rambled softly, "Mom, are you okay? I had a scary dream that something really bad happened to you... Something bad happened, and then you were gone, and it was just me, David, and Dad. Please, Mom, tell me you're okay!"

She finishes the last sentence in what was almost a shout of terror. It utterly breaks my heart to hear the dramatic, vivid dreams that she is having. Surely it is the result of what she has seen over all of these years from me and Johnny causing her these nightmares—this is her stress response.

I took a deep breath before I fully turned around to acknowledge my forlorn brunette, big-brown-eyed girl. I was already scared of the reaction my children would have upon seeing my face swollen with red blisters and filled with pus.

Sadly, they have seen my face plenty of times with a black eye swollen shut or a lip busted open, making it difficult for me to eat, but they have never seen it in *this* condition. I only took a very short look at myself in the mirror this morning, and it scared me seeing my own reflection.

"Honey, of course I'm okay. I'm fine, you're safe, darling. Don't you fear, I'll always protect you." As I went closer to give Lisa a hug and reassure her of my words, I could hear as I stepped nearer to her, her gasp when she could more clearly see my face.

"Oh, Mom, your face looks... It looks so... bad. I mean, uh, painful. Can I get you a warm washcloth to wipe it with? Maybe it will help? I can go with you to see a doctor today, they'll help you for sure."

My eyes started to burn as the tears began to fill them. Hearing my daughter's endearing offer to help take care of my injuries felt gut-wrenching.

This is yet another reminder that I needed to get Lisa out of this life and David too, if he would agree to come of course.

CHAPTER 3

Lisa

July 1975 Age: 14

Growing up in the small town of Lemard was great, but sometimes, as great as it was, it was equally as unfulfilling.

The Connors next door had two children who were closer to David's age than mine. Kitty-corner from our house on Main Street was a two-story white home owned by the Tullys, and compared to our house, it seemed much larger.

James and Mary Tully had three children; Scott, Jerry, and Denise.

Scott was two years older than me and was the typical jock of Lemard High. He was muscular with jet-black hair and dark brown eyes, easy on the eyes to all the young girls, so naturally, they flocked to him. He knew what he had to offer, and he played his cards to his advantage.

But to me, I could see right through him. I knew that

while he may be good-looking on the outside, that's where it all began and ended. I was confident I could surpass him on an arithmetic exam any day.

Next in line was Jerry. He was in my class at Lemard High, and we were both in our freshman year. New year, new school and having lived so close growing up, we hung around the same crowd of friends. We had a lot of fun together. Jerry was funny, yet knowledgeable about a variety of topics, and everyone seemed to enjoy being around him since he almost always had something to say, and it was something most everyone wanted to hear. You were guaranteed to either relate to his story or laugh listening to his captivating, humorous, and thought-provoking depiction.

Finally, there was Denise, she was the youngest of the Tully family and was entering the 6th grade.

In Lemard, we do not have much to do for entertainment with the town being so small. Each summer David and I ride our bikes over a few times a week to the Tully's and grab the three of them and ride around town. Some afternoons we'd spend on their front lawn sipping lemonade from Mrs. Tully and when one of us thought we heard the rumble of a car coming down the road, we'd jump one on top of the other and make a pyramid of us with David and Scott on the bottom, Jerry and I on top of their backs, and Denise on the very top.

We always let Denise, since she was the youngest and the smallest, be on top of the pyramid and wave to the passersby. We'd cheer and shout and sometimes they'd notice us and give us a honk and a wave back. This was a big day for us when we got a reaction from a car going by!

Lemard was considered mostly an agricultural-based town. We didn't even have a stoplight. People would joke that if you blinked while driving through Lemard, you'd completely miss it.

Over the course of the year, there were different attractions that brought people to our town or through it.

The main traffic during the summer months were kids and young adults playing on our memorial baseball diamond for an intramural league. Directly behind the baseball diamonds were the grain bins.

The baseball diamond was built in memory of Andrew Johnson, who was killed in an accident at the Lemard Grain Bins where he slipped while walking the catwalk and fell into the grain. The grain suffocated him to death and the ambulance didn't make it in time to rescue him.

Many high schoolers and young adults came to support the memory of Andrew and play in a league.

During the fall, the farmers headed in their grain semis to drop their grain into the bins from their harvest.

But all year round, traffic could be counted on to come to visit the infamous meat locker, Meats and Beets. It gained its name because the owners, Mr. and Mrs. Dockinson, owned a small hobby farm where they raised cows, goats, and chickens but their biggest and most well-known item they grew were their beets.

They canned and sold them in their store along with their meat. When they first opened their storefront, only locals came in to buy meat; however, it didn't take long for the secret of the deliciously sweet yet tender beets to get out to the surrounding small towns.

They were consistently selling out of them in less and

less time once they had restocked their shelves. The reputation of Meats and Beets quickly spread.

Soon, it was considered a privilege to buy from Meats and Beets and even more special to have meat from your animals sold in their store.

The outside of their storefront was painted all white with their "Meats and Beets" lettering painted in brown and red, respectively.

Living on Main Street, we'd see all of the trailers with cows and pigs go through town heading to be let out at Meats and Beets, the animals having no clue this would be their last view of the earth as they knew it.

Last summer, with nothing better to do, we snuck in —myself, David, Scott, Jerry, and Denise, as well as a few of the kids from around town. We watched how they butchered the animals.

First, they led the cow into the room and had it squared up over the 'x' on the floor. Next, hung from the tall ceiling, was a big stone in a loop through the band strung from above. One of the butchers would release the stone from one side of the room, and we watched it as it swung across the room and crashed forcefully into the cow's head, making contact directly between the eyes.

When I looked at that cow in the face and could see its eyes lose the glimmer of life behind them, I wondered if that's how my mother felt when my father would hit her.

Did she lose her zest for life inside of her when he beat her?

After the cow was hit, it would tip over, and at that point, they deemed it 'brain dead'.

Was this the reaction my father looked to see from my mother when he'd struck her?

I am taken back in time to a flashback when I once heard my dad threaten her by saying, "This time you won't make it out alive, San. I bring you to death's doorstep, I can also take you to the other side of that door..."

The thought of this memory sent chills down my spine even though it was 82 degrees out that summer day.

Next, the butcher came over and sliced through the neck of the cow from just under one ear all the way to the other ear. They removed the stone from the ceiling strap and then loosened and fastened the strap around the cow. Using the mechanical controls, the butcher lifted the cow up to the ceiling over massive drains in the floor for the cow to bleed out. According to the butcher, this process took quite a while before they could start cutting the cow apart and extracting the meat.

David, Scott, and Jerry watched with wide eyes and full of young-boy excitement at what they were seeing. Meanwhile, Denise was silent as the tears streamed down her face.

I was a bit in shock at the process but wasn't entirely surprised, albeit I was sad for the poor, helpless animal. Seeing Denise's face, I nudged the boys and nodded back to the door we had come in, signaling them to go. We all ran out the back door to our bikes and rode back up town.

Scott hollered to Jerry, "That was cool, Jer! Especially when they hung it up from the ceiling!"

Jerry replied, "Yeah, I'd like to be the one that gets to

release the stone and hit that sucker dead between the eyes. How satisfying would it be to know that you were the one who killed the animal?"

In reply, I yelled out from four feet behind on my bike, "Jerry! How could you want to be the one that hits and hurts the animal?"

Jerry pedaled off ahead and I watched as the wind ripped through his thick jet-black hair as his baggy t-shirt flapped in the breeze against his back.

I couldn't help but wonder why Jerry was so intrigued by the slaughtering process and how he could want and even more so, have the courage to kill a large and innocent animal. I probably shouldn't have been so honed-in on what Jerry said and I *should* have been more concerned about Denise's and my well-being after witnessing the slaughtering of a cow for the first time in our lives as she was pedaling slowly behind me wearing a long face, but I was taken aback by Jerry's reaction and comment.

It's one thing to think watching something like this is "cool," but it's quite another to want to do the killing yourself. That takes a very special person, and not *special* in a good way.

Someone who lacks empathy and enjoys blood, guts, and all the gore. This was a side I'd never seen of Jerry— the smart, funny, quick-witted, and liked-by-all kid.

Did I like that about him, or did I find this new side to him eerily unsettling?

As of now, I didn't have a good feeling about it but maybe I was reading into it too much. I had a tendency to do that, after all.

CHAPTER 4
Sandy

June 1975 Age: 35

It has been a few weeks since the last incident in our family, but to me, it feels like it was just yesterday since most nights, last night being one of them, when I actually could get some restful sleep with Johnny being home, but I woke up in a panic.

I awakened sweating and short of breath from another nightmare of him taking me past the point he's ever taken me before during a violent beating. As if that wasn't bad enough, leaving my children to subsequently be raised by him should I die... the thought of that whole scenario caused me to have a full-fledged panic attack.

I walk to the living room and lay down on my back on the sofa. I close my eyes tightly and tell myself that I can get out of this. I have it within me, and I owe it to my children. I pray to God to help me find the courage to make a

THE END IS THE BEGINNING   23

plan to make it there—to the other side, the happy side of life.

Rarely I would have dreams reflecting on what my children's life (and my own life) would be like without my husband.

Wouldn't all of our troubles be gone? No more fighting, no more bruises, no black eyes—amongst other injuries. I am already doing all of the housework and caring after the children. There is just one small problem... income. I do not work since I have always raised the children and kept up the house.

Whenever I have brought up getting a job to Johnny, he is less than enthusiastic or supportive of the idea.

He has said to me, "You do not need to be outside of the house. A woman's place is in the kitchen and raising the children. It's the man's job to be outside of the house making the money and enjoying his life. You don't need to be making friends and drawing unneeded attention to yourself working at some factory or grocery store. That would distract you from your duties in this house...and to me, Sandra."

Whenever he uses my full name, I know he means business. I also can sense that he is the jealous kind and does not want any attention brought on me. I often wonder if I did have a job, maybe we would have more money, and then there would be less stress in the household. If there was less stress and more money to buy food and pay the bills, then maybe, just maybe, Johnny wouldn't become so angry with me.

But no, that isn't right. I know that his anger typically doesn't stem from the stress of money since I pay all the bills and buy all of the groceries. He probably doesn't even know that we are actually tight on funds.

His anger comes from the alcohol, and if we *did* have more money, maybe that would have a bad outcome after all. Having more money might further feed his addiction because then he would have more money to buy the alcohol, which would lead to him drinking even more.

Either way, what are my options if I don't work? I will never stock enough money away for us to make an escape successfully on Johnny's income alone.

I decide that my first step in coming up with an exit plan is to go to my parents, Marge and Max, who live just a few miles away and see if they have any advice for me and also, asking without *actually* asking, that if needed, could me and the kids could come stay with them if all else fails.

After making sure the kids get on the bus to school as usual, since the weather is supposed to be fairly decent today—70 degrees and partly sunny, I can walk to my parents to have the conversation.

Johnny and I only have one vehicle and he took it to work today so I don't have a vehicle to use but even if I did, if it isn't for me going to the grocery store or running errands for the family, Johnny doesn't seem to like me going out for much. He is always questioning me as to where I am going and how long it will be until I will be back.

Briefly, the thought crosses my mind of having my parents come to the house during the day, but I am fearful that Johnny could be off early or come home for lunch and see them or that one of the neighbors would tell him that they were here. Most likely, it would be Jimmy who would tell him since he probably will be drinking with Johnny a night this week, if not multiple nights, so I don't want to risk that happening.

I bundle myself up since even though the sun is peeking out, it is still early in the morning, and I need protection from the wind. I have to walk down two long country roads to get to my parents' house, which is on Greenville Road, and the winds can easily make it up to 20-30 mph out there.

It takes me around 45 minutes to make it there on foot, but I finally do.

As I walk up to the door, I hear my mother holler to my father, "Sandra's here to visit, Max! Come on out to the kitchen, and I'll make us all a pot of coffee." I enter their home, and the screen door slams shut behind me.

The same familiar smell of their kitchen hits me, and I'm at home coming here. Something warm comes over me, I know that I am safe.

Until my father mutters, "What in the sam-hell do you want from us now? We told you that when you married that boy, you were getting into something you'd want out of later on. Well... I'll be damned if that is what you have come here for today."

As I walk further into the house to sit at my 'old' spot at their kitchen table, foolishness and embarrassment wash over me. I am doubting why I have come.

It is very quick how my feelings change from stepping foot in their house. Initially, I felt safe and warm, and everything felt familiar, but that all shifted within the first 30 seconds after hearing my father's unwelcoming and negative commentary.

Although my father was right, I knew when I was going to marry Johnny that he had his imperfections...but I was young, only 17. I thought our love would stand the test of time. I couldn't wait to be a married woman to my high school sweetheart.

We grew up attending Lemard High together, where I was the captain of the cheerleading squad, and he was the quarterback of the football team. We were both on the homecoming court and voted "The Couple Most Likely to Marry" with a photo of us together—him in his letterman jacket and me in my cheerleading uniform printed in our class yearbook.

Our high school relationship was fun and relaxed. We would spend every night after the football games together with a group of friends having bonfires and drinking. It would usually end up with Johnny and me in the backseat of his *very* used Chevy Bel Air, which had some mild rust around each door and tire, fogging up the windows with a steamy make-out session.

I thought that we had a lot in common back then, albeit the material we were working with (shared love of sports, specifically football, social groups, Friday night bonfires, and being together in arithmetic and history class) was on the surface level, that seemed to be where it began and ended.

Although my parents didn't have much to provide for me, they had much more than Johnny's family had for him. He never wanted anyone to know, but he was actually quite poor. I would bring him leftovers from our dinner the night before to give to him for lunch the next day at school or else I would give him my school lunch, and I would eat the leftovers. He tried to put on a happy face and a strong persona, being the funny and masculine guy while at school, but it all made sense when I went to his house and met his parents one day during my senior year.

Johnny didn't have much of an example in his house while growing up when it came to family. His dad was a drunk and didn't have a single nice word to say about his wife or to me whenever I would come over. He would outwardly tell Johnny to not shack up with a woman like me, that I'd leave him once I realized he didn't have a pot to piss in since I came from something.

Looking back now, it all makes sense that he became who he is. He simply grew up to fit the shoes that he was shown to be by his very own father. He rarely ever showed that side of himself to me until after we were married— it's like he let his guard down. It was only then that I could clearly see his true colors and realized he was a carbon copy of his father.

Yes, Johnny would lose his temper sometimes back then, but he never laid a hand on me. He only would raise his voice when he was really passionate about something. It never went beyond that, and I never had a worry that it would. He seemed so genuine and acted as if he wanted to break away from his rough home life to make a better future for himself. I couldn't imagine what it was like for him being raised in the condition he was in, and I wanted to share with him some of the things I was given.

Hearing my father's remark today, though, it triggered my mind back to when my parents sat me down after Johnny asked for my hand in marriage, and they explained that they strongly advised me against it.

My mother, Margie, said, "Now darling, honey, don't you know how much I love you? Your father and I both do, dear. I don't want to see you rushin' off and marryin' that boy. You two haven't been together much longer than eight months, and furthermore, I know I've heard him raise his voice around you, and I'm not all too fond of that. He doesn't come from the best family, and I don't want you getting into something that you'll later want out of, sweetheart."

Before I could speak, my father spoke up and said, "Sandra, your mother is right on all that she has said. I especially don't want you marrying that boy. His family is rough around the edges, and you won't be living a life like what you have with your mother and I. We're not rich by any means, but we've worked very hard to provide for you. There's a rule in the family that has been passed on through the generations that I'm a reckonin' I ought to share with you. Once you've chosen who you're marrying, you will have made your bed, and then you'll have to lie in it. Once you commit yourself to that boy and you lie down with him, which I'll tell you again, we strongly urge you not to. You will be committed to him for life, and if you need anything, we will not be able to help you. We will treat you as a grown adult."

It has been so many years since they said that to me that I had almost forgotten, but noticing my dad mutter a negative comment upon my arrival at their house brought it back to the forefront of my memory as if it was just yesterday.

I sunk deeply into *my old* dark wooden chair that wrapped around my torso at both sides at their oval shaped cherry wood kitchen table. I clasped my hands nervously around the hot, small white coffee cup my mother placed in front of me.

My father then sits down to my left and my mother sits to my right, just exactly as they used to do when I was growing up.

I am torn between a wistful nostalgia and an unsettled nervousness with what I am about to discuss with them. After a moment has passed which feels like an eternity to me, my mother breaks the awkward silence first.

"My dear, what are you in need of, honey? Are you doing alright?" she asks in a calm and soft voice while holding a concerned facial expression.

As I open my mouth to speak in response to my mother's inquisitive question, my father interjects and responds on my behalf.

"Marge, we can see from the long and hopeless expression upon Sandra's face why she's here." He turns and looks at me with a scowl. "We know that you're struggling in your marriage to that asshole of a man we told you not to shack up with."

My mother rapidly responds, "Now, Maxwell! Certainly, Sandra didn't come all this way on foot to listen to you disrespect her for her past decisions. If you can't keep quiet, then leave the room. We are here to listen, dear. Go ahead."

I squeeze my hands tighter around the coffee mug as I

swallow, making a palpable gulping sound. My mouth feels like someone has stuffed it completely full of cotton and I notice a bead of sweat begin to trickle down the side of my hairline toward my ear.

I am not even hot, I am nervous and have no idea how to begin to explain my situation or ask for help. I can't even quite put together what I actually came for or what I expected my parents to do for me.

I open my mouth again, but I can't find the words, so I stutter, "I uh, I was hoping to share with you some information about my uh, my marriage."

My father looks down and fixes his eyes on his coffee mug on the table. He holds a blank stare and a clenched jaw, but I already know that his anger is building, and it is taking everything in him to keep himself composed. I can sense the tension emanating off of him like rolls of steam. They aren't visible from the eye, but my heart can easily sense it.

My mother still holds a concerned expression on her face as her eyes widen with empathy and sadness.

"In short, Johnny and I aren't getting along as well as I thought we always would. He's not the best version of himself to me and the children, and as they're growing older, I'm concerned about their upbringing and what this type of exposure will do to them."

Without lifting his gaze from his coffee mug, in a stern, clipped tone, I hear my father, "You're not telling us anything we didn't already suspect, Sandra. You made a poor choice, we tried warning you."

My mother speaks rapidly and in a high-pitched tone, "Max, this is no time for making her feel bad for a past decision. You are not perfect yourself, and everyone deserves to have a loving and supportive family surrounding them, especially when they're going through a tough time. We are listening, Sandra."

I respond hurriedly with a bit of impatience in my tone, "I don't really know what I'm here to say or what I'm hoping you can do for me, but I thought you should know what's going on in my life. I'm unhappy, and to put it frankly, I'm disgusted with the life I'm raising my children in. I need to find a way out of this sooner rather than later so that I can be present to see my children grow."

As a tear trickles down my face, I look down at my lap, feeling ashamed and embarrassed.

My mother replies, "My darling, dear, you look up at me right now. If Johnny has laid a hand on you or your children, you know you can always come with your children for safety. We do not want to see you be treated less than you deserve. We want you all safe and to be protected."

As the tears stream down my face, one after another, I let out a small whimper of a cry attempting to hold back the lump in my throat.

"Marge, you know the rules in this household. Sandra, you proceeded to marry that bastard after we gave you warning after warning. You have chosen this life, and now you need to figure it out all on your own. At some point, children need to be treated as the adult that they are. Sandra is no longer our 'baby' and she shouldn't be treated as one either."

With that, he lifts his eyes from his coffee mug and makes eye contact first at me, then to my mother. He slides his mug away from him, scoots his chair back, gets up and walks out of the room.

Seeing this makes me go into a full-fledged breakdown. I hold my head in my hands as my shoulders shrug from the heavy tears and gasps of breaths I take between the sobs.

My mother quickly comes over, pulling my father's chair over close to mine and begins to rub the middle of my back in a circular motion.

She slowly whispers in my ear, "You will succeed in anything you set your mind to, my dear. You are stronger than these circumstances, and you know I am always here for you. Your father is, too. He simply takes longer to come around to these kinds of things. You know how he can be."

After a few moments, I gather my composure, lean into my mom's side-hug and whisper, "Thank you, Mom. Your support and encouragement are everything to me. My children deserve more, and it is my job to protect them. I have failed them thus far, and that needs to change."

With that, I grab a hold of my coffee mug, lift it to my mouth, and chug it without taking a single breath.

I set it back on the table forcefully, grab my mother's hand, and gave it a tight yet brief squeeze. "I love you, Mom. I have to go."

I rise from my chair and go out the front door with my mind full of thoughts and my face still damp from the tears I had shed.

As I begin walking back home, it seems I arrive much quicker than it took me to walk there, but I am sure that it is because my mind swirled in thoughts of making an exit plan.

But no matter how I come up with my plan, and what I need to do in my life next, the first step is I need to find a job so I can have a steady income source to raise my children on my own.

But how will I find a job when I have never worked and have no resume or networking? I have no idea if anyone will hire me, but I am bound and determined to get my name out there and prove my work ethic. My children need that from me and although I can't take back the past, I owe it to them to do this for their future and that is that.

Breaking away from Johnny and setting my kids up for a more positive life is no longer a dream for my life, it is going to become a reality. Even if my dad isn't going to support or help me, I will use his negativity as motivation and the newfound strength that I need for moving on and proving him wrong.

CHAPTER 5
Lisa

July 1975 Age: 14

It is like any other typical weeknight in the Hansen household except for one thing. I'm walking over to the Clark's house to babysit their children, Eloise and Michael, for the night. I've watched their kids before when they've gone out to dinner parties or out with friends to the movies, but I haven't yet watched them when they're coming to my house for a party. The party tonight is to celebrate Jimmy's birthday.

I'm not sure why Jimmy's party is being hosted by my parents instead of at their own house, but nonetheless, I am heading to their house to babysit their kids, and then they will walk over to my house for the party. A few of the neighborhood families in Lemard were invited to celebrate Jimmy's birthday. I overheard my mom calling around to some of the houses in town this week.

The odd thing about the party for tonight is it isn't a

THE END IS THE BEGINNING   35

Saturday night. It's Wednesday night, and I have school tomorrow. Eloise and Michael do too, not to mention most of the adults have work. I don't know why they couldn't celebrate his birthday this coming weekend, but I guess someone must have plans and couldn't make it.

When I arrive, Mr. and Mrs. Clark are all dressed up. Mrs. Clark is in black stiletto heels wearing bright red lipstick. While Mr. Clark is wearing a button down shirt and a jacket.

It is rare that I have seen them dressed up at all, let alone to this caliber. As I attempt to look them up and down in incognito style, I notice that Mrs. Clark is wearing black tights that look like netting pulled over her legs.

I have heard the upperclassmen girls on the school bus talk about fishnet tights. I wonder if maybe this is what those are? Why would she be wearing those to her husband's birthday party though?

I sense that they caught me looking them over when Mr. Clark loudly clears his throat.

After a moment, he clears his throat. "I suppose we should get going, Lisa. Thanks for coming by, we shouldn't be too late since it's a school night."

Jimmy turns his head and sends a quick wink with his right eye to Marianne and with that, he slips his arm around her waist and snugly pulls her close to him. She smiles up at him with her teeth brightly shining through her red lipstick.

The lipstick makes her teeth look extra white, and I think, *Wow, I hope my teeth look that way when I am a grown-up.* Hopefully, my love of sweets doesn't derail that aspiration. Maybe I should cut back on the Bubblicious gum and Laffy Taffy.

I pause in a bit of shock as I think about their clothing choices and the flirtatious interaction I just witnessed between Mr. and Mrs. Clark. I still find it odd that this party is happening on a Wednesday night. Why would an adult feel the need to have a party that is apparently a 'dress up party' on a school or work night?

I finally reply to them, "Okay, thank you. Have fun."

Why did I tell them to have fun? It's not that I *don't* want them to have fun, it's just a little bizarre this whole evening. It almost feels like I am acting as the parent and they are the teenager.

As I swing the front door closed, Eloise, who is five, and Michael, who is seven, come running down the hallway, snapping my mind out of my thoughts and back into the current moment.

"Miss Lisa! Miss Lisa!" cries Eloise. "Come into my bedroom! I want to show you my Barbies!"

"No, Miss Lisa, I'd first like to show you the new game I got for my birthday last month. We can all play it together!" Michael pleads in a whiny tone.

Bending forward at the hips and placing my hands on my knees in an attempt to get on their level, I reply, "Can we do both, you guys? Can I see Eloise's Barbies first, and then we play the game you have with her Barbies, Michael?"

They both nod in agreement simultaneously and seem to be elated that I'm here for the evening. They skip joyfully down the hallway, standing in the doorway of their bedrooms awaiting for me to step in their direction.

Although it is strange babysitting on a weeknight, it is fun to be around these kids and getting out of the house for something different.

My brother, David, went to his friend, Ron's house for the evening. Ron lives south of Lemard in the country. David enjoys going there since they have animals, dogs, and cats, and Ron has his own pet gerbil that he keeps in his room.

Dad doesn't like for us to have any pets so we have never been allowed to have a dog. Even when I begged and pleaded for one growing up since age five, the answer was always a stern, "No."

We first play with Eloise's Barbies while Michael patiently waits in the doorway of his room and when she begins to show signs of losing interest in them and makes her way across her bedroom to a new toy, Michael jumps on the opportunity to take us to play his game.

He motions me silently to come toward him as if he knows speaking about us transitioning from the activity with his sister to his bedroom to do something else will set her down a slippery slope into a temper tantrum. I slowly rise up from my knees to get off of the floor and follow him to his bedroom, urging Eloise to follow me there with an arm wave, although she is too immersed in searching for a new toy to notice my exit.

We arrive at Michael's room and he gets out his board game for us to play. It is a brand new game of Trouble with the newest version of the dice popper in the middle. I actually love this game from when I've played it at friends' houses before. We sit down to play the game together as we hear loud footsteps rounding the corner.

We turn to the doorway and Eloise is standing, frowning holding her Barbies.

"You guys left me all alone to play Barbies. I thought we were playing all together, and you left. I don't want to play this Trouble game!" Eloise exclaims through tear-filled eyes as her voice rises more high-pitched with each word she shouts.

"Oh, Eloise, it's okay! We can play Barbies while we also play Trouble. Come sit next to me, and I'll show you how we can do that," I offer to her in a soft and gentle tone.

Eloise walks slowly across the room as if she's contemplating if she really wants to do this or if she is going to have a meltdown instead. Without giving her the chance to react negatively, I move quickly over and tap my hand on the floor next to me, inviting her to sit beside me.

We play Trouble and Barbies for some time, laughing every so often over us all rolling the dice popper to the same number of two multiple times in a row.

Michael has won the last two games and now we are beginning to play the third game before we move on to playing a new game. The time has gone by so quickly and when I look up to the wall clock just to the right of Michael's bedroom door, I notice red and blue lights on the glass of his clock reflecting through his window. The time is now 8:25 pm.

My stomach flips like it is falling, similar to how it does when I ride a roller coaster and the ride goes over a big drop. The sweat starts to form on the palms of my hands as I rise from the floor to make my way to Michael's bedroom window to look out to see if the police are stopped close by or if, hopefully, they are just passing through town.

I can see the lights are no longer moving down the street and appear to be in the driveway of...my house. Why would the police be at my parents' house for the party? Uncontrollably, my hands start trembling and sweating more than just a general dampness, so I wipe them on my jeans as I peer out the window longer.

What am I going to tell these kids? Should I call back home or go there and see what is going on? Do I leave the kids or bring them along?

So many thoughts are flooding my mind it makes my heart start racing. I hope this doesn't involve my dad again and having had too much to drink, how embarrassing would that be?

I turn around, and Eloise asks, "Miss Lisa, what are you looking out the window for? Did someone walk by that you recognized? I hope Mom and Dad aren't coming back yet, we're having so much fun, aren't we, Miss Lisa?"

I quickly try to hide the angst that has to be showing on my face and force a half-hearted smile back to Eloisa.

"I'm going to step out for a moment, you guys. You two play this next round of Trouble, I'll be right back!" I announce as I slip by Michael sitting on the floor on his knees. I walk as quickly as I can without running to the kitchen and grab the phone and dial my home number through trembling fingers, 287-9737.

The phone rings for three rings and then a fourth. I mutter under my breath, "Come on, Mom, pick up, pick up."

Finally, someone answers the phone and I hear the sound of a deep voice of a man in the background. The voice isn't someone that I recognize, which causes me to experience what I refer to as 'the nervous-nausea'.

I hear this man express, "How did it start? Okay, and then what happened?"

Finally, someone starts to speak on the line, "Hello there?"

The voice coming through the phone is not my mother nor is it my father. It is Mrs. Connor from next door.

"Hello? Is this Mrs. Connor?"

"Yes, dear. Is this Lisa?"

After I pause for a moment to register whom I'm speaking with and wondering why it's not my mother on the other end of the line, I question, "Is everything alright?"

"No, honey, it's not. Your parents had a party tonight for Jimmy's birthday, I guess. I wasn't invited to the party, but I came over when I heard loud noises coming from the house, and I was worried. When no one came to the door, I entered the house, and your mother was on the kitchen floor. Don't come home right now, dear. It's not the best time."

"Mrs. Connor, what should I do?" I ask, the lump in my throat forming overhearing those words, "It's not the best time."

That means it's not safe. What could have happened? Especially at a party around other people?

"Stay where you are, dear. It'll be some time to get

things taken care of at home. Are you somewhere you can stay for a while?" she asks.

"I'm at Mr. and Mrs. Clark's house watching Eloise and Michael."

"Ah, yes," she utters, her voice inflection changing to sound relieved, now knowing I have somewhere to stay. "Jimmy and Marianne are here as well. You just stay put, honey. We'll all be alright." The line goes dead.

"Mrs. Connor, are you there? What's going on?" As I turn to put the phone back on the receiver, Michael comes around the corner.

"Is everything alright, Miss Lisa? Elle and I have finished our third round of Trouble, and you won't believe it. I won again! Let's go play it together, Miss Lisa!"

I try my best to force a smile back to Michael, but a tear escapes from my eye and trickles down my cheek. I lower myself down to my knees and grab Michael's hands.

"Michael, I want you to get your sister and your game of Trouble and bring it to the living room. Pick out your favorite movie, and I will put it on for you both. I have to run back home for a few minutes, but I will be right back. Can you keep an eye on your sister for me while I do that, please?"

"Sure, Miss Lisa! My favorite movie is *Willy Wonka and The Chocolate Factory*. I know right where it is too. I'll grab it for you."

I rush into the living room and pop the *Willy Wonka and The Chocolate Factory* tape into the Philips VCR Player. Once they are both coming around the corner, Michael carrying Trouble and Eloise carrying her Barbies, I know I can head out.

"I'll be back in a jiffy, you two. Don't do anything you wouldn't do without your parents here," I declare as I sneak out the front door, not waiting to hear their reply.

I run as fast as I can down the sidewalk two houses down from The Clark's and across the street, almost forgetting to check for cars but since there's hardly anyone that comes through our sleepy town, I figure I would have heard it before I crossed.

When I make it to the house, there is the police car right in my driveway but the police officer is just climbing in and closing the door. My heart is beating out of my chest, and the adrenaline is spiking in my veins as I run to the front door and burst into the house.

I see my mother is wearing her black high heels and a formfitting dress—something I've never seen her in before and she is lying on the couch with her feet propped up on the coffee table. Also, something I've never seen her do—wear her shoes in the house, let alone high heels and have them on the coffee table. This is bizarre. She's holding an ice pack to her eye with her right hand and sipping some sort of beverage that looks to me like whiskey over ice cubes.

I rush over to her and mutter in a hushed tone, "Mom, are you alright? What happened here tonight? Where's Dad?"

She takes her time looking over at me and acts as if she almost doesn't quite see me, or maybe she just isn't registering who I am. What is wrong with her? Her eyes

THE END IS THE BEGINNING   43

look shiny, like someone gave her eye drops to make them extra glossy, and her cheeks are red and flushed.

"We're having a fun time celebrating Jimmy for his birthday bash, dear. The party is still going on, actually, so let's live it up. Let me show you to some of our guests, Leese," she exclaims loudly through slurred words.

Leese? I've never been given a nickname by anyone in my entire life, let alone 'Leese' by my mother. Is this supposed to be a shortened kind of nickname for my already short four-letter name?

This evening is more and more peculiar by the minute, I swear. Mom doesn't even acknowledge that she clearly has an injury to her eye and is using an ice pack for it. She just acts like nothing has gone on and the party is reaching its peak.

She grabs my arm to do what she thinks is show me around, but I quickly realize it is for me to help her off of the couch and steady her to walk around the party. If the police were here five minutes ago, you surely wouldn't know it by how she or anyone in this house is acting. She guides me around the corner, and there is music playing in the background and a few couples around the room sitting on different pieces of furniture.

What is weird is that the couples aren't with their partner. They are all sitting with someone else. Mr. Clark has his arm around Mrs. Wallen and Mrs. Wallen is leaning back on the couch with her legs up across Mr. Jenson's lap. What the heck is this? Where is Dad and where is Mrs. Clark? As I scan the room, I can't seem to spot either of them.

When they see I'm here with my mother, they all

straighten up a bit. Well, some of them do, the ones with their eyes shiny and glossy like my mom's, just keep at it, whatever it is that they're doing.

"You all can relax, my daughter is here to help us keep the party alive! We're having so much fun we're not going to stop now just because we had a uh... dull moment. Leese, give our guests here a party favor and flash them your big boobs. They *are* your best asset and they just seem to keep growing. Show these folks you know how to use those perky things!"

I think that I am going to puke, jarred by my mother's absurd words. Did my mother just ask me to show my boobs? What the hell is happening tonight? I look around the room with wide eyes and everyone seems to stop what they're doing and look over at me as if they are actually expecting me to do it.

What the hell?

Is this what peer pressure feels like? I look back at my mom and she is gauging the room, seeing how interested the guests are in me as if she is pondering over what she can ask me to do next should I go along with this first request.

I shout, "I don't know what the fuck you all are doing here, but it is disgusting and I want nothing to do with it."

I turn to my mom as I take in a deep inhalation. "Clearly you've been hurt Mom, probably by Dad as usual, and where is he? Did the cops take him in tonight?"

She laughs as if this is the funniest thing that she has heard all night or maybe even all year. I don't know that I've ever heard my mom laugh like this. It is loud and high-pitched and purely from her gut.

"No, Leese, our birthday bash just got a little bit wild there for a moment. It was an accident. Initially, your father wasn't interested in these 'games' and became upset seeing me with Jimmy, and the other guests became worried, and someone called the police. It's Jimmy and Marianne who got us started in doing this sort of swing-swap—whatever you call it. At first, Johnny was hesitant, but once he saw Marianne's... ahem, saw her...he couldn't resist, and after a few drinks, he decided we'd start a new game down the hall. It's so relaxing to just let loose and live a bit—I don't think I've laughed this hard in all my life! So that's where your father is—he's in our bedroom with Mrs. Clark. We're each taking our turns for 7 minutes of heaven. We were hoping you'd show us a little something to keep everyone in the 'mood'!" she blurts out as she nudges me in the side and moves her shimmering eyes from my eyes down to my chest and back up again.

I look around the room one last time in sheer horror. Everyone is now making out with whoever is next to them, apparently, since they gave up on me doing a 'trick'.

Mom walks over and leans to whisper something to Mr. Clark and Mrs. Wallen. I can't hear what they say, but I see Mr. Clark put his arm out and reach around my mother's waist as he pulls her down in the chair with them, and then Mrs. Wallen and my mom erupt in laughter while Mr. Clark grins.

I turn around and run out of the house as fast as I can, running across the road and back up to the Clark's.

As I come through the front door, I remember I left these two children alone and unattended, and immediately, the guilt washes over me.

But I feel guilty? Their parents are having sexual relations with other married individuals at MY house, and I feel guilty? What the hell!

Both kids are on the floor staring at the movie. Thank God they didn't move, and nothing bad happened while I was away. I hear the line from the movie, "Don't argue, my dear child, please don't argue!" cries Mr. Wonka. "It's such a waste of precious time!"

For some reason, it seems again tonight that I am the parent... this is overwhelming. What is this, my third time acting 'parental' tonight? I run down the hallway and into their bathroom where I lock the door, turn the faucet on high, and sink down to the floor and sob.

What in the hell are my parents doing, and what did I just witness?

CHAPTER 6
Sandy

June 1975 Age: 35

I t's been a week since I had the discussion with my parents expressing my need for leaving my marriage and saving my kids. Although it wasn't apparent that I had full support from them, I need to look for a job to support my exit strategy.

I also am dreading telling Johnny about it but he needs to know so that he can grapple with the idea of me being in the working world and hopefully come to terms with it.

It is Monday, and after I've gotten the kids off to school, I decide to walk downtown to the Phillips 66 gas station to fill out an application for employment.

Upon entering the Phillips 66, I notice that there is a sign posted on the door that reads "Help Wanted, please apply inside". Immediately, a jolt of excitement goes through me, knowing that they are actually looking for someone, maybe someone just like me to work here.

I swing the door open with excitement. The door is much lighter than I had anticipated so it opens quickly and crashes on the cinder block wall situated behind it.

Instantly, embarrassment hits me as I walk through the door. Why would anyone want to hire me to keep this place up after I just almost broke the front door of the place off? I walk up to the counter and smile up at the man standing on the other side timidly.

"Hello, ma'am, how may I be of service to you today?" he exclaims jovially.

"Hello there, sir. My name is Sandy and I saw your sign that you are looking for help. I was hoping I could fill out an application to be considered for work here," I reply in a soft and self-conscious tone avoiding as much eye contact as possible.

"Well, uh, ma'am, do you understand the job description?" The shift in the man's tone is palpable. He's no longer as upbeat but is more serious now, and I can tell that he's staring right at me, waiting for me to look up at him.

"I believe, I do, sir. Clean the facilities, stock the shelves, and check out customers," I announce in reply, trying to sound confident even though inside, I'm shaking like a leaf. I've never applied for a job like this or had a conversation with someone to this depth about how to perform a job.

"That's not an all-inclusive list. You would also be responsible for pumping the gas for customers upon their arrival at our station as well as cleaning their windows, amongst other duties. I don't mean to be rude to you, uh, Susan, was that your name? But we've never had a woman work here in that capacity. I'm not sure you could do all of that work to the ability that a man-filling station attendant can."

It took just that statement from him of not getting my name right and assuming I'm incapable of performing the job to shift my gaze to meet his eyes as I adjust my shoulders back and stand up a little taller. A rush comes over me that I don't even recognize—something that I don't even have the time to process or filter through before the words just start to come out.

"Listen, Mr. Phillips 66, is that your name? Oh no, that's right I didn't catch it since you didn't introduce yourself after I told you mine. I'm a mother of two children and keep a very tidy home and do all that is needed for them. I don't see how doing the work in your facility is any more difficult than what I am currently doing at home. I don't appreciate your presumptuous assumption about my work abilities before you even know anything about me or have given me a chance to show you that I am more than capable. I'd really appreciate you to reconsider how you speak to others, specifically women, before you comment on my inabilities for which you are wildly inaccurate about."

The man stands with his jaw open and just blankly stares at me. A moment passes and he crouches over to search nervously around his desk. Finally, when he stands back up, he passes the employment application to me across the counter.

"Here is an application for employment. I'll be sure to

get it to the owners right away, Sandy." He lifts his trembling hand from the pen and he places it on top for me to complete the form with.

"I'm sure you will do just that, Mr. Phillips 66."

Although I highly doubt they'll even consider hiring me because he's right, these roles are usually fulfilled by males, but why should I not be considered just because I'm a female and don't have a work history? It's not like it takes a degree in gasoline filling to work here, for Pete's sake.

I fill out the form and slide it back across the counter.

"Thank you, sir." I swivel on my heel and leave the gas station, pushing the door just as firmly as I did upon entry, but this time, I do it with intention.

He deserves to feel a bit small and shaken up slightly from my confrontation.

Honestly, it is like I just bullied someone into hiring me, and I am befuddled at my explosive yet articulate commentary to him. Where in the heck did that come from?

Maybe I'm turning into a 'mama bear'. If I am, I think I like that about myself. However, I've rarely seen myself fly off the handle over being offended so quickly. My emotions seem to be getting the best of me lately, and *that* I'm not sure I am as proud of.

CHAPTER 7
Lisa

July 1975 Age: 14

After I spent what seemed like a good 10 minutes or so in the bathroom of the Clark's house, I decided I needed to get myself together and stop sulking in my disgusted emotions. I washed my face with warm water and went back out to the living room to see how the kids were doing.

Luckily, they are still sitting in the same spots they were 10 minutes ago, with eyes glued to the screen. Thank God for good movies to sidetrack their minds. If only I could sit down and have the movie take the same effect on me as it is on them.

I check the time and it's now 10 pm, much later than these kids should be staying up, especially on a school night. I decide I'll give them a two-minute warning and then attempt to get them to their beds.

The intense thoughts I've been having tonight creep

back into my mind. The main thought is that I have had to be the parent to what feels like everyone today. I'm also hoping The Clarks don't even come back home tonight, I really don't want to see their faces. I have lost all respect for them after seeing Mr. Clark on Mrs. Wallen and then... there was my mother. I can't even think back to that scene, it's actually disturbing.

"Okay, kids, two-minute warning to finish up the movie, and then we've got to make our way to your bedrooms. It's getting quite late and we need to get our rest before school tomorrow."

"Aw man! Miss Lisa, can we please stay up to finish the movie? You'd be the best babysitter if you let us. Please?" pleads Michael with his hands clasped together in front of his chest as if he's praying.

"You two have already stayed up way past your bedtime and your parents won't be too pleased with me if they find out I let you stay up as late as it is. Sorry guys, bedtime it is. We're down to the last minute."

Michael and Eloise frown simultaneously but seem to silently accept my rationale. They both stare at the screen until I walk to the television to turn it off. I motion my arm to direct them down the hallway toward their bedrooms. They take their time walking but go into their rooms, and I help them put their pajamas on and get into bed. I tell them, "Good night," and mosey my way back to the living room.

Before I sit down on the couch, I take a peek out the front window and see the lights still lit all around my parents' house. Clearly, they're still partying. This is unbelievable.

Maybe I should call David to tell him not to go home tonight? But I don't know the number to Ron's house to get ahold of him. I just hope he doesn't walk into what I did tonight—no one should have to witness a swinger fiasco at all, let alone one of your *own* parents.

I close the blinds on the front window and turn the movie back on, and I take a seat on the couch and absent-mindedly stare at the screen, allowing my mind to drift into the land of *Charlie and The Chocolate Factory* until I drift off to sleep.

CHAPTER 8
Sandy

June 1975 Age: 35

Since I didn't have the best experience with Mr. Phillips 66, I decided it might be a good option to put some of my eggs in other baskets and because I'm a little fired up from that last encounter, it has boosted my confidence in finding a job in this town.

It is a beautiful, sunny 75 degree day today with a light breeze so I decide to further enjoy this weather and walk down another block to my favorite, Meats and Beets.

As I walk in the front door, it smells like bacon, beef jerky, and sweet beets. The scent is delightful and fills my soul with nostalgia from coming here periodically over the years to buy a special cut of meat for a holiday.

I take a few steps toward the counter, and a heavy-set, dark-haired woman with a dingy, what was once white, now off-white apron that is visibly soiled, probably with blood from a slaughtered cow, greets me at the counter

THE END IS THE BEGINNING 55

and, from glancing at her apron, my stomach turns slightly.

How can I work in a place like this if the sight of blood on an apron makes me queasy? Maybe I *would* be a better fit for the gas station.

"Hello there, darling, what can I help you find today? I'm Mary, and I am the store owner. Would you like a sweet honey-cured ham?" she asks with a smile. She reaches forward to grab a jar of her beets on display on the counter and asks, "Or how about a jar of our lovely beets? Happy to help you!"

She is smiling such a genuine yet gentle smile to me. You know, the kind that just puts you at ease in the presence of someone, so welcome. I immediately notice the tension in my shoulders fade away as I do a small roll of my shoulders and take a step closer to the counter in hopes I can reciprocate a fourth of the kindness shown by this woman.

"Hello, Mary, thank you for your offer to help me. I'd like to take you up on it. I'm here to see if I can apply to work here," I answer her while looking down at her apron and the wooden countertop and then slowly bringing my eyes up to meet hers.

"Oh darling, I'd love to hire someone like you. But I'm not so sure you could handle working in the slaughter room from the sheer look of terror and disgust upon your face when you saw my apron. We need someone who can work both, in the back with the animals and do our meat processing but also in the storefront to greet customers as I've greeted you. I don't want to offend you, dear, but you seem rather shy."

Why is everyone judging me by my looks today? Am I looking extra feminine or frail where it appears I'm utterly incapable of doing any work outside of my home? This is beginning to infuriate me.

"Mary, with all due respect, I'm fully capable of performing the job. I enjoy organization and can easily stock your shelves and keep track of your inventory, including the sales of your meat. I can be taught working in the back and grow into that role as I'm sure most do when they start here and don't have the experience."

Mary looks aghast with her mouth hanging wide open while staring at me. She closes her mouth and clears her throat before responding.

"I'm sure you can, ma'am. I apologize for judging you without getting to know you further. May I ask your name? I'd like to give you my contact information and have you fill out an application so we can stay in touch."

"My name is Sandra. I go by Sandy, and I live just up the road, so I could easily make it here for my shifts. I'm looking to work here while my children are in school during the daytime if possible."

"Ah, I see, Sandy. Please complete this application and bring it back to us," she states with a soft smile.

I take my right hand and reach up to the counter to get the application and business card and am met with a warm hand on top of the back of mine.

I quickly pull my arm away, failing to grab the application. A jolt of energy courses through me, and I'm immediately uncomfortable. My stomach does a flip—like the adrenaline when you almost get into a car accident, but you don't, and amazingly enough, you continue driving unharmed and free. I feel it down to my core.

"Sandy, dear." Her eyes shift side to side checking that no one is around us.

She lowers her voice to a whisper. "I know we just met, but I can't help but notice some bruises on your arm here and your eye appears to be puffy. I'm not asking for any details. It's none of my business, but please, with the application, I've put my business card, and on the back here, I've written my home phone number. Take my card and feel free to call for anything you may need. I live just south of Lemard and can be of help to you."

I stand shocked with my mouth slightly open, thinking of how to respond. My knee-jerk reaction is to be embarrassed that she even noticed them of course, and offended that she had the audacity to mention it to me, especially her first time meeting me. However, with her calming presence, I find it hard to actually become angry with her. I certainly can't afford to mouth off to her like I did to Mr. Phillips 66.

The front door swings open, and the bell rings, notifying us of a new customer entering the storefront.

"Well, if it isn't the one, the only, Mrs. Hansen. The beautiful Mrs. Hansen, if I might add. What is a gal like you doing in Meats and Beets on this wonderful day?" Jimmy Clark smirks while winking at me as he casually looks through the beef jerky box on the opposing check out station counter.

I notice that there is heat rising up my back from between my shoulder blades, but I'm trying to push it away so that it doesn't reach my cheeks and he can sense my emotions.

Because I take a moment to respond, Mary starts to speak on my behalf.

"Oh, the lovely Sandy is here today to look into employ—"

I interject after clearing my throat. "I'm here looking at food options for a meal I'm preparing in a few weeks for Johnny's family and the kids."

I fear that Mary is going to question why I'm wearing a wedding ring, and I just made reference to making a meal for Johnny and our children, but Jimmy is in here clearly hitting on me. Why did he of all people, have to be the one to waltz in through the doors during the 10 minutes that I'm here?

"Thank you, Mary, for the information. I'll be on my way now." I grab the application and her business card and shove them both into my purse. I swiftly walk from the counter to the door, but am met with Jimmy stepping toward me so I cannot leave.

He whispers down to me, "If you have free time this afternoon, I'd love to spend a few moments with you. You know where to find me."

I move past him without looking up to him. I don't want him to see the blushing of my cheeks despite my inability to control them.

I also don't want Mary to have further questions about my situation. She already has concerns since she gave me her personal phone number and empathetically told me she could see my bruises. I don't need her thinking that I'm deserving of my 'treatment' from

Johnny because I'm fooling around on my husband with another man... That's the LAST thing I need for her to think of me.

I push the door to exit Meats and Beets and take my sunglasses from my purse and place them on my eyes as I start to walk toward home. I hope I can get a job there after that awkward encounter... Why has this day been such a shit day?

CHAPTER 9

Lisa

July 1975 Age: 14

Where in the heck am I? I wake up and look around. The panic begins to set in, and I start to sweat a little bit as I look around, trying to recognize something in this room.

Oh yeah, I'm at the Clark's from babysitting last night. I can't believe I stayed here all night and they haven't come home yet.

I rise from the couch and walk across the dark room to find a light switch so that I can see what time it is. It has got to be the early morning, but it is still mostly dark out.

Finally, after fumbling across the room in the dark, I find the light switch and can walk to the kitchen.

The clock above the sink says that it is 5:30 am. Am I supposed to get the kids ready for school today too? I am SO sick of being the 'parent'. It feels like I am the one and only 'parent' for multiple families.

THE END IS THE BEGINNING   61

I look through the refrigerator and decide I'll try to make the kids eggs and see if there is some fruit I can put together for a makeshift breakfast. As I start to pull the egg carton out from the refrigerator, trying to be as quiet as a mouse, I hear the knob of the front door start to wiggle and the sound of keys clinking together on a keychain.

Hearing this, I am met with an enormous wave of nervousness and uncomfortability. I try to make myself look busy and avoid noticing their entrance, although they aren't trying to be as quiet as I am being, it seems.

As they enter through the door, Marianne softly whispers, "Hi Lisa, how are you?"

How am I? Are you kidding me, she wants to make small talk after they pulled the stunt that they did last night? I'm beyond annoyed and sleep-deprived. I'm disappointed in them and everyone at that party.

"I've been better, Marianne," I mutter through closed teeth trying to withhold my anger and voice too.

She makes her way to the kitchen and places her hand on the middle of my back. Is she trying to be comforting or consoling? Does she really *not* know I was there last night and saw with my own two eyes the disgusting behavior they were all engaging in? The thought of it all makes my skin crawl in unforgivable horror.

"Darling, thank you for watching the children for us. I'm so sorry we kept you so late, especially on a school night. What can we do for you? Do you want to be off of school today so you can catch up on some sleep? I could call you in?" she asks with a wry smile.

What is wrong with her, seriously? After the abominable conduct I witnessed last night, I can't believe she's not trying to be a better person today. But instead, she's furthering her inexcusable efforts by offering to call me off of school because *they* stayed out too late? Does she actually think that is some sort of admirable gesture?

"No, thank you, Marianne. I'll be going to school today even though I'm short on sleep. Maybe Mom will let me have a few sips of her coffee before I catch the bus." I abruptly try to get my point across.

"Are you sure, dear? Your mother wouldn't mind if I called you in, I already spoke with her about it this morning. We're so sorry to have kept you so long into the night... ahem... The morning I should say, I suppose."

Of course she spoke to my mother this morning. I wouldn't be entirely surprised if she had kissed her too before she left in following the suit of their party scheme.

"No, I'll be alright. I'll be on my way now, then, Marianne." I make my way out of the kitchen trying to look around and get anything I might have forgotten.

Marianne grabs my arm to spin me around. I become stiff by the mere touch of her hand on my arm. She could be passing sexually transmitted germs onto me from her hand on my arm which sends shivers down my spine.

In a pleading tone, I hear, "Lisa! Is everything alright, dear? I need to grab the money to pay you from Jimmy."

"I don't need any money, Marianne. I'd really like to be on my way," I respond, looking down at the floor, feeling my anger begin to show through my short tone.

"Lisa, what is the matter? I'm sorry we were so late."

Is she playing dumb or does she *really* not know that I

was there last night for their swinger swap shenanigans or whatever it may be called?

"Marianne, I know that I'm only 14, and I may not know much or have much worldly experience, and it is not technically my business. However, I do know that what I witnessed last night was just plain wrong. I don't know how you could live with yourself behaving in such a way."

Marianne stands flabbergasted, staring back at me as she drops my arm and takes a step backward.

My God, she really must not have known I was there. She was upstairs with my father, according to what my apparently, very drunken mother said.

I take four more steps to the door, grab the handle, open the door swinging it wide, and slam it shut behind me.

I don't want their pity money. I just want to go home and erase this whole night from my mind.

CHAPTER 10
Sandy

June 1975 Age: 35

"Hi, Mom!" exclaims Lisa cheerfully once she has exited the school bus and is far enough away for her friends not to hear her.

I wave to motion 'hello' as I haven't even made it inside to set my purse down from coming home from Meats and Beets. I only walked a few blocks from the meat locker to the house, but I am so exhausted, I wish I could lay down for a while.

I enter the house and begin fixing the kids an after-school snack as well as prep dinner. We are short on money right now so we don't have much for groceries, so I'm not sure what I'll be able to put together for tonight. I'll have to ask Johnny when he gets home for some money to go to the store tomorrow.

I enter the living room with a small tray with crackers, some leftover cheese I found in the back of the refriger-

THE END IS THE BEGINNING 65

ator that I cut, and a few slices of a tomato that I could salvage while having to throw the rest away.

"David and Lisa, here's a snack for you guys. Come on in the living room, I want to hear about your day while you get your homework out."

Both kids come running down the hallway, but their faces fall when they see the snack I have put together for them.

"Aw, Mom, this is what you made? I don't even like tomatoes or cheese. Ugh... gross!" announces Lisa.

"Just eat it, Lisa. Mom put together whatever we had. You know it's probably not much, so just make it easy on her and eat it, will ya?" David blurts out, seemingly having a short-tempered tone with her.

Hearing this from David makes my heart ache, knowing how privy yet accurate he is of our current food situation. But I'm also concerned over his delivery of the message to Lisa. It sounds so much like his father's irritation toward me at times I'm a bit shocked. Putting this correlation together makes my head start to hurt and a wave of nausea runs through me. I can't look at the tomatoes, or else I think I may just vomit right here across the coffee table. I swallow the lump forming in my throat and walk to the kitchen for fresh air and a glass of water.

"Lisa, how was your day, dear? And David, did you make new friends in your class today?"

Lisa replies first with a question. "Mom, is your arm okay? It looks bruised and is different colored in spots..."

David interjects with, "Lisa, lay off of Mom today. She has a lot going on, can you just answer her question about school? Gosh... She doesn't need to be interrogated by you."

"David, honey, thank you for recognizing I'm busy lately, but I'm always here for you kids, you know that, dear." I flash a reassuring smile toward him while he reciprocates a half-smile back at me.

"I'm just fine, Lisa. Thank you for being so caring about your mother. Let's look at your books and what we have to get working on before I start to fix up some dinner, huh?"

I come back into the living room, but it takes everything in me to not look at those tomatoes. What is it with those? I love tomatoes, maybe it's the fact that I had to throw some out that had rotted so it makes my stomach churn.

Lisa and David get their books out for their homework for the evening, and I help point them in the right direction—Lisa with arithmetic and David with social studies.

I make my way back to the kitchen to try to come up with something creative to make for dinner. Of course, not because I want to be extra thought-provoked but rather because I have to be based upon what we have in the house.

I decide I'll make a pasta dish with canned shredded chicken with leftover vegetables sautéed to be put on top. I add a little garlic and butter to the sautéed vegetables, and the flavor comes together nicely, luckily. This doesn't always happen since I'm cooking with whatever scraps I can salvage in the house.

When Johnny arrives home, he smells the aroma of the dinner I've prepared and seems pleased, which immediately puts me at ease, and my shoulders release the tension that was pent up between them, waiting to gauge his mood this evening.

He makes his way to the counter, where he places his work cooler and sets it beside my purse. He bumps my purse, which ruffles some things around. As I rush over to grab my purse to relocate it, he has already spotted the card that fell off the top of my purse—the business card from Mrs. Dockinson, owner of Meats and Beets. Seeing him hold it in his hand makes me stiff with anxiety, as if I have just gone rigor mortis.

Why did I not put that somewhere else once I got home? I've been so absent-minded lately!

I quickly explain, "Oh, I can take that. It's just another random business card."

"Is it random though, Sandra?" he questions, accusing me with his stern no-break-in eye contact look.

Oh no, he's questioning the randomness, and he used my full name. This can't elicit a good outcome. What can I possibly do to turn this around?

Honesty.

My mother always said that honesty was the best policy.

"No, it's not random, you're right, Johnny. I've mentioned to you before that I want to get a job to support our family so we can have a better quality of life. I thought I could work a few hours during the week while the kids are at school."

"Were you going to tell me about it before I found this card, Sandra?

"Of course, I planned to tell you this evening," I tell him with a small smile.

"Okay. I believe you, darlin'. But you know that I make enough money to support this family without you being out in the workforce. We don't need the both of us out working. But I'll give it some thought... for you." With a half-hearted smile, he swoops in for a peck of a kiss.

Then, with that, the anxiety is relieved again, and I attempt to spike up the mood even further with a mention of getting groceries tomorrow and needing money.

"Johnny honey." That's something I haven't referenced him as, the 'honey' part, in probably months, if not years. "I need to get groceries tomorrow. Do you have some extra money to spare for me to get them, please?"

Sensing some hesitation from him in wanting to give up some money, I add in some extra pleading commentary. "I can make your favorite dishes, chicken pot pie and beef stroganoff?"

He tenses and his jaw clenches at the same time his fists do.

"Sandra, I don't have much extra money, you know that. You always ask for money at the most inopportune times, woman."

He reaches into the front pouch of his work cooler, where he keeps his extra change from the week and tosses out a few coins.

He moves his gaze up at me slowly as he explains unapologetically, "This is all I can spare for now, Sandy. Surely you can make do with it until I get paid again next week."

THE END IS THE BEGINNING   69

I can see him search his cooler as if he's looking for more money to give to me, but he doesn't think I notice when he stuffs a five-dollar bill deeper into it. He is such a prick, prioritizing his selfish drinking addiction over his family being fed and his children's needs being met.

Oh no, here it comes again. I am weak at the knees, and my stomach churns. I look around, but I don't see any tomatoes nearby to have made me feel this way. Why is my head starting to pound? Is it stress-induced nausea and weakness? I reach to the countertop to grab a hold of it until this wave passes.

I turn around and gingerly seat myself at the table with the kids while Johnny continues to get unpacked from returning home from work. I begin eating feverishly in hopes of making my nausea and fatigue go away so I can straighten up.

We finish dinner, and all the while, I'm contemplating what I can possibly buy to get us through a few more meals with less than $5. I could buy 2-3 pounds of chuck-roast meat, one loaf of bread, and perhaps one vegetable, but that would be all I could afford with tax included, and I'd have to make it last two days.

The mere thought of having to scrimp with food for our family over the next few days makes my blood pressure rise. I can feel the sensation of my vessels tightening around the blood pulsing through my veins as my headache pounds stronger.

Johnny reaches a hand over to mine once dinner is complete and gives it a small squeeze with a wink. I know the message he's trying to send and I know it has been a few weeks since *it* happened last.

Oh shit, how long has it been since we last had sex? Two weeks? Maybe three? Oh no, I don't even know for certain. It can't be...

What if my headaches, nausea, fatigue, and smell aversions are all signs of.... A pregnancy looming in my womb? How could I have possibly missed this? Why couldn't I have just turned him down that night?

In this moment, I am instantly brought back to that night. It feels wrong to be thinking of Johnny forcing himself upon me while at the dinner table with my children, but that is when it happened, well, if *it* even happened at all.

There is no way I could have turned him down that night unless I wanted to no longer have a life at all. But maybe that is what I should have done. Maybe not having a life at all would be better than the possibility of bringing a *new* life into this world in this incredibly dysfunctional and abusive family?

Should I even take a pregnancy test, or is ignorance my best option? I honestly don't even want to know.

As we head to bed for the night, I can't fall asleep with thoughts of having another child with this man I despise with whom I can't even get enough money out of for a week's worth of groceries for our family of four.

How will I ever be able to get away from him now? How will I be able to feed possibly three children instead of just two? I wish I would have left months or even years ago.

I'm filled with so many negative and overwhelming emotions tonight.

As the tears begin to stream down my cheek onto my

pillow, I pray to God that He will help me through this. If He gave me this miraculous child, if I am even pregnant, that is, He'll help me get out of this mess of a life I've created, right?

I can only hope and pray for that to be true.

CHAPTER 11

Lisa

July 1975 Age: 14

I run in the front door of the house feeling eager to be back home and out of the Clark's house after that exhausting night but coming in the front door, I am overcome with equal parts awe and outrage.

There are probably about 20 beer cans scattered throughout the kitchen and living room, mixed with half-empty glasses of wine and small plates with leftover food scattered on the floor and tables. The ashtrays are over-flowing with ashes and half-smoked cigarette butts. The smell of this house is taking everything in me to not puke and add to the complete disarray of this room.

As I walk farther into the house and turn my attention to the living room, I'm met with a sight I have never seen, and something tells me I'll never forget.

There is blood splattered and dried on the two throw

pillows which are no longer on the couch but instead on the floor. Mom is lying on the couch with blood dried on her lips, and her right eye is black and blue—completely swollen shut.

She did not look like this last night when I was here. She did have a bit of a swollen eye at that time but this, this is much worse. She had to have been hit again later in the night.

I rush over to her and gently touch her arm. She doesn't move or flinch.

Oh My God. Is she dead?

What should I do? Do I touch her and try waking her or moving her? Should I call 911?

Damnit, I can't even ask her about what the hell that shit was last night if she can't even move. Damn it!

Where is my dad and David? Why am I the only one here dealing with this mess of a situation?

I start to sweat, my heart is racing as I grab her shoulder and start to shake her.

"Mom, Mom! Wake up, Mom!"

There is yet no movement. I am shouting her name and yelling for help so loudly that anyone within a mile radius of this house should be able to hear me. I remember I learned in health class that you can place your fingers to find a pulse on someone, so I place my hand on her neck to the right of her throat and press down firmly.

I think there is a pulse, or is it the fact that I'm shaking so much that I'm feeling my own movement?

I can't even tell. Shit! Why did I even care about

asking her about what happened last night when I can't even make out if she is alive or dead—how self-centered of me! Who cares what it was, if Mom got to have a bit of fun for *once* in her life, then good for her. I just hope she's alive.

Maybe she is just knocked unconscious. She couldn't be dead, there's no way that she could be.

My mom is so strong. She has been through so many fights and she always makes it out. Should I have stayed here last night instead of going back for the kids? If I did, maybe none of this would have escalated to the point that it apparently did. I had intended to ask Mom what the hell that all was last night but perhaps I'll never get the chance to...

Oh my GOD.

I decide I'll go to the kitchen and get a cold wash-cloth to place on her head and try shaking her even harder this time. I don't remember all the details from health class but this feels like the right thing to do. I'll place this cold water-covered washcloth on her head and shake her shoulders really hard this time. Surely she'll respond.

I run to the kitchen as fast as I can and I place it on her head and shake her shoulders with all my might. I grab her face forcefully, having my hands on both sides of her cheeks and shake her head while screaming through tears.

"Mom, wake up! You have to be in there. Wake up! Wake up! Wake up! Mom!"

As I look closely at her eyes, her left eye begins to crack open ever so slightly. Oh My God, she's in there! I begin to shake her more, but now more gently, as I realize she's alive.

Thank God, she's alive!

I reach for her arm, which is dangling off the couch, to find a pulse near her wrist. Maybe I'll have better luck than I did at the neck. As I place my pointer and middle finger over her wrist I feel the daintiest of pulsation.

God, I'm so thankful she's alive.

I start to shout for my dad and David to no avail. Where the hell ARE they?

This is my greatest moment of need—this house is trashed, my mother is nearly dead, and I'm left here alone to deal with this?

I need to be getting ready for school. But maybe I won't actually be going today. Who cares, forget it. I've got too much going on today to make it. I should have just allowed Marianne to call me in like she wanted to.

Wait a minute, Marianne said she spoke to my mom before she came home this morning, and my mom supposedly gave her permission to call me into school today. If that is true, this beating has JUST happened.

Where are David and Dad? Is Dad hurting David somewhere? Or did David get involved and try to protect Mom, and this is what happened to Mom and now David is in danger for stepping in?

Oh my God, what is happening?

I run to the kitchen to grab the phone hung on the wall to dial 911 for Mom. Clearly, she is in need of emergent help.

As the dispatcher picks up the line saying in a calm and methodical voice, "911, what is your emergency?" I hear the screen door start to open with its same old creaking sound and followed by footsteps, one... then another... and another.

Next, I hear a 'click-click' sound.

What is that? Is someone here with a... gun? The lump in my throat is growing larger and I don't know how much more I can handle.

CHAPTER 12
Sandy

June 1975 Age: 35

I begin to drift off to sleep through my tears, but I've prayed to God, and that's all I can do. He will guide me upon the path that is best for me and my children. I trust that and know it to be true, I just can't see how I will make my escape... alive.

Just as I'm in that last awake drowsy stage before falling asleep, I notice a hand on my arm. Oh no, not this again...I try to pretend I'm actually asleep but he starts to shake me to try to awaken me. I hear his raspy voice whisper to the back of my hair.

"San, are you up? It's been a while since I've had my way with you, can you do your thing for me tonight, darling?"

Well, at least he wasn't being a complete jerk, and he's not in a drunken stupor tonight like last time.

Then it dawns on me, if I do decide to take a pregnancy test and if by some odd chance of God, I am pregnant, my body is going to undergo all of the changes it does in pregnancy, and I may truly be unable to have sex, or I will probably be sick like I have been in the past which would also make me not able to do it much.

Maybe my best option is to do it tonight but this time, change my mentality and emotions around it. Maybe I'll actually try to get into it.

"I'm here, Johnny," I reply in a quiet and hesitant whisper.

He pulls me closer to him, and I start undressing him in a way I haven't felt myself do in years—many, many years. Am I feeling more open to this tonight because he's actually not drunk? A slight amount of guilt washes over me as I contemplate the fact that I want to leave him.

Is he really all that bad? Why am I going down this path of mental agony? I need to focus on this moment, not what I've been working on leading up to this.

We start kissing slowly and softly, and I actually start to become aroused. Oh my God. I haven't felt sexually turned on by this man in so long.

Why do I feel this way this time? Is it a hormonal shift, or am I actually feeling this way all on my own?

This isn't just having sex, this is making love. I haven't felt this connection with him probably since the night I had sex with him when we conceived David.

What is happening right now? Is this him, or is it me? Because I'm actually trying to find enjoyment and connection in this experience tonight? I'm shocked by my own reaction, and I'm going to enjoy this. I'm going to make this about me just as much as it is about him...

Typically, in drunken Johnny sex fashion, he'd want me to be on top and doing all of the maneuvering and work, but this time, I am on the bottom, and he has his arm around the middle of my back wrapped around to my waist to steady himself. It feels so good to be held by him, so close and wanted and needed.

I can practically smell the desire emanating off of him like it is a true pheromone scent in the air. What is really different this time, though, is that he actually took his time and put *my* wants ahead of his own.

There isn't any rushing or sense of urgency about it but rather, his approach is so calm and gentle. I am actually able to become aroused for a change and enjoy the sensations—the soft teasing kisses, the sweet building, and then the release of my climax just before his. It truly feels heavenly to me.

Immediately after our rendezvous, I catch myself... What the hell? How was I just crying moments ago over a man who has been so awful to me, and now I'm feeling angelic from the best orgasm I've had in nearly a decade with that SAME man?

Afterward, I rush to the bathroom to take a quick shower but more than anything, I really need to pee.

Why do I feel that sensation so often? I peed just before I got into the bed, and I haven't had anything to drink in that half-hour time frame.

Oh God, it's probably another early pregnancy sign. Or it could be that I drank extra water this afternoon, and it took longer to digest. But as much as I don't want to admit it to myself, I did experience an increased urgency to pee with both pregnancies with the kids very early on.

Maybe I should take a test tomorrow when the kids are off to school.

But do I really want to know? What will I do? Who will I tell?

I have so many emotions, and after tonight's love-making session—a reignited flame seems to have been lit. But, there is also a nagging bit of worry that I'm letting my guard down when I shouldn't be, although I'm feeling the most optimistic I've been in years with Johnny.

It's making me rethink everything I've been working on lately. Is the problem between us...me? Or has the strife between us been exacerbated *because* of me?

I walk myself back to the bed, and I actually notice a sense of ease tonight in the same room as Johnny. There is a sort of peace that has come over me for this evening— for this moment in time.

I'm surprised because typically, when he comes into the room, just his mere presence makes me have a sense of heightened anxiety. I am not going to completely let my guard down because I've seen how quickly he can turn —he can be like Jekyll and Hyde.

But for tonight and maybe even tomorrow, I'm going to look at the bright side and enjoy this time.

CHAPTER 13
Lisa

July 1975 Age: 14

I turn to face the front door but proceed to listen to the phone line I've got with the 911 dispatcher as the anxiety rolls through me like a wave. I know that because I have them on the line, they cannot hang up, so even if something happens to me or my mom, they'll be coming for us, which is, strangely enough, comforting.

I start to speak and cut the dispatcher off before she can finish asking, "What's your emergency?"

In a fast and staccato tone of voice, I tell her, "My name is Lisa... My mother is badly injured, she needs immediate help. She has a very faint pulse and seems to be unconscious with a swollen eye. Someone is also here at my house with what I think is a... gun. Please send help. Please!" I speak with each word becoming faster yet quieter, not wanting to let the intruder know that I'm suspecting their gun.

I hear more footsteps, but they are slowing as if whoever it is, is listening to me before they decide what their next action will be.

Who is this that is here? Is it my dad coming back to finish the job with my mother, or is it someone else coming to sweep in and rescue us all?

I wish I could run around the corner and see who it is, but at the same time, I want to run and hide because if my senses are correct that it is a gun that this mystery person has, we could all be in serious imminent danger.

I hold my breath in waiting to see who it is. When will they come around the corner? I hear the dispatcher respond to me with such calmness.

"Lisa, I've got a crew on the way to you. Rest assured, you and your mother will be safe very soon. Please stay on the line, I will direct you as I can until the crews arrive. Are you able to check the consciousness of your mother again to tell me her status? Have you confirmed if there is anyone else in the house with you?"

I'm afraid to answer her in fear that the more words I speak will cause this intruder to reveal themselves to me in a not-so-good sort of way. I try to deliberately breathe into the phone speaker so that she can hear me and know that I'm still here.

I'm secretly hoping my breathing is telling her I'm afraid, very afraid right now.

I try to tippy-toe softly as I step forward to look around the corner and see if there is someone still there, but the phone cord won't give me enough leash. I begin to hear the shuffling of footsteps.

Oh my God, who is it? Won't they come around the corner already? This terrifying suspense is killing me. I can hardly slow my breathing to make it quiet anymore.

Finally, the toe of a boot begins to round the corner from the entryway, and as I squint, I think I can make out an idea of whose shoe it is.

It looks a lot like my brother, David's boots that he wore last night when he went out to Ron's while Mom and Dad had the party for Mr. Clark's birthday. I want to yell at David to make him step around the corner and reveal himself, but I'm still too scared. What if it's not actually him, and whoever it is, pulls the gun out on me before the emergency responders arrive?

"Da da da David... Is it you? It's just me and Mom home. I don't know where Dad is. Are you here to help us? Please don't do something you'll regret," I whisper through my plea.

I went with my gut on recognizing his boot, but doubt is creeping in, awaiting hearing a response. Even though I hope that it is him, fear courses through me at the thought of what he is capable of doing if his mind isn't in the right place.

I don't hear a response from the intruder as I stand as still as I've ever stood in this kitchen, still holding the phone to my ear on the call with the 911 dispatcher. I'm grateful that this dispatcher hasn't tried asking me more questions. It's as if she knows the fear has me paralyzed and unable to reassess my mother to address her questions.

I see the boot of his shoe move a bit more, as if he is contemplating whether to flee the premises or make his identity known. He takes a full step out from the entryway, and as I identify the pant leg fully, I can tell it is, in fact, David.

Instantly, relief washes over me. It is definitely my brother that is rounding this corner, but whatever more has happened in this household before my arrival, I worry it may have sent him over the edge.

CHAPTER 14

Sandy

June 1975 Age: 35

The next morning when I wake up, exhaustion makes it nearly impossible to open my eyes fully and see the sunlight creep in through the windows. It is the kind of exhaustion that comes from having very little sleep, but also, a sense of peace overcomes me. It's a very out-of-body experience for me to actually experience calmness in the presence of Johnny, even if he's sound asleep.

I rush to the kitchen to get breakfast started for the kids and get their sack lunches packed.

An hour later, Johnny awakens, and he and the kids rush around the corner. "Mom! What's for breakfast today?" I'm so hungry, I really hope you made us pancakes or toast!" Lisa yells as she grabs her sack lunch and gets her backpack to catch the bus in a few minutes.

"Yes, honey, I did, and there are a few slices of apples

and strawberries on top of your lunch sacks you can take with you to eat on the bus if you don't have enough time this morning."

No matter how early I wake these rascals, it seems they're always running late.

Johnny flashes a genuine smile at me, one that sends the message of a deeper, intimate connection.

I haven't felt this in so long, I can't even recall when I last had the pleasure of feeling that from a man, especially my husband. How pitiful is that? I love that he's being so affectionate and treating me more nicely.

If only it would last, but I've got to take the good while I can and soak it in. I never know when he'll flip, and his wrath will be unleashed against my body like the sharp burn from a hot piece of coal—one moment, my skin is cool, the next, it is scalded and charred forever.

Once the kids are off to school and Johnny is off to work, I decide I'll call the doctor's office to get me in for a urine sample pregnancy test. It has been well over a month since my last cycle, I honestly can't even remember when I last had it, which probably isn't too good of a sign.

I can still remember when they came out with the urine tests to detect pregnancies. They didn't have them when I was pregnant with Lisa and David, so I'm glad they have the tests today. I'll have to call my general practitioner to consult him since I haven't seen a gynecologist since I had Lisa 14 years ago.

I walk to the kitchen and reach up to the cabinet to the right of the refrigerator in search of the telephone book. After thumbing through old papers and magazines, I finally stumble upon it.

I'm not sure how I didn't find it sooner, considering it has a bright yellow and black bookend. I open it up and flip the very thin almost transparent pages in search of Lemard Community Health Clinic.

Ah, there's his phone number—Dr. Cunningham. As I turn from the countertop to walk toward the phone and reach his office, I stop dead in my tracks. Full chills run down my back, traveling the length of my arms coursing fiercely to my feet.

I can't believe I'm calling my doctor when I have a 16 and 14-year-old to ask about getting a pregnancy test. What the hell is wrong with me? How did I get here?

The mere thought of having to start over with raising a baby basically alone, since Johnny won't be of much help, especially when the child is younger, is equally terrifying and depressing. The sleepless nights, addressing their constant need to eat, and calming their cries.

When raising Lisa and David, I always felt like the real connection didn't begin to form until they were about 4-6 months old when they can form facial expressions back to you and they're on a bit more of a consistent routine as far as eating and sleeping goes which makes it life-changing as a parent.

That connection only multiplies exponentially as they grow up, of course, but those first few months, while they're sweet to look at, that's about where it begins and ends.

If I am actually pregnant, how am I possibly going to

manage this alone with minimal income and an uninvolved and abusive husband?

I dial the number, and as the phone rings, the unsettled anxiety in my stomach creeps upward, and I worry I might actually puke before anyone picks up on the other end. As the receptionist answers, I explain to her my request.

She explains that the earliest availability for a urine pregnancy test isn't until next week, but for me, that is fine. I tell her that I'll take that appointment for now. As I hang up the phone back onto the receiver on the wall, my heart racing through my chest and my stomach churning with anxiety from what I think is early pregnancy nausea, the phone immediately rings. Who in the world would be calling me on a Tuesday morning at 9 am?

"Hello?" I answer hesitantly.

"Yes, may I speak with Mrs. Sandra Hansen, please?" a polite woman requests.

"Hi, yes, this is her. What can I do for you?" I reply.

"This is Mary Dockinson, the owner of Meats and Beets, and I was checking to see if you were still interested in employment in our store, dear. I haven't seen or heard from you in a few days and wanted to follow up with you and see if I could have you back in our store to get you started on some training if you're still interested?"

Mary Dockinson, the owner of Meats and Beets, is actually calling *me* to discuss options for me to work there? I'm surprised that *she* is following up with *me*. This is crazy, right?

Isn't it usually the inquiring and optimistic potential staff member who does the footwork to obtain and secure the job? Is this a good thing because she really wants to hire me, or rather, is it because they're short-staffed and in need of a warm body?

Or even worse, the thought crosses my mind— perhaps she's concerned and feeling sorry for me from our first encounter at her store with creepy Mr. Clark.

"Ah yes, Mrs. Dockinson. Thank you so much for calling me to follow up. I am definitely still interested in the position. I'd love to come by and talk about more details. When are you available?" I cheerfully respond.

"Well, today, dear. We're open and there's plenty to do if you are available. Just come down when it works for you and I'd be happy to go through some initial paperwork to get the process started," she extends her invitation to me with a welcoming tone.

Well this is such a shock.

"Uh, okay, thank you, Mrs Dockinson. I'll come down later this afternoon. Thank you very much."

As I hang up the phone, I think, this is so unreal. I'm so thankful for her calling and offering me the job, but it is so odd that she called me, right? I can't believe that I will actually be a working mother.

However, with this nagging feeling that I am pregnant, how will I do this with three children, one being very small? I no sooner finish that thought when the phone rings again.

What is this place? An operating control center for directing calls?

"Hello?" I answer the phone with an annoyed short voice.

"Hello, yes, is this Mrs. Hansen? This is Lemard

Community Health calling you back from our conversation earlier. We have an earlier opening today due to a cancellation if you would like to come in for your urine pregnancy test?"

"Yes, this is her. Uh... what time?"

I really am uncomfortable with her offering me to come in today. Why does everything always have to happen on the same day?

I get offered a job and could also potentially find out if I am pregnant on the same day? I was liking the idea of waiting a week or so to find out and also to see if my symptoms that I've been having subside. Hopefully, they will, and it's just a fluke. But now that I called them this morning, I feel like a burden, so I have to go today for the opening, right?

"We have an opening today at 1 pm if you can make it?"

"Yes, I can make it at 1. Thank you for calling and offering me an earlier appointment," I reply quickly.

As I hang up the phone, I am left feeling torn with so many emotions—emotions that are in complete opposition to one another. The largest of these is feeling overwhelmed by the potential for so many new experiences beginning today.

It is exciting but also... terrifying. I am so rushed trying to make it to all of the commitments before my children get home from school.

I rush out the door and head to Lemard Community Health Clinic. I recite a prayer that the Lord's will be done but hopefully His will is for me to NOT be pregnant.

CHAPTER 15
Lisa

July 1975 Age: 14

"David! Come out here and let's talk," I demand in a stern yet gentle tone, not wanting to upset him any further. There is a long bout of silence, and my hands begin to tremble.

Am I wrong in my intuition that it is him around this corner? Who else could it be? I know that it is not my father. Those aren't his boots, and the color doesn't even match his.

David finally takes a firm step around the corner as he faces me with blood streaming down his face between his eyes from his head. He also has a cut open lip and his eyes appear varying colors of black and blue, like he has been very recently beaten up.

He is standing in the entryway with the same clothes he wore last night when he left to go to Ron's, and I went to the Clark's to babysit. He has one hand behind his back as if he is trying to hide something.

"David, what has happened to you? Come in here so I can help you. I've called an ambulance for Mom, they'll be here any minute. I can't get her to wake up."

"You called the authorities? Why would you do that, you know that they come here too often as it is. You're such a fucking idiot, Lisa," he responds abruptly, sounding annoyed with me.

"I called 911, David. Not the police, although the 911 dispatcher said they'll tell them too. Mom is hurt very badly and seems to be unconscious and unresponsive. The 911 dispatcher asked me to check her status and pulse, and from what I can tell, due to my inexperience, she has a very weak pulse. What other options did I have? You weren't in here to help nor was the villain and master of all of our tragedies, our father," I retort back snarkily.

How dare he question my judgment on calling an ambulance for our mother. She does everything for us and deserves none of her beatings, it's the least I could do to take care of her in her most dire moment. However, after what I saw last night, I am utterly confused about the true dynamic of my mother and my father's relationship and to what lengths my mother will go. No one should ever be physically abused like she is.

"God damn you, Lisa," he scolds as he wipes his forehead pushing his strawberry blond hair out of his face. "Shit, we've gotta do something really quick. Put that phone down and get out here."

What is wrong with him? He is behaving like he's strung out on too much caffeine and is about to crash into a well-needed 24-hour-long hibernating sleep. His swearing is something he's never done, at least not around me. It is making me very uncomfortable to be around. I've only ever heard Dad swear from time to time, and that is bad enough.

"What the hell is wrong with you, David? What could you possibly need to do right now besides help save our mother and make sure she is okay?" I bark at him with a furrowed brow and anger spewing through every word.

"Lisa, enough with the questions and resistance, damn it. We need to get outside and take care of something. Set the phone down on the floor and get outside with me... NOW," he demands, yelling across the room, still holding his hand behind his back.

I do as he has commanded for fear that if I don't, something bad could potentially happen to me next. After all, I don't see my dad around anywhere. God only knows what has really gone on here. As awkward as it was at the Clarks, maybe staying there would have been better than coming home.

As we're walking out the screen door of the house, we can hear the siren of the ambulance coming from just down the road. David begins to run to the sideyard, and I follow suit, not knowing where we're going. We take a few short steps, and then I notice Dad is lying in the grass, black and blue covering his swollen face.

"Dad and I got into a bad fight when I came home this morning to find him beating Mom to death. I tried to protect Mom and stepped in, and Dad pulled his gun on me and threatened to kill me if I got in his way. I got in his face, and we ended up taking our fight outside. As he was chasing me off the porch onto the front yard, I clothes-lined him and got him on the ground so hard it knocked the wind out of him. Then...I beat him. I fucking beat his ass as hard as I could, throwing punches all over his face and chest. The bastard deserved every single punch I threw at him, but now I don't know if he's alive or not. After he no longer tried to fight back, I was able to grab his gun to protect you and me."

"David... What the hell? What are we doing out here?" I ask naively.

"We need to figure out what we're going to do with him. If he is alive or not and whether or not to have the ambulance take him."

We both walk up to him as he's lying on the grass in the side yard and stare down at him as we try to decide what we're going to do with him. Does he have a pulse?

Good thing their fight happened on the opposite side of the house from the Connors because surely Alice would have witnessed it and called the police long before I came home had it been in her line of sight.

The small amount of light coming from the sunrise is reflecting off of the wet dew-covered grass. It is still mostly dark outside, yet seeing the sunrise that is quickly coming—David and I have to do something to figure out this debacle we're in... and we've got to do it fast.

CHAPTER 16
Sandy

June 1975 Age: 35

I walk into Lemard Community Health Clinic and am feeling silly for going to the doctor's office for a pregnancy test. I am probably not even pregnant so am I just wasting everyone's time? How much will this test likely cost me? And then, if I am not pregnant... what will I tell Johnny as to why I got the test done without having a conversation with him before I came here?

He will tell me that I should have waited more time and discussed it with him first, I just know it. And then, depending on his mood and alcohol intake that day... ugh, that will determine his behavior toward me. I really wish I wasn't even here now.

I slowly push through the glass entryway door and make my way to the registration desk. The receptionist is a petite blonde with big blue eyes and a warm, welcoming smile, wearing light pink lipstick on her lips. I'm not sure why she's working here. She could be working anywhere else with her round, ocean-colored eyes that sink you in and her captivating perfect hourglass figure, that's for sure.

"Hello, I'm Sandra Hansen here for a urine pregnancy test. Someone just called and said there was an opening for me, last minute today?" Immediately I feel intimidated by her swoon-worthy looks.

"Ah, yes, hello, Mrs. Hansen. I'm Anna, and I am pleased to meet you. Here is the urine sample cup." She hands me a small brown paper bag where the cup must be inside, across the registration desk.

"Please follow the instructions and bring it back to me. The doctor will review the results and will call you within a few days, dear." She then takes her right hand pointer finger and points across the waiting room to where the restrooms are located. "Right across the way, Mrs. Hanson. We will be here waiting for you." She again speaks calmly and methodically through that beautiful smile of hers.

I'm not sure why, but I was thinking I would be brought back into an exam room and could have a discussion before having the test. Guess not... As I walk through the waiting room, I take a look around. There are at least five other people here. The guilt begins to build more inside of me, feeling as though I am taking up resources at this clinic that could be used on people that *actually* need care.

I walk into the restroom and open up the paper bag. Inside there is a medicine cup with a light blue lid and a small piece of paper that explains the instructions of how to collect a 'clean catch urine sample'. I still can't believe I'm even here doing this.

When I finish, I walk back to the lobby and hand my brown paper bag discreetly back to the receptionist, Anna. She smiles at me again and waves goodbye.

I don't know exactly why, but shouldn't there have been more of a conversation at this visit? Maybe about my symptoms of why I think I'm pregnant? But I don't question anything since I am embarrassed for being here in the first place, let alone by the model woman of a receptionist. I look like a pauper off of the street in my getup. I simply wave back to Anna and head out the glass door.

As I'm exiting the clinic, I notice the clock on the wall showing that it is 1:30 pm. Dang it, I really need to rush down to Meats and Beets to meet Mrs. Dockinson for the preliminary job information. When I told her I'd come down today, I wasn't planning on having to come to the clinic first, I better get over there before it's 2:00. This day has sure turned from ordinary to unordinary in record time, that's for sure.

What if I am pregnant, can I start a new job if I know I'm expecting? Do I have to tell my employer? Oh my gosh, I don't even know the basics of how to handle these sorts of things. How did I ever think I could take all of this on?

I walk in the front door of Meats and Beets and expect to see another worker at the front desk, but it is Mrs. Dockinson herself. Upon her eyes meeting mine, she smiles a large, soft smile and waves me right over to her and behind the front register. I walk over and I immediately start to tell her how grateful I am for this opportunity.

"Mrs. Dockinson, I wanted to tell you how thankful I am that you called and offered me this—" Before I could finish my sentence of gratitude she cuts me off interjecting.

"No time for chatting, dear. There is much work to do and a lot for you to learn, especially since you have to be home early to meet your children. I'm glad you're happy to be here, now let's get to it. Oh, and Sandy, you can call me Mary," she states with less excitement than I was hoping our first conversation would be. She sounds so matter-of-fact, not quite like she did on our call earlier.

I am completely zapped of any excited energy that I had walking in here today and instead am anxious for all there is to learn and a bit of a burden for needing to leave at an earlier time than what the other workers probably leave at, I assume.

Rather than responding with anything back to her, I give a small nod of my head and follow her. It feels so weird and almost disrespectful to refer to her by her first name. I'm trailing behind like a lost puppy as she turns to quickly walk to the back through a white saloon swinging door with a small window in the center of it for the workers to see through.

"Now, for starters, we are going to review the process from beginning to end of what we do here. This will show you what will be expected of you as you begin to work with us. That is why we are in the back now. All animals are brought in by their owners first, and the process begins. They drop them off from their trailer after they've had their last meal on their farm. They are kept here overnight until we slaughter them the next morning," she explains, pointing outside to a small corral where the pigs and cows are kept.

Next, we walk to a floor with a large drain in the middle, and it appears to be wet.

"In here is what we call the kill floor...for obvious reasons. This is where we bring the animals in, knock them out, kill them, and then they're hung to bleed out until we take them down and cut out the meat. You won't be doing any of this portion for a long time unless you really want to for some reason; however, it is important to know what goes on in here."

I nod and feel slightly nauseated by the thought of animals being slaughtered here and the smell of the room. It has a strange aroma, like a mixture of iron, which is probably blood, and a rotten smell that reminds me of roadkill.

My knees are starting to be weak, and I am willing myself to stay standing up straight.

Then it dawns on me, did I even eat any lunch today? Maybe my blood sugar is low, and that's why I'm not feeling very well. I don't want to say anything to Mary to make her think I'm unfit for the job, though. What could be worse?

It is my first few minutes of a new job, and I can't even handle the smell of the kill floor when I've raised two children and handled their poop-filled diapers and vomit on me, yet this is what gets me? She probably would tell me, "Here's the door," and then I would have successfully set the record for holding the shortest-term job ever.

I've got to find a way to make it through this. I need this job more than anything to start stashing away some money to make the getaway with my kids that I know I need to do. I am strong, I can do this.

As I follow Mary through the white saloon-style swing-through door, I take in a deep breath while tucking my nose inside the opening of my crew neck top to try to catch a whiff that's not of this nauseating kill room in hopes of feeling a bit more refreshed and less woozy so I can focus on what there is to learn instead of how I feel.

CHAPTER 17
Lisa

July 1975 Age: 14

The police arrive with the ambulance just behind it, and the EMTs jump out and rush to the front yard when they see us and ask where our mom is. I wave them over as they follow me, and we run inside.

While sprinting, I hear one of them shouting up toward us, "Son, do you need any lookin' over? You look like you've seen better days."

As we open the creaking porch door, David hollers, "No, I'll be alright. Just please take care of our mother. She is in great need."

I see them try to assess her just as I have done but I don't see her responding much at all.

A slight bit of relief sweeps through me when I hear them announce, "We have a weak radial pulse on the right wrist coming in at 35 bpm. We are going to need oxygen for her as we are en route to the hospital. From the looks of these injuries, we won't want to give her anything more until she has been fully worked up. We want to make sure to prevent further damage internally."

Although I don't know much of what they're talking about, I'm glad to know that she's alive and in good hands now. I want to ask if I can ride along, but I'm afraid that they'll tell me that I'm not allowed. I also think that we need to have them assess Dad, but I'm scared to ask them to in case David doesn't want me to since he practically came unglued when I told him that I called 911.

We both stand there on the front porch as we watch them load the stretcher into the back of the ambulance. A police officer spots us and takes the opportunity to approach us. He is about 6 feet tall and, strangely enough, resembles our dad.

"You kids care to share some details of the happenings of this morning's incident with your Lemard Police Officer, Danny?" He tips his hat as if to say, "Top of the mornin' to ya."

I thought I was already standing as still as could be, but I now seem to be paralyzed and don't know what to say, so instead, I slowly look over to David.

I remember Mom told us years ago that Dad had some cop buddies in town, and if we were ever asked if we wanted to file a report, to always say no, no matter how bad it was. She was so fearful of the potential for retaliation should Johnny find out.

David shakes his head. "Not at this time, thank you, Officer."

Officer Danny nods his head, places the cap back on

THE END IS THE BEGINNING   103

his pen and sticks it behind his ear while he swivels on the heel of his boot to make his way off of the porch.

I look over at David, but he doesn't look back at me. He's standing there, staring with a blank expression as they put the oxygen mask over Mom's face. Out of all the fights that we have witnessed between Mom and Dad, there's never been one where either of them have had to go to the hospital. For some reason, I get the feeling that this moment will be one of those that I will never forget.

I wait for as long as I can before they are about to drive off in the ambulance when I run up to the passenger side door of the ambulance and wave my hand to get the EMT's attention. She rolls down her window with an annoyed look on her face as if I am holding them up, which I probably am.

"Sorry to bother you, but I think my father is injured as well. Can one of you look at him or send another ambulance for him, please?"

She looks at me initially with shock, and then her expression changes to empathy. It's as if she can read right through my soul, seeing all the fights that I have witnessed between my parents and the toll it has taken on me, knowing this isn't the first. It seems that she's looking at me and thinking how much older I am on the inside compared to how I look on the outside because of my life experiences. All within this moment, her demeanor completely shifts as she responds to me.

"Yes, absolutely. I'm so sorry you're going through this. Where is your father? We will assess him, and I'll have Brian here call for another ambulance for him," she responds as she motions her left arm toward the man in the driver's seat. "My name is Sheila, by the way."

I nod my head in understanding as I turn away from the ambulance and walk toward the side yard of where he is as my eyes start to well up with tears. She follows close behind me, not speaking a word as we listen to our boots squeak with each step we take on the dew-covered grass.

We arrive at where he was—lying in the grass with arms spread away from his sides. He appears unmoved from when I last saw him. I stand there staring blankly down at him while she crouches down to assess him for what I think is a pulse at the neck.

After a brief moment of her fingers on his neck, she shouts, "We're going to need another ambulance en route here ASAP, Brian. Do we have an extra oxygen tank you can bring over to me? He's got labored breathing and faint pulses."

Brian nods as he exits the ambulance after grabbing a few things and walking hurriedly over to us. He leans over quickly and passes the requested items to Sheila. They begin muttering softly to one another, and for a moment, I wonder what it is they are saying, but I know that even if I could fully hear them. I wouldn't understand the medical lingo. It crosses my mind that maybe what they are speaking about isn't good, but all I can do is know that both he and my mom are getting the help they need.

I look around and realize that I don't know where David went. Last I knew, he was standing next to me. I begin to walk back toward the house, thinking maybe he went back inside, but as I glance up at the porch and through the front door, I don't see him in the kitchen area.

A flood of panic rushes through me, and the pounding of my heart starts to quicken with every beat that comes through my chest. What if he's feeling guilty for having the fight with Dad and he ran away? He did have a gun on him. What else might he be doing?

I turn to the ambulance to check on Mom. Since both of the EMTs are with Dad, I want to make sure she's doing okay. As I round the corner on the back of the ambulance, I see my mom on the stretcher. She is hooked up to a machine, and I can hear beeping probably every few seconds, which I'm assuming is probably her heartbeat.

Sitting next to her is David. He is holding her hand and weeping over her, whispering something in her left ear as his arm is wrapped around her, holding her right shoulder.

This site completely destroys me as I stand there and silently watch as the tears stream down my cheeks.

CHAPTER 18
Lisa

July 1975 Age: 14

I stand frozen for a moment, not sure what to do. It's as if I'm watching a movie, and everything is happening in slow motion. David's crying while leaning over Mom in the ambulance intensifies, and he looks up at me with bloodshot eyes.

It is hard to discern his expression, but I can tell that he's hurting.

I can't help but feel a twinge of perplexed confusion as I watch David and my mom share this moment. I've never seen him like this before—vulnerable and emotional. I've always known him as the tough and stoic older brother who never showed his emotions. It's strange to see him cry like this, but it's also comforting to see that he cares so deeply for our mom.

His head is bowed, and his body is shaking with sobs.

THE END IS THE BEGINNING   107

It's as if he's completely broken. This isn't the same David I saw earlier, who was so full of anger and aggression.

My heart is breaking for him as I walk up to the side of the ambulance and tap on the window to get his attention. He looks up at me with puffy red eyes and runs his hand across his face to wipe away the tears. I can see the pain and guilt in his eyes.

"Are you okay?" I ask him, not really knowing what else to ask.

He shakes his head slowly and looks back down at our mom. "I don't know, Lisa... I don't know."

I want to offer him some words to comfort him, but they won't come out. Instead, I reach out and place my hand on his shoulder, offering him some form of support. He leans into my touch, and it is then that I notice him shaking with emotion.

We stay like that for what feels like an eternity, just standing in silence, watching over our mom.

He looks up at me with red, puffy eyes. "I'm sorry," he whispers to me.

"For what?" I ask, confused.

"For everything. For the fight with Dad. For not being there for you and Mom. For not being a good brother," he whispers, his voice breaking with emotion.

I reach out and take his hand, giving it a squeeze. "You're a great brother," I tell him. "And none of this is your fault."

He nods, but I can see the guilt still etched on his face.

"Hey, can I talk to Mom for a minute?" I ask him wanting to give him the break that he needs.

I walk around to the other side of the stretcher and take my mother's hand in mine.

It feels cold and lifeless, and I can't help but feel a sense of dread wash over me. I close my eyes and try to push away the negative thoughts, focusing instead on the sound of her heartbeat and the beeping of the machine.

David stands there for a moment, watching us before finally turning away and walking toward the house. I don't know what he's thinking, but I know he's hurting just as much as I am.

As I sit there, holding my mother's hand, I can't help but think about all the times she's been there for me. The times she hugged me when I was sad over something someone said to me at school or cooked my favorite meal when I was feeling sad as a source of comfort when we probably could barely afford it in the first place, but she did it just to make sure I felt loved that day by her. I can't imagine my life without her, and the thought of losing her is too much to bear.

The sound of sirens in the distance snaps me out of my thoughts, and I look up to see another ambulance pulling up in front of the house. The EMTs rush to begin tending to our dad, and I can hear them talking about his status.

Eventually, David walks back to me, and as he's approaching the ambulance, I see him wiping his eyes.

"I'm going to go check on Dad." His voice is hoarse. "You stay here with Mom."

I nod, not trusting myself to speak and watch as he walks away toward our dad. It's only then that I notice the gun lying on the ground a few feet away from where

THE END IS THE BEGINNING   109

he had been sitting with Mom. It's a small handgun, but it looks deadly in the grass.

My heart starts to race again as I realize just how close we came to losing both of our parents... the anchors to our family.

As I let out the breath that I didn't realize I had been holding, I turn my attention back to our mom. She looks so fragile lying there on the stretcher, hooked up to all these machines. A wave of guilt and responsibility takes over my mind from what happened.

Maybe if I had just intervened earlier or had come home sooner from the Clarks, things wouldn't have escalated to this point?

But then I remind myself that it's not my fault. It's not David's fault, either. Our father is the one who made the choices that led to this moment. We're just the lucky ones who are left to pick up the pieces.

As they load my father into the second ambulance, I turn to David, who is standing off to the side, watching everything with a blank expression.

"We should go to the hospital." My voice is barely above a whisper.

David nods, and we both climb into the back of the ambulance, sitting silently as we watch the world rush by outside the windows.

The world seems different somehow, as if everything has changed. We arrive at the hospital, and I watch as the medical staff rush to take care of my parents.

As the hours tick by, David and I sit in the waiting room, trying to process everything that's happened.

Eventually, after what feels like an entire week has passed, a doctor comes out to speak with us.

"Your mother is stable," he tells us, "but she's sustained some serious injuries. We'll need to keep her here for stabilization and observation, but she should make a full recovery. Your father, on the other hand, is in critical condition. We're doing everything we can for him, but it's touch and go right now."

I nod as the large lump forms in my throat.

I want to reach out and hug David, to tell him that it's going to be okay, but I can't find the words. Instead, I stand there awkwardly, watching as he wipes away his tears with the back of his hand.

David nods his head, but I can tell he's still struggling with his guilt. I reach my hand over to his and give it a squeeze reassuringly, trying to convey my support and love for him.

As we continue to hold each other's hands as we watch the doctor turn and leave the waiting room, a sense of closeness and connection forms between us. I know that if we lose our father, at least I'll have him.

CHAPTER 19
Sandy

July 1975 Age: 35

I wake up alone without Johnny next to me. It feels so good knowing he can't harm me, but more than anything, I'm safe right now, yet I am lonesome. I never thought I would miss his presence in any capacity.

I almost want to slap myself across the face or pinch my arm—anything to snap out of these irrational thoughts. I suffered a broken facial bone, a concussion, and several internal injuries. Jimmy's birthday party turned into a nightmare... a brutal attack that left me fighting for my life.

I don't remember much of that night due to the intense alcohol consumption and whatever else the Clarks brought over and offered to us all, but I do vaguely recall Lisa being there for some reason. I know I should bring it up to her and clear the air, she was never meant to see any of that scene—but I just can't bring myself to reminisce about the events that occurred that night if I don't have to. Perhaps if Lisa has questions, she'll just come to me with them, and if not, we can all just lay that damn night to rest.

As grateful as I am to have survived, I simply can't go back to that life. Living in fear, always looking over my shoulder, wondering when the next attack will come... That's not for me anymore, nor is it for my children.

After a few days in the hospital, where they performed many tests, including X-rays and labs, among others, I was discharged with strict instructions to rest and heal.

"Rest and heal." That sounded great to me. I'd love to lay around and relax, but unfortunately, that isn't something I can do while raising my kids and trying to make money for them and our future.

Despite Johnny being in a much worse condition than I am, I am happy to be alive and back home, where I can try to find our new normalcy.

Although my mom offered to take me and the kids in, I knew I needed to start fresh on my own.

Not to mention, my father wouldn't be thrilled at that. Even though I am disappointed in my father's lack of support and willingness to take me and the kids in should we need it, I am also thankful for it. It is my biggest motivation to prove to him I don't need their help as I navigate this time in my life.

I have to support my family without sacrificing my safety and well-being. I have to fight for my right to live without fear.

As I rise out of bed, the nausea hits me with each inch that I stand taller. I run to the bathroom, barely making it to the toilet bowl in time before stomach bile comes up and out. I know that I didn't eat anything out of the ordinary last night, and the fact that it's just bile coming up makes me realize that I am about 98% sure I am pregnant. Damn it. I guess I didn't even need to take that test at the doctor's office... my body is telling me loud and clear.

Maybe I should go look at the calendar and see if I can pin down the date that Johnny and I last had sex to have an idea of how far along I could be. The thought of having to recall that night causes me to wretch again, and this time, it is a forceful vomiting episode. Shit, I hate throwing up, especially when I know it only brings a very temporary feeling of relief. Afterward, I feel a bit refreshed and walk to the sink and splash water on my face to wake myself up.

I mosey to the kitchen, shuffling my feet along, and open the cupboard above the refrigerator in search of some saltines to settle my stomach for the morning. Surprisingly, I find a sleeve that has been opened, but as I take a bite of one, even though they are, without a doubt, stale, the cardboard taste with a little bit of salt seems to be soothing to my overwhelmingly watery mouth and dry throat.

As I turn around, Lisa is standing there, staring at me with a blank yet quizzical look.

When did she get in here? Has she been standing here this whole time, watching me move as slow as a snail?

Before I can address her, she questions me with her arms crossed at her chest, "Mom, are you okay? You don't look like you feel well, and I think I heard you throwing up?"

Well, shit. How am I going to explain this to her? She is really on it for it to be only 7:45 am on a Saturday morning. Since I haven't even gotten the doctor's confirmation, there is nothing for me to share, right? And if I *did* get the call from the doctor's office, I would first have to tell Johnny. But how would I even go about that? The thought of the whole situation begins to make me feel nauseous and overwhelmed.

"Thanks for your concern, dear. Maybe I ate something last night that didn't settle with my stomach. I'm sure I will be better as the day goes on. Do you want me to fix you some breakfast?" I ask while forcing myself to smile as the nausea creeps back in slowly as I swallow my saltine cracker and my stomach begins to let out a loud rumble.

I slowly walk toward the counter to get the pan out and make some scrambled eggs. As I crack the eggs into the pan, my mind can't help but wander back to my morning sickness episode and the looming pregnancy my body is trying to communicate to me.

How am I going to raise another child with Johnny, whom I am working my escape away from? The timing of this couldn't be worse. I take a deep breath as I try to focus on making breakfast for Lisa and David.

Suddenly, the phone rings, startling me out of my thoughts. I wipe my hands on my apron and rush to answer it.

"Hello?" I answer, still trying to catch my breath.

"Hi, is this Mrs. Hansen?" a female voice asks on the other end.

"Yes, this is her," I reply, my heart already pounding in my chest.

"It's about Johnny. I'm sorry to tell you that his condition has worsened. We're doing all we can to stabilize his vitals, but we're not sure he's going to make it," the nurse informs me.

My knees weaken and I grip the edge of the counter for support. "What do you mean? Is he going to be okay?" I plead, tears starting to form in my eyes.

"I'm sorry, Mrs. Hansen. We're doing everything we can. Please come to the hospital as soon as possible," the nurse tells me quickly before hanging up the phone.

I stand for a moment, feeling helpless and alone, paralyzed by thought. Johnny's life is in danger, and I don't know what to do. I'm torn between wanting a new life for me and the kids and never seeing him again after what he has done to me on one hand. But on the other, there is the deep pang of guilt for wanting to be away from someone who I know once loved me, and I think, hopefully, still does.

I know I need to visit Johnny, especially given the recent call, but I can't afford not to work. How will we make ends meet? How will we make our escape from this life?

I can't let Lisa and David see me like this, so I quickly compose myself and finish making breakfast. I serve Lisa and David their eggs and sit down with them at the table, working hard to pretend that everything is normal.

After breakfast, I get dressed for work at Meats and Beets. I'm still new to this job, and already, I'm dreading it. But I need to work to support my potentially growing family.

As I leave the house, I give Lisa and David a hug, promising them that everything will be okay.

The remorsefulness creeps into my mind heavily as I make my way to work and throughout the day, but I really need the money. I know that as a 'good wife', I should go see my husband, especially after that call, but what good will seeing him actually do? That nurse doesn't know our situation and how he has treated me.

If I went to see him, he might not even like that I'm there, and I'd leave feeling worse than I already feel without going.

Luckily, when I arrive at Meats and Beets, Mrs. Dockinson doesn't ask any questions. She allows me to work in the back of the store and to be seated to rest my body when I can. I love how she treats me and makes me feel welcome and at ease around her.

While working, I try to focus on my tasks, but my mind keeps drifting back to Johnny and the potential baby. I can't shake off this feeling of dread, and thoughts over what the future holds are all-consuming.

As the day drags on and I'm learning the ins and outs of the store, including how to stock the shelves, I'm relieved when it's finally time to go home.

But when I walk in the door, I'm met with chaos. David and Lisa are fighting about Johnny and who is at fault for his current state. I try to intervene by yelling at them to calm down, and I attempt to break up the fight, feeling exhausted and under-prepared.

Suddenly, the phone rings and we all jump in surprise. My heart races as I pick it up.

"Hello?" I answer nervously. "Hi, is this Mrs. Hansen? This is Dr. Cunningham," his deep voice asks on the other end.

"Yes," I reply, my hands shaking slightly.

"I have your results, and... you're pregnant," he informs me.

My eyes widen in shock as the tears stream down my face.

"What? Are you sure?" I ask, my voice trembling and cracking with the last word.

"Yes, Mrs. Hansen. The test confirms it," he announces without reservation.

I take a deep breath, trying to steady myself. I can't let my emotions get the best of me, not here, not now.

"Okay...Thank you." My voice sounds firm despite how I'm *actually* feeling.

After hanging up the phone, I turn to see Lisa and David looking at me with anticipation, waiting for me to tell them who was on the phone.

"It's okay. Everything's fine," I explain, trying to sound confident and make myself believe the words that are coming out of my mouth.

My mind begins to race as I try to make sense of everything, while the mixed and overwhelming emotions take over.

Who can I tell this to? Who can I share this news with? I don't know where to begin. All I know is that our lives are about to change forever, and I'm not sure if I'm ready for it.

The tears start streaming down my face, and I can't seem to stop them, so I rush to the bathroom to get ahold of myself. Even though I had every suspicion that I was pregnant, I still didn't want to *actually* believe it.

I take a deep breath and remind myself to take it one moment at a time. I can't change the past, but I really wish that I could.

I can't say that I am exactly happy to be pregnant, but I can say that it must truly be meant to be and God's plan for my life, considering the cruel beating I took from Johnny and the significant battle my body went through to survive it let alone grow another human. Of all of the things Johnny has taken from me in this life, I am thankful that he did not take this child from me.

Although, there is no way that I am prepared to raise a third child. Not under these conditions. Not to mention, will Johnny even make it out alive? How will I work and raise my children with a newborn in the house too?

The questions are a constant swirl in my mind as the anxiety takes over. I have no idea how I will do any of this, but somehow, some way, I will figure it out and hopefully become a mother of three.

CHAPTER 20
Sandy

July 1975 Age: 35

As I sit in my car, taking deep breaths as I prepare to start another shift at Meats and Beets, I can't help but be overwhelmed and scared about my future... all the unknowns. My husband has been in the hospital since the fight with David. He was only trying to protect me from Johnny, which now has left me alone to recover from my injuries and care for our two children. I know that I need to work to support us, but I honestly don't know how I am going to manage everything.

After a few moments and a lot of deep breaths, I finally muster up the courage to get out of the car and head in. As I walk in, I am greeted by a new and handsome customer, a man with ocean-blue eyes and jet-black hair combed to the side to perfection—not one hair out of place. When he smiles, he looks a bit like Frank Sinatra—

showcasing his pearly white and straight teeth, and when he speaks, his voice is low and calming.

"Hi there, new face! Good morning, darlin'," he announces with a smile.

"Hi, hello, good morning, sir," I reply, trying to mask my nerves and meet his level of cheeriness.

"My name is William, but you can call me Bill. May I ask your name?" He walks slowly with both hands in his pockets while appearing confident with his chest lifted as he follows behind me up to the counter while I'm nervously searching the top drawer of the desk for my apron.

I look up and my eyes meet his. "Hello, Bill. My name is Sandra, but you can call me Sandy. Is there something I can do for you, sir... uh, Bill? Sorry."

I try to offer a smile back toward him, but I honestly can hardly function in his presence. Why is he wanting to speak with me as he can obviously see I'm just getting in for the day? What is wrong with me for being so frazzled by him?

As I try to fasten my apron, reaching my arms behind my back and begin going about my work, this man, supposedly Bill, who is undoubtedly, probably the most attractive man I've ever laid eyes on in my entire life, seems to have nothing better to do than to linger around this store as if he is needing something from me.

Suddenly, the phone rings and my heart jumps to my throat. I answer it quickly, turning away from the storefront where Bill is standing and I can tell right away that it is my mom, her voice dripping with concern.

"Sweetheart, are you okay? I've been trying to reach

you all morning. I've called the house and figured I should try your new workplace next. I'm glad I could finally reach you."

"I'm just tired, Mom. Sorry, I haven't called you back. Working while trying to raise the kids and everything else that is going on... it's just really taking it out of me, I guess," I respond, trying to sound more upbeat than I feel.

"I'm sorry to hear that, honey. But I'm proud of you for working so hard to provide for your children. How are David and Lisa doing?" she asks.

"They're okay. It's just hard being away from them so much," I admit shortly, wanting to get off the phone as quickly as I can.

"I know, dear. But remember, you're doing this for them. And if you need any help, just let me know. I'm always here for you," she reassures me.

Her words bring tears to my eyes, and I realize how much I miss having someone to lean on. But then, as if fate intervened, I hear his voice behind me.

"Excuse me, miss. Could you help me find the beef tenderloin?" he asks.

I turn around to see him looking back at me with a warm smile leaning with one forearm resting on the countertop. My heart races as I abruptly hang up the phone and lead him to the meat case where all of the beef is located. Although I am perplexed as to why he couldn't have perused the store himself to locate what he is looking for and is insistent on asking for my assistance, I do feel slightly guilty that I haven't given him my full attention while he's been at the store thus far. If Mrs.

Dockinson saw me, I'm sure she wouldn't be pleased with my customer service skills right now.

"You're a really strong woman, you know that?" he mentions, his eyes meeting mine.

I blush, becoming quickly embarrassed but also, oddly enough, appreciated. His kind words make me feel alive again, but how does he know that I am 'strong'? Surely I don't look like I lift weights, for Pete's sake.

"Oh... thanks, uh... Bill," I reply, not feeling comfortable calling him by his first name. Honestly, I'm not comfortable in his presence, period—it's gotta be his captivatingly good looks and suave demeanor. He wastes no time in cutting right to the chase. He reaches right into the meat cooler, grabs the first beef tenderloin he sees and turns back to me once the door has closed, his hand still resting on the door handle.

"I can see that you're healing from some rather serious injuries, Sandy, but you should know that I don't take it lightly that you're doing so much for those around you," he comments without breaking eye contact or even blinking. Not even once.

Becoming increasingly uncomfortable by his comment and lingering in the store while I am unaware of how this man seems to know so much about my life when I've just met him is unsettling.

"What exactly are you referring to, Bill?" I ask sternly, looking back up at him, reflecting his consistent eye contact.

Why are his eyes so gorgeous? There is this strange pull, almost like electricity between us, which causes me to become awkward and unsure of myself.

"Sandy, I know you come from a troubled home life, most anyone from this town knows that about you. It ain't no secret. You're out here working hard to provide for your family, and it is one of the most commendable acts I've seen a woman do. It shows your innermost true strength. You have a beauty that shines from the inside out like the brightest rays of sunshine on a cool day. No matter if you're looking at the sun or not, you can feel that light strike wherever you are."

Is this the nicest thing anyone has ever said to me? I can't help but be drawn to him. I hesitate before responding, but something about him makes me want to open up about my life.

"Thank you, Bill. You're right, I *am* working to provide for my family while I am undergoing a few things in my personal life. I appreciate your recognition of me. I should be getting back to work now," I tell him sharply, breaking eye contact while trying to send a message of finality to this conversation to him, but he presses on.

"Sandy, I know that it is certainly none of my business, but I just would like to know because quite frankly, darlin', I find you beautiful and your work ethic rather inspiring. Are you married to that... fella still?" he asks as he drops his hand from the door of the cooler and holds his beef tenderloin as he leads the way back to the storefront.

I follow like I am a lost puppy dog following their owner to get a treat. I am not only pathetic, but I am behaving a bit out of control.

I guess I'll share it with him... No one else has taken the time to talk with me about my home situation, and quite frankly, talking about it creates a therapeutic effect on me to discuss this. Luckily, there are no other shoppers in here at this time.

"Yes, I have a husband, Johnny, but we're uh... separated right now," I explain slowly.

"I'm sorry to hear that. May I ask what happened?" he asks, his tone turned from lightweight and airy to serious.

"He was abusive, and my eldest son stood up for me, and now my husband is hospitalized in critical condition." I hear my voice become quieter with each word I share with him, feeling the pain rise up in me again.

"I'm so sorry, that's terrible. Are you and your children safe now?" he asks, concern evident in his voice.

I nod, feeling grateful for his understanding.

"We're okay now. But it's been hard, you know? Trying to take care of everything by myself," I reply.

"I can only imagine. But you're doing an incredible job, Sandy. You deserve so much better than what you've been through." Empathy pierces through his eyes as they lock onto mine again as we reach the checkout counter and he places his beef on the countertop.

His words ignite something in me. A desire stirs up inside of me and my chest and back start to heat up. I get the sensation that I'm about to break out into a sweat. Out of nowhere, I am asking him a question that I didn't even know that I was going to ask until after it came out.

"Are you making this beef tenderloin for a special occasion this evening?" I ask in a soft and inquisitive tone as I punch in the numbers to ring it up.

He smiles up at me as he pulls out cash to pay for it.

"You mean as a date with a woman? No, darlin', it's

THE END IS THE BEGINNING 125

just me at my house. Well, me and my dog, Red," he replies with a small smirk.

I don't even acknowledge his response to my question because the embarrassment rises up in me, and my face and neck begin to blush, so I try to keep looking down as I take his cash and put it into the register. I am so flustered. I hope I am making the right change for him.

I hand him his change back, and my fingers brush against the palm of his hand. As I drop the coins into his hand, there is something that strikes me. A jolt of energy courses through my fingers as they pull away from his palm, and it runs up to my chest.

We lock eyes for what feels like an eternity. He simply nods his head as he grabs his beef from the counter and exits the store in one swift motion.

What was that? I feel the most 'seen' I have felt in my entire life by a complete stranger in a matter of moments.

What in the hell just happened, and who was that man? Immediately I am hoping he comes back tomorrow when I work. What is wrong with me? I am technically a married woman still, and the last thing I need on my plate is a distraction from another man I can't trust.

I need to maintain my focus, and now, I hope I never see that man again. I don't know if I could control myself... Clearly, I can't since I asked him if he was going to have a date tonight. How embarrassing.

I shake my head and walk back to start stocking the shelves.

CHAPTER 21
Lisa

July 1975 Age: 14

As we leave the hospital after a visit to Dad in the Intensive Care Unit, it has been two weeks since the incident, I notice that Mom seems to be less concerned about Dad's well-being than she was when the fight initially happened. I get the sense that something seems off with her; she seems to be sick a lot lately. It's as if the stress of everything that's happened has taken a toll on her.

As I reflect on my relationship with David, I realize that we have grown much closer since the fight. Despite our differences in personality and interests, we have found a newfound understanding and appreciation for each other.

I'm amazed by David's sensitivity. It is something I have not seen in him before, and I am grateful for the time we have spent together comforting one another and trying to make sense of everything we are all going through.

It is unfortunate that it may have taken this large of a traumatic experience in our family to bring us closer. I'm glad we now have a stronger bond, and I hope to continue building on this newfound closeness.

Although, I've been noticing some concerning behavior from David lately when it comes to our visits to see Dad. He doesn't come with Mom and me as often as I thought he would, and it's been making me worried. I can't help but wonder if he holds resentment or blame toward Dad for what happened, which I definitely wouldn't blame him if he did.

It's been difficult for me to understand why David would distance himself from Dad like he is at a time like this, and it seems like I'm caught in the middle. I'm not sure how to approach the situation or provide support for both David while also being there for my Dad, even though I too, am resentful toward him.

Perhaps David is grieving the potential future loss of our father, given the state he is in with his injuries, and maybe he is processing his feelings in his own way. But seeing him sit at home and not go with us feels like he is taking the easy way out. It's not like Mom and I want to see him this way, hooked up to all of the machines, and he's barely able to communicate with us, let alone know we're even there.

It is frustrating not knowing what's going on with David. One minute, he's opening up and showing his sensitive side; the next, he's closed up like a tulip in the dark of night, and I worry that this issue may be indicative of a larger problem in our family.

Maybe the incident is revealing the ongoing tension between David and Dad, and he knows he may never be able to reconcile with him, and that makes him very uneasy. Whatever the cause may be, I think it's important for us to talk about what's going on and work through our emotions together.

After we've returned home from visiting Dad tonight (this time David did come along) and we just finished dinner, I walk into the living room to find David sitting on the couch with a book in his hand. He looks up at me as I enter, and I can see the sadness in his eyes.

Saying, "Hey," I take a seat next to him.

He sets the book down and leans back into the couch.

"Hey," he replies in a monotone voice.

"How are you holding up?" I ask him.

"I don't know," he admits. "It's hard to see Dad like that, you know? And Mom...I don't know what's going on with her, but it's like she's not even here sometimes."

I nod, knowing exactly what he means. "Yeah, I've noticed that too."

David looks at me, his eyes searching mine. "Do you ever wonder if things will ever go back to the way they were before?"

I sigh, knowing that the answer to that question is no. "I don't think so. I mean, things will get better, but they'll never be the same... and maybe that's a good thing."

David nods, and we sit in silence for a few moments, lost in our own thoughts. I can see that he's struggling with something, and I want to be there for him.

"Hey, can I ask you something?"

Breaking the silence, he looks at me, waiting for me to continue.

"Why don't you come with us to visit Dad more often? I mean, it was great to have you there tonight, but just wondering why so often you don't come along with Mom and I," I ask, curious.

David looks away, his eyes focusing on something in the distance. "I don't know. It's hard to see him like that, you know? And it's not like he was ever there for us when we were growing up."

I nod, understanding his point of view. Dad wasn't always the best father, but he did what he thought was right at the time.

"But he's still our dad," I remind him. "And he needs us right now."

David looks at me, his expression softening.

"I know," he acknowledges, his voice barely above a whisper.

We sit in silence for a few more moments, lost in our own thoughts. The weight of everything that's happened bears down on me, and I know that David feels it too.

"We'll get through this," I comment, trying to offer him some comfort.

David looks at me, a small smile forming on his face. "Yeah, we will."

I can see that he's starting to open up to me more, and I'm grateful for that. We may not be able to fix everything that's happened, but at least we have each other to lean on.

CHAPTER 22
Sandy

July 1975 Age: 35

I take a deep breath, trying to calm the racing of my heart. Bill's behavior has been getting to me lately, and I can't seem to shake that there is some unease that comes with it.

But at the same time, I can't deny my attempts to conceal the attraction that I have toward him. He's charming, handsome, and always seems to know just what to say to make me smile.

It doesn't help that I'm technically still married and pregnant, but Bill doesn't know that...

Heat starts rising to my cheeks from the mere thoughts of the curiosity I have for him... how would it feel to have his lips on mine or his hands on my body...

Oh my God, what am I doing thinking of him in a lustful way? But why does he have to be so damn good-looking?

THE END IS THE BEGINNING   131

I can't ignore the nagging worry in the back of my mind about him and his intentions with me.

Every time he comes into the store, I know that he's watching me, studying me, trying to figure me out. And the way he looks at me, with those intense, hypnotic eyes, it is like he's seeing straight through to who I am.

What I can't figure out though, is it lingering on the verge of creepy or is it endearing?

While restocking the shelves at Meats and Beets, I catch him staring at me from across the store. His eyes are staring at me, making no effort to look away.

For a moment, I too, can't look away.

But then, as he starts walking toward me, my heart skips a beat and I snap out of it as I watch his lips curling into a grin.

Is time moving in slow motion? I am met with a scent that must be his cologne-musky and strong, as he leans in close.

"Hey, Sandy. Can I ask you something?" His voice is low and smooth.

"Uh, sure. What is it?" I reply, trying to sound casual.

"I was wondering if you'd like to grab a drink with me sometime?" he asks while his lips purse together, attempting to hold back a larger smile.

I freeze, unsure of how to respond. Part of me wants to scream yes, to experience the thrill of someone wanting to spend time with me by someone so desirable. But the other part of me is worried...

Worried that he's too intense, too possessive, too much like a... stalker. I'll try to let him down gently, telling him I'm married and have kids.

I take a deep breath and try to steady my voice.

"Bill, I appreciate your interest, but I'm not comfortable with the idea of going out with you. I'm married, and I have kids. It simply wouldn't be right."

Bill's eyes darken, and he steps closer speaking in his low and slow whisper tone.

"Come on, Sandy. Don't be like that. We could just grab a drink and talk. It's not like we have to do anything more than that."

I step back, trying to put some distance between us. "I'm sorry, Bill, but I can't. I'm not interested in anything more than friendship at this time."

Bill's expression turns sour, and he takes a step toward me again.

"You're making a mistake, Sandy. I know we could have something special. Don't let your fears get in the way of that."

I try to take a step backward as I realize just how close he is to me and the reality that he's right, I do have a fear.

"Bill, please, I really need to get back to work."

He touches my arm, sending shivers down my spine, I'm trapped. I don't want to lead him on, but I also don't want to push him away. It's like I'm stuck in this limbo, caught between my desires and my fears.

He leans in even closer, and his breath on my cheek causes my skin to form goosebumps. "I'll be back, Sandy. And when I am, I hope you'll have changed your mind. We're too good of people to not spend more time together to see... what there could be."

With that, he looks up at me and winks through his gorgeous eyes as he turns and walks away, leaving me feeling shaken, exposed, and weak at the knees while also wanted and attractive.

I try to escape the dread that settles in my stomach, but it's no use. Considering how often he comes into the store, Bill's behavior is teetering on feeling more like that of a... stalker? Despite his beautiful looks, I don't know how to make him stop or that I even truly want to?

The vulnerability within me lingers, and I can't rid myself of the worry that he's still watching me, still waiting for his chance to make a move. What would I do if he did? Turn him away like I know that I should, or embrace it because I have such curiosity over what it would be like to be coveted by a man... this man?

CHAPTER 23

Lisa

July 1975 Age: 14

As David and I continue to engage in conversation, we are abruptly interrupted as we notice the distinct footsteps echoing down the hall. Mom emerges with a notable difference from her usual appearance—she is much more put together. She is even wearing makeup, which is such a rarity that I can count on one hand how often I've seen that.

Her dirty-dishwater blonde hair is styled elegantly with half pulled back to reveal her visage and striking dark brown eyes. But the most remarkable sight is seeing her in the dress that she is in. It's not just any dress. It is a formfitting black dress with long sleeves boasting a neckline deeper than her typical mid-chest tops.

In my recollection, I struggle to recall a single occasion where my mother flaunted her figure so boldly, or dressed with such an air of elegance. She generally

THE END IS THE BEGINNING 135

avoids dressing up or applying makeup, and I cannot pinpoint the last instance she did more with her hair than tie it into a simple ponytail, whether for housework or her job.

David and I exchange puzzled glances, our curiosity piqued, yet Mom offers hardly any explanation. Her departure is swift, telling us that she's going out with a friend and she asked Alice next door to keep an eye on us periodically. As she leaves, she swiftly takes her purse, and we hear the quiet click of the door as she departs, leaving us in silent bewilderment.

"Where do you think she's going?" David asks me, his perplexity mirroring my own.

"I have no idea," I reply, my voice low in a hushed tone. "But it's not like her to leave us without telling us where she's going. It is also strange how peculiarly sophisticated she was dressed, and we still do not know for what purpose."

Our shared unease lingers as we ponder this situation until, finally, David breaks the silence.

"Do you think something's going on?" David asks, his voice low.

"I don't know." My heart is pounding in my chest. "But I have a bad feeling about this."

We sit in silence for a few more moments in contemplation until the sound of the doorbell pulls us out of our reverie.

David gets up to answer it, and I can hear the faint sound of a woman's voice. A few seconds later, he comes back into the room with an unsettled look on his face.

"Who is it?" I ask him.

"It's uh... Alice, like Mom said. She's just checking in on us, I guess," he announces, his voice low."

A lump forms in my throat. It's not like our mother to leave us like this, especially when Dad is in the hospital. Something is definitely not right with all of this.

"Why would she ask Alice to come by, especially for us at our age?" I ask, my voice barely above a whisper to David, not wanting to offend Alice, who is standing in the doorway to 'watch us' or for my rather unwelcoming words to cause her to go back and tell my mother that we were questioning her whereabouts.

David shrugs, clearly just as confused as I am. "I don't know." His eyes are searching mine. "But I don't like it."

We sit in silence for a few more moments, the tension in the room almost palpable. I can't help but wonder where our mother could be going and why she's being so secretive about it. David and I exchange another look, both of us looking like we can't just sit here. We need to take action about the situation.

"What do we do?" David asks, his voice low.

I take a deep breath, seeking to steady my thoughts and my nerves alike.

"I don't know." My voice is barely above a whisper. "But I think we need to find out what's going on."

David nods, and we both get up from the couch, determined to get to the bottom of this.

We make our way to the front door leaving Alice in the living room talking to us. My heart is pounding in my chest as we step out into the cool night air to talk privately, where a sense of urgency courses through us.

"Where do we start?" David asks once we are on the front porch, just the two of us, with a quiet whisper.

I take a deep breath, trying to calm my nerves.

"Let's start by checking her bedroom. Maybe we can find some clues as to where she's going."

David nods, and we both make our way back into the house, our hearts pounding as we are consumed with adrenaline, anxiety, and searching for answers.

Something is certainly off, and we need to find out what it is before Mom gets home or... it's too late.

CHAPTER 24

Lisa

July 1975 Age: 14

We quietly make our way down the hall and enter into our mother's bedroom with a sense of unease at trespassing her private space. It feels strange to be in here without her permission, but we know that something is off, and we need to find out what it is.

We start by checking her closet, but all we find are the usual clothes she wears to work and around the house. We move on to her dresser, opening each drawer and sifting through her belongings.

"What are we looking for, exactly?" David asks, his voice low.

"I don't know," I reply, as my eyes scan the room. "Anything that might tell us where she's gone or who she's with."

David nods and continues to search, but I can tell he's

THE END IS THE BEGINNING   139

just as confused and worried as I am. After a few minutes of searching, David stops and holds up a small, rectangular piece of paper.

It's a note paper clipped to Mom's personal calendar book that reads, "7/6 Gibson's Dinner at 6 pm".

Today is 7/6! But Gibson's... What the heck?

Gibson's is the caliber of restaurant where they have starchy white tablecloths with white napkins everyone places on their laps while they eat, and they even have two forks placed at each table setting. I still don't know when you use which one for what part of the meal, but I probably never will know—we don't eat at such places. Gibson's is in the next town over—Edwardstown.

My heart sinks as I have a heavy hunch that our mother is more than likely out on a date with someone. But who?

We continue searching through her things, hoping to find another clue, but we come up empty.

As we leave the room, David turns to me with a determined look in his eye.

Before he can speak, I tell him, "It just doesn't feel right. Why would she dress up like that, have Alice, of all people, come be with us at our age especially and not tell us what she is doing in more detail? We need to follow her. We need to know who she's with and what's going on."

He shrugs, but I can see the worry etched in his face.

"I don't know, but maybe we should just wait for her to come back. We don't want to jump to conclusions."

I nod, but I can't ignore this nagging feeling in my gut.

"I don't think I can wait. I have to know what's going on."

David looks at me for a moment, then with hesitation, he nods in agreement. "Okay, but we have to be careful. We don't want to get in trouble."

I give a swift confirmatory look with my eyes, and we make our way out of the bedroom and back to the living room. As we pass through the hallway, we hear the sound of Alice's voice coming from the kitchen.

"Do you think we should talk to her?" David asks, his voice low in a whisper.

I shake my head.

"No, let's not involve her. We don't want to cause any problems. Hopefully, she'll think we just stepped outside for some fresh air. So let's try to be quick!"

We make our way out the front door and into the cool night air. My heart is racing as we step onto the porch while my mind floods with possibilities.

We start to walk down the street, the darkness enveloping us as we go.

"Where should we go?" David asks, his voice low.

I take a deep breath, trying to calm my nerves.

"Let's just walk heading toward Edwardstown and see if we can find her."

I nod in agreement without saying a word as the sense of urgency overwhelms me. We can't just sit here and wait for our mother to come back and explain herself. We need to take action.

After a few minutes of walking, we run into Jerry, our old neighborhood friend. He looks surprised to see us, but his face breaks into a smile.

THE END IS THE BEGINNING   141

"Hey, guys! What are you doing out here so late?" Jerry asks, his eyes scanning between the both of us.

We hesitate for a moment, unsure of whether we should tell Jerry what's going on. David looks at me, and I look at him and shrug my shoulders.

"We're out for a walk tonight looking for our mom. She left the house dressed up without telling us where she was going, and we're looking to see where she might be."

"Oh... hope you guys find her so you can figure out what's going on. Hey, uh, Lisa, would you want to hang out sometime? I've been meaning to ask you at school but haven't gotten the chance."

My cheeks start to blush and my knees become weak. Is he asking me out? What the... Is he asking me out *in front of my brother*? This is a first for both.

"Uh, sure, Jerry. We could hang out sometime. We better get going, we'll see you later." I try to put a harsh end to this very awkward conversation. I take steps to go around him without looking back to see if David is following. Luckily, within a few moments, I can hear his footsteps, and I'm hoping he won't bring up what just happened.

What is worse than being asked out for the first time while it being in front of your brother? Having your brother harass you about it afterward.

"Jerry's got a crush on Lisa, Jerry's got a crush on Lisa!" I can hear David in his mocking tone of voice just as he walks up next to me. I walk even faster, hoping he'll stop saying it soon. Can this be any more embarrassing?

CHAPTER 25
Sandy

July 1975 Age: 35

As the days pass, I can't help but be drawn to Bill, even as his behavior becomes more unsettling. His persistence in pursuing me and now officially having asked me out is both thrilling and terrifying. I know it's wrong, but the attention he's giving me makes me feel wanted and desired in a way that I haven't felt in years.

So... should I just do it? It's just one date, right?

There is a voice in my head that tells me to be careful, to keep my guard up. The notes and gifts of flowers and chocolate he has been leaving for me at work, only adds to the sense of foreboding that's been growing inside me.

Is this what it feels like to be stalked, or worse...is this him showing his love for me? I wish I only knew.

The sun is setting over the field as I get into my car after

THE END IS THE BEGINNING   143

my shift at Meats and Beets. I turn the car onto Main Street to head toward home, and out of the corner of my eye, I notice a car pull out from a side street. It is now directly behind me, having wasted no time in getting this close to my bumper, the headlights shining into my rearview mirror, causing me to have to squint to see clearly. Already feeling anxiety bubbling within me from the recent events, I am positive this is Bill.

What is wrong with this man? Why is he obsessed with me? Have I not been clear enough with him? He must be sensing my attraction to him as meaning more than what it is. I turn onto a side street and drive down a few blocks before I pull over and he follows behind closely. This needs to be confronted. I slam my car door as I walk toward his car with rage filling each step I take toward him, my arms swinging forcefully by my sides. Before he is even out of his car, I am yelling at him over the silent soundtrack in this sleepy town; surely anyone within a mile radius of us can hear me.

"What are you doing, Bill? Why are you following me?" My voice is shaking with fear and anger, but I hope it comes off as confident and sends the message, "Don't mess with me."

He smiles as if he's amused by my reaction and has my attention. "I just wanted to make sure you got home safely, Sandy. Is that so wrong? I sent you the gifts at work and didn't hear from you all day, so I had to check on you."

"No, you can't be doing this without my permission. This is wrong. I don't know you, and I don't want to get to know you like you do me. Please, just leave me alone," I request, as my voice rises and I worry it's revealing my fear.

He shrugs and backs away, giving the impression that he is backing down, but I can tell he's not giving up.

There's a darkness that takes over his eyes that scares me while simultaneously drawing me in, a sense that he's capable of anything. A mix of panic and excitement courses through me. I want to push him away, to tell him to leave me alone, but there is a part of me that craves his attention... and his touch. I am scared to learn what his mysteriousness could reveal but it is just that— that same mysteriousness that pulls me in and wanting more.

His intense, hypnotizing eye contact I can't seem to avoid, it draws my eyes to his eyes. His suave demeanor and his gifts of admiration which demonstrate his affection and his unending relentlessness... When it comes to getting my attention and showing me how he feels about me, he makes no mistake about it. All of these things are *the* things that I never knew I was longing for until he walked into my life. All of the unknowns that 'could be' with him are exactly what makes me want to get to know him more to see what actually could be.

But I can't let him know any of this. I can't let on that I may be emotionally and physically attracted to him. I am a married woman with two, soon to be three children with another man who is hospitalized for Pete's sake.

Feeling embarrassed from the realization of my reality, I withdraw my eyes from his, breaking the eye contact.

But his eyes darken while his gaze intensifies, and it makes me wonder if I'm in over my head. There's a sense of danger that emanates from him, a warning that tells me to stay away.

Bill steps back away from me, sending the message that he is hearing me and will respect my wishes if what I say *is* what I really want.

"I will only let you be if you tell me right now that I am the only one who feels what I feel between us. Tell me that I'm wrong. Tell me that you don't feel it too, Sandy," he whispers.

He says this while his eyes move rapidly between my eyes to my lips and back again, over and over. His mouth is open just slightly as he gently licks his lips, and I notice a fluttering sensation deep inside my stomach as I lean in closer to him.

He takes his hands and grabs mine while his thumbs caress the backside of my knuckles, gently rubbing them in a circular motion. A pulsing sensation begins between my thighs, and my heart rate quickens even more than it was already, and I also have to open my mouth just to breathe with more ease.

I hesitate before answering him. I have never been a good liar. How can I look him in the eye and tell him I don't feel and want this, too? How can my head want nothing to do with him but my heart, my body is physically aching and yearning for his touch, his voice upon my ear, his eyes locked with mine, his... before I can finish my thought, his lips are on mine. Pressing ever so gently, his tongue, so soft and smooth, enters my mouth as he takes his hand to my neck and pulls me toward him.

My back lights up with a heat wave that runs from my hips to my neck, where he is touching me ever so softly yet without a doubt, lustfully and intentionally. Without an ounce of control, I let out a moan that I don't even recognize as coming from me. I have never made this noise in my entire life, certainly not while doing this. His hand moves up under my shirt and rests on the crease of my lower back, but his fingertips ever so softly massage my skin, and my knees begin to weaken.

I know that I need to pull away and put a stop to this, but it's like I am in a deep REM sleep cycle dream where I want out of the dream because it is so bad, but my body is fully paralyzed, and I have absolutely no control over it. That is me at this very moment. I have less than zero control over my physical actions.

Between my thighs is growing warmer, and it seems as if all my blood has been drained from my extremities and is pulsating... there. I reciprocate his physical touch with my hand wrapping around his waist, and as it pulls him closer to me, I can feel... it.

Oh God, I am completely out of control. I have never wanted something more in my life than I do right now. I want him to caress every inch of my body, to have it all. To take my nipples into his hands and massage them like he is my back. I want him to experience every part of me and me, every part of him. I want to know where every single hair on his body is and to have touched it, kissed it. I want to return the feelings of love he has given to me in gifts and persistence to him—but physically and... I want it right NOW.

He slowly pulls me toward him as I follow his lead foot by foot to his car, where he opens the door and motions for me to get into his backseat with him.

By now, the sun has completely set, and there are only a few stars out, making the night sky pitch black and dark. I get into his car and he begins pulling at my clothes and me at his.

The next thing he does is the best part of all of this, he pauses for only a moment and kisses me on the forehead, demonstrating his admiration, and then takes each of my hands and kisses them with adoration so gently that instinctively, my legs fall open wider as he presses against me.

I moan again, but this time louder. I can't hold this back any longer. I know that I should stop this. I really need to stop this from going any further, but... I just can't. It feels too good and too right to be wrong. I run my hands down his back, and all of his back muscles tense, and I feel the most relaxed and at ease I think I have ever felt in the presence of a man in my most vulnerable form —completely naked, in his backseat.

He whispers in my ear, "Is it alright that we do this?"

I don't even respond with words. I decisively insert my tongue so deeply into his mouth that I think it completely takes his breath away as I pull him toward me, and he thrusts inside of me. I have to pull away from him just to breathe from the force of him filling me so tightly. He takes his time and never stops looking into my eyes to make sure I am enjoying it as much as he is.

I am fairly confident that I am enjoying this *more* than he is. I have never felt this way before about someone— this desired, this sexy, this cared for. When he is finished, he makes sure I am too, and he can tell by my breathing that I am not satisfied like he is. He moves himself down and caresses his tongue in all the right spots for only a few seconds until I let out the loudest moan while I let. It. All. Go.

Holy shit. It has either got to be pregnancy hormones, or else my body is infatuated with this man because I have never you-know-whated that quickly or for that long like I just did with him. His mouth knew exactly where to go and for how long to be there. It was as if he was reading my mind in the deepest ways, locating my private anatomical pleasure map of *how to* and *where to*.

We lay in his backseat, arms around one another while we breathe in and out, coming down from... whatever that was. The windows are fogged up and even if someone wanted to, they couldn't see in here.

We don't speak a word, there is nothing to say. Our bodies have just said it all, and for this moment, I have never felt better.

Not just within my body, not only inside my heart, and certainly not in my head, but somewhere in between all those places, this all makes sense. Right now, I feel like the luckiest woman on this planet.

CHAPTER 26
Sandy

July 1975 Age: 35

The pull of Bill's attention continues to grow stronger, even as my lustful attraction grows, concerns about his behavior only intensifies. The notes, gifts, and his relentless pursuit both thrill and terrify me. I know deep down that this isn't right, that I shouldn't be entertaining his advances, but the allure of feeling desired and wanted after years of neglect is incredibly difficult to resist.

This evening, after my shift at Meats and Beets, as I turn to close the door and lock it with my set of keys, I hear footsteps and an "mmhmm" of someone clearing their throat. I turn to look and there he is... Bill. He is holding a bouquet of roses with his arms stretching out toward me.

"Hello, darling, I thought you might like these... and I wanted to ask you something."

I try to hold in my mix of emotions of being worried someone will see us together with these roses, but also, I am so excited to be given these flowers. I absolutely love the smell of fresh flowers, but I love it even more when they're from someone who holds me in such high regard.

Taking the bouquet from him, I arch my head toward the bright red roses and slowly inhale their beautiful yet soft aroma on this humid, July evening and smile a smirk up at him.

"And what is this 'something' you'd like to ask me, Bill? You're clearly up to something, surprising me at work again, and this time with these gorgeous flowers."

Bill clears his throat and responds stoically as if he is concerned about what my response will be, which naturally makes me nervous to hear what he is about to ask.

"I'd like to ask you out on a formal date. A date to Gibson's, perhaps this Saturday night?"

I hesitate at the thought of going out in public with him. The weight of judgment and the fear of how it would look nags me in the back of my mind.

But since Gibson's is in the next town over, it would probably be safe to do without running into anyone as long as we don't stay too long. Don't I deserve a nice meal that isn't prepared by me once every decade or so?

"I suppose we could do that sometime, Bill. I'm not so sure as to when though. There is a lot of planning that would need to go into that. Not to mention, I am still very much a married woman. I really don't know about all of this as tempting as it is. It is not that I don't want to it's just—"

Before I can finish my thought, Bill is interrupting me.

THE END IS THE BEGINNING   151

"Sandy, I know all of your concerns and reasons not to, but how about the reasons TO. Clearly, we have something that has proven to be strong and captivated both of us in more ways than one. I will respectfully follow all of your wishes around when we go, day of the week, time of day, even seating location. Or, if you'd prefer, we can go somewhere more casual; however, you deserve to be wined and dined. Something tells me that you haven't been in quite some time."

There is something about his persistence, his unwavering desire for me, that makes me want to say yes. He is standing there looking back at me without hardly blinking. I can tell he's hanging on my response. Perhaps my contemplation over this offer is the thrill of doing something daring, of stepping out of my comfort zone for once. Or maybe it is my own desire to feel alive again, to experience something different from my daily routine.

"Yes, you are correct, I haven't been wined and dined probably...ever," I reply seriously with a huff as if to come off that I am offended he would point that out.

"Oh, Bill, you sure know how to put things into perspective. The perspective *you* want me to see, of course. I have actually never been to Gibson's—only ever heard of it. Yes, we can go sometime. Maybe this Saturday. Give me a little time to see if there's a neighbor who can check on the kids while I'm gone."

I can't look back up at him without a smile spreading across my face as my eyes lock with his baby blues, and that's all it takes.

Bill steps toward me, wraps his heavy, strong arms around my shoulders, and holds me tightly for a hug.

He whispers in my ear, "I'll cover the cost of someone to come be with your kids. Whatever the rate is, I don't care. I just want to do this one thing for you. That's it."

I don't respond. There's really no need.

Our lips connect as if we are two magnets of opposite poles. As if he is the South Pole and I'm the North, we're locked together like we are meant to be, like we were always meant to be. His lips taste sweet and are ever so soft against mine. His tongue swirling with mine feels so delicate yet gently playful tonight... The romance between us is growing stronger than it ever has.

———

Luckily I was able to get someone to keep an eye on the kids and worked extra hard to get all of my housework done to make it to tonight's date with Bill.

The night quickly approached, and the anxiety bubbled within the core of my stomach. How will I explain my whereabouts to David and Lisa? They are already dealing with their father being away healing, and my absence again tonight will only add to their worries. I have thought of canceling on Bill, but I just can't bring myself to do it. I need this escape, even if it is temporary.

I am dressed in a simple and elegant dress, trying to balance the desire to impress Bill with the need to appear as though I am not trying too hard. As I walk out the door, David and Lisa are looking at me with curious eyes questioning where I am going.

I take in a deep breath being sure to fill my lungs fully and release some tension, gathering my thoughts before telling them, "I'm going out for dinner with a friend, kids. I won't be long. I've got Alice coming to keep an eye on you both. I know you don't necessarily need it, but I thought it would be best. She is parking her car out front."

Their gazes hold a mixture of worry and confusion. I hate seeing that in their eyes, but I can't bring myself to tell them the truth—that I am seeing another man while I am still married to their father. That I am sleeping with this *other* man. This will be a secret I keep locked away, a forbidden chapter in my life that I don't think I will ever be ready to share with them.

With a forced smile, I add nervously, "You'll be okay. The gal, uh, Alice, she will take good care of you."

As I close the door behind me, their concerned expressions stay with me. Guilt begins to eat at me as it does whenever I have left my children, but tonight's guilt is much heavier than other times. I push it aside with each step I take away from the door, reminding myself that I deserve this night for myself.

Gibson's restaurant is as elegant as I had imagined. Soft lighting, beautiful décor, and a lively atmosphere greets us as we enter. Bill holds the door open for me, a charming smile on his face, and I can't help but feel a flutter of excitement despite the reservations wavering in the back of my mind.

We are seated at a cozy table in a quiet corner, away from prying eyes. I am grateful to be seated in a secluded spot so that no one will recognize me being here with him. I am dressed much nicer than I typically dress so if anyone does happen to see me, I doubt they'd recognize who I am.

The conversation flows easily between Bill and me, and for a brief moment, I allow myself to forget about my responsibilities, my children, and the consequences of my actions. The guilt washes away when I am in his presence —he makes me believe that I really am the only woman alive for him.

We talk about my work and how much I have learned in my short time of being there. I tell him that I have learned to love the job and meeting new people. Which of course, Bill segways this comment to being about having met him and how it was simply, "fate of course", according to him.

As the evening progresses, Bill showers me with compliments, and I can tell that he has a genuine interest in getting to know me on a much deeper level. He asks about my childhood, my dreams, and even my future goals and ambitions. His attentive nature makes me feel 'seen' and valued in a way I haven't experienced in a long time, I'd even venture to say ever... as bad as that is to admit.

The conversation flows so naturally that I even slip and tell him about my pregnancy, something I don't particularly like talking about, considering that it is a stark reminder of my ongoing marriage to another man. I don't want to be reminded that I am actively cheating on my husband, I already have the guilt layered on as thick as a foundation that is tacked with rows and rows of cinder blocks—the weight of it is nearly suffocating to me.

He asks me how far along I am in the pregnancy and what he can do to help. He goes on to specifically ask how

THE END IS THE BEGINNING   155

I have been feeling mentally and emotionally managing all the stress I am under.

When was the last time anyone cared to ask how I am doing with *anything* in my life? The awareness of this initially fills me with excitement and admiration for Bill since it clearly demonstrates his deep feelings toward me and his concern for my well-being. Bill's question also fills me with sadness over the realization that I have spent so much of my life surrounding myself with Johnny, who has never actually cared for me in any form—physically, mentally, emotionally, and certainly not sexually.

Bill continues. "I'd be more than happy to provide financial assistance to cover doctor appointments and such, Sandy," he offers with a tone of sincerity and steady eye contact—the kind he does when he is doing his best to show he genuinely means what he is saying. Whenever he does this, the pressure to respond to him right away overwhelms me.

"You shouldn't have to worry about anything during this special time," he explains urgently as if to not allow a beat in the conversation so I won't respond by telling him "no" right away.

"The uniqueness of you being pregnant with your third child should be a time that is joyful, but for you, it has been tainted with such stress and negativity—all of which you don't deserve. Let me take care of you, your children, and the new baby, Sandy. I care about you too much to watch you go through all of this alone."

His offer catches me off guard, but in my vulnerable state, the idea of having some support is certainly tempting. The weight of financial responsibilities has always been a constant burden on my shoulders, and the thought of someone willing to ease that stress is certainly hard to resist.

I hesitate for a moment, torn between the need for independence and the practicality of accepting help. Finally, I muster the courage to respond, "Uh, Bill, I appreciate your generosity, but I want to make sure I'm not taking advantage of your kindness. I need to think about it."

Bill nods understandingly, his gaze filled with warmth and honesty. "Of course, Sandy. Take your time. Just know that I truly want to help, and I'll be here whenever you're ready."

His reassurance melts away some of my doubts, and I find myself grateful for his support. It is a new sensation, having someone willing to step up and be there for me and my children, even if it is the result of a complicated situation.

As the evening drew to a close, Bill walked me back to my car. The night air was cool, and a gentle breeze brushed against our faces.

It was in that moment, standing under the soft glow of the streetlights, that a surge of desire coursed through me.

Bill's lips met mine with an intensity that sent shivers down my spine. His hands caressed my back, pulling me closer. The weight of our connection, the passion that had been building throughout the evening, consumed us both.

Caught up in the moment, I reciprocated his advances, my own desire overwhelming any lingering doubts or hesitations. In that embrace, the world faded away, leaving only the raw, primal, and physical connection between us.

Kissing him felt so soft, so sensual, and strangely, also meaningful. It felt as if he was telling me through each flick and swirl of his tongue and his pulling of me closer to him, that he valued me.

Not just that he values me on the surface level, but everything that makes me uniquely me. Like if he could see into my soul and was not only accepting it, but admiring and loving it.

Our tongues slide together, and there is a heat emanating off of his body like a pulse in his veins. It just keeps going and going getting stronger and hotter with each second that passes. This does something to me... like the hot blaze steaming from a fireplace on a snowy day and the coziness of being tucked inside so warm... The embers are sparking from the flames and swirling with one another just like our souls seem to be tonight.

While my body is being pulled lustfully toward his and my heart is feeling a type of love and connection it has never felt before, my mind is traveling down the road of thoughts around my duties as a married woman and the vows I took. Although Johnny hasn't held up his, I should still be holding up mine and setting an example for the kids.

The kids... what am I doing to them, leaving them alone with Alice so I can go out on a date as a married woman and get worked up connecting to this man whom I've hardly known for more than a few weeks?

As quickly as this flame ignited between Bill and I, the

flame of passion extinguished. Reality crashed down upon me, and I pulled away from him—a mixture of confusion and regret flooding my senses.

What am I doing with Bill? How could I have allowed myself to be swept away like this? I am embarrassed and ashamed of my actions. I am in a seemingly impossible situation—one where not a single person doesn't get hurt by my actions. If Johnny ever found out, not only would he be hurt, but I'm unsure if I'd make it out alive, and if I left Bill to stay with Johnny, not only would Bill be hurt, but so would I.

How could I ever explain this to anyone? I hope that I never have to.

"Bill, I really should be getting home to my kids. I've been out plenty long enough, and they are probably worried about my whereabouts. Thank you for a wonderful meal and...conversation."

I turn and begin walking to my car, not waiting to hear his response.

We bid each other a tense and silent goodbye, the air thick with unspoken words. With a heavy heart, I make my way home, my mind a whirlwind of emotions.

CHAPTER 27
Sandy

July 1975 Age: 35

As I step through the front door, David and Lisa's eyes meet mine—their expressions a mix of concern and disappointment. They obviously had been waiting for me, worried about my whereabouts. Their questions hang in the air, demanding answers I am definitely not ready to give.

Taking a deep breath, I face them, my voice trembling slightly. "I'm sorry for worrying you, my darlings. I went out to dinner with a friend. It was just a chance to get some time for myself."

Their expressions harden, their disappointment palpable.

"But Mom, you've been spending so much time away lately. We need you. Dad needs you. We haven't gone to visit him in a while," Lisa says, her voice laced with frustration.

Tears well up in my eyes as I struggle to find the right words to explain my actions. "I know, honey. I've been trying to balance everything, but sometimes I need a break too. I promise I'll do better."

Their young faces, a reflection of the pain I have caused, tears at my heart. How can I make them understand the complexities of my choices? How can I justify the path I have embarked on? I really don't think that I can. Not now, not ever.

But amidst their hurt, I know I have to find a way to rebuild the trust I have broken. I have to go visit Johnny again soon and be more present with him in his current state at a rehab facility now. They transitioned him from the hospital there, and I haven't been to see him.

To put it simply, I am ashamed. The version of myself that I have become I hardly recognize. While flirting and falling for Bill, I've managed to completely neglect my children and put their needs behind my own. I have set the example (hopefully they will never learn about) that it is acceptable to date while being a married woman, and I have not checked on or visited my husband in over two weeks' time.

With a shrug of the shoulders, willing myself to let these feelings of guilt brush off, I gather Lisa and David close, embracing them tightly.

"I love you both more than words can express. From now on, I'll be more present, more attentive. You're my priority, and I won't let you down."

The weight of their forgiveness seems distant, but I know it is a journey we need to embark on together.

The next morning is Sunday, following my date with

Bill, and I spend the day at the house with the kids having lunch and making a true and concerted effort to be present. It makes me realize how much they have changed even throughout this short time while I have been preoccupied.

Having this realization makes it even more clear: I have made quite a mess for myself... I have become my own homewrecker.

It has been a challenge to find enough money to buy our groceries. Even though there always is some struggle in my life, whether it is my unexpected pregnancy or trying to put together funds for purchasing groceries, I still am less stressed and my happiness has increased with Johnny not being here.

However, when it comes to food, I can't bring myself to make meatloaf anymore. I just can't see it the same way I used to, even knowing the recipe for it is delicious and the deep meaning that it has to me since it has been passed down from two generations before me.

Heck, I can hardly even look at a package of ground beef in the grocery store without remnants of flashbacks flooding my mind. The shock and pain I felt that night when the plate struck my face to the pain later that night in our bedroom... The reminder of it sends a shiver down my spine.

On Monday after work, I decide I'm going to get the kids and we're going to visit their father. As we walk into the rehab facility and the staff guides us into his room, I am amazed to see him sitting up in a chair, looking out the window at the sunny day.

As Lisa walks beside him, he looks up at her with a

small smile, but when he looks at me... his eyes flicker between two emotions: anger and disappointment. I can't entirely blame him—he probably feels betrayed. I haven't seen him in over two weeks, and he has changed so much.

Lisa hugs him and David stands beside her as they look out the window and take in the scene of his room and the view. His room looks tidy, but it feels lonely. I noticed when we walked down the halls of the facility the other patients had photos and flowers in their rooms, but not Johnny, his room has starch-white walls and yellowing-colored drapes. No photos, flowers, balloons, or cards wishing him well and a fast recovery. The guilt sets in. Guilt that I have let him down and haven't been by his side during all of this. My stomach feels like it's going to turn, and I might puke as I contemplate, wondering if he has any notion that I have been cheating on him.

I sit down beside him, and with a quiet and delicate voice, I whisper, "Hello." He continues to look out the window before he slowly shifts his attention and looks back at me. When his head faces me, he doesn't speak a word; he just stares deep into my eyes, searching for answers to all of his questions. My breath is taken away just as quickly as my words are. I stare back breathlessly as I try to hide the nervousness that is coursing through me.

He finally breaks the stare and looks back at the window with the kids. I try to pretend that what just happened didn't and make small talk. "You look great." I try to raise my voice to sound uplifting and genuine. When there is no response from him, I comment, "It looks like you have come a long way."

THE END IS THE BEGINNING   163

He barks back much faster than I had anticipated him to. "Yes. I have. You would know if you cared to come around."

I just nod my head and look down at my hands as I'm fidgeting with my skirt. As I look up, he is staring at me again. I really don't know what to say, do I apologize? Do I tell him the truth?

"Did they say when they think you can get out of here and come back home?" I ask, avoiding the inevitable.

"Yeah, if my healing continues and my therapy stays on track. They think I should be getting out of here, hopefully soon. But they won't commit to anything as of yet. They first have to know that I have a place to go after this."

Shit. What am I to tell him? Of course he has a place in our home, but does he know that my heart is not with him anymore? That the home he once knew isn't much of a home anymore but more of a house?

I clear my throat, putting off my response to him.

"Of course you do. Why wouldn't you?" I look down at the floor, avoiding eye contact in hopes that he won't be able to read through my eyes what I am thinking.

As Johnny begins to speak, I am reminded of the truest version of himself.

"That is my house. Those are my children. You are my wife—no one else's. Does everyone in this small ass town think that I'm an idiot? Do they think that word isn't going to make it back to me of what goes on when I'm not around? Apparently, you do. You are no more than the dumb whore that I thought you were when I married you."

These words cross his lips with such a growl and anger that it causes Lisa and David to look back from the window at us. Their eyes jump between the two of us, searching for answers as to what has just gone on. With that, I wave them over so that we can leave. But, of course, Johnny isn't going to let me off that easily.

He looks at the kids with his finger raised to their faces and begins to shout. "And the both of you... acting as if you haven't been in the know about what's been going on in our household while I've been cooped up and recovering! You both are no better than your SLUT of a mother."

Lisa gasps, and the tension rising between David and Johnny once again is now palpable. David takes a step closer to Johnny, and as he crouches down to look him directly in the eyes like he is going to 'have words', as if it were fate, a nurse casually walks in to check on us.

"Is everything alright in here? Are you guys having a nice visit?" she asks cheerfully with a bright smile.

I can't respond to her. None of us can.

We all collectively turn and exit the room leaving the nurse standing there with her mouth hanging open in confusion and perplexed as to what has just happened between us. If she only knew the life we have lived and who Johnny *really* is.

CHAPTER 28

Lisa

July 1975 Age: 14

I can't believe that Mom was out with someone and didn't think to tell us who and where she was going beforehand. It makes me wonder what else she may be up to that she hasn't told us about. Was she *really* just meeting up with a friend? And if so, who is this *friend*? Is it a man? I have more questions that haven't yet been answered, but I didn't necessarily want to ask them in front of David.

And then there were the weird comments that Dad was making when we visited him about what he thinks is going on in our home when he is not there. I couldn't tell if that was him being a little out of it from pain medicine or if he actually knew something that neither I nor David knew.

The last few days at home and school have been just plain peculiar. I'm still trying to discern what Mom is really up to when we are not around and reading into her motions and actions more heavily than I probably should and snooping around her things when I get the chance.

At school, I've run into Jerry a few times while passing in the hallway, and he smiles a longer-than-normal sort of smile at me. I can feel that as I walk past him, and if I were to look back, he would still be looking at me. It's like that feeling of being watched—you don't have to actually look to confirm. You know it's already happening; you can feel it.

I am worried Jerry is going to bring up my agreeing to meet up with him for a date. It's not that I don't want to, I'm just a little apprehensive about what to expect since I've never been on an official date with anyone before.

I don't know that I've even ever thought of Jerry as much more than a friend. But maybe he only meant asking me to 'go out with him' to be simply in a friendly way. How will I know which way he meant it if I never go?

When it comes to school, I really enjoy going, but lately, it's felt a bit nerve-racking waiting to see if Jerry will say something to me.

What I love about school, though, is that it allows me to make friends and be involved in activities like Key Club and the Spirit Squad. It's always been my way of maintaining the positivity in my life with the constant turmoil at home between Mom and Dad.

I thought things would seem lighter at home now that Dad hasn't been around since the accident, but I still feel the weight of the situation even during his absence. I imagine on Sunday nights, when most adults are preparing to go back to work and they have the Sunday night 'blues', I have a Sunday night sweetness because I know that come Monday morning, I'll be able to go to school and be around people who really care about me. Focusing on the schoolwork to work hard to build a better life for myself than what I have been raised in has always been my motivation to study hard. However, lately, it has been increasingly difficult to focus on the schoolwork since Jerry has served as an intriguing distraction.

As I walk into the library on the second floor of the school for the Key Club meeting, I see Jerry. He nods at me as he waves me over and pulls out a seat next to him.

I quickly glance around the room in hopes that no one noticed him making a spot for me.

I sit down next to him as he starts to speak. "Hey Lisa, how has your day been? Did you and your brother end up finding your mom this weekend?"

"Hi, Jerry, so we actually never ended up finding her that night, but she did come home and said she just met up with a friend. She told us she was trying to make time for herself since there is a lot going on at home with dad being in the rehab facility."

"Oh, that sounds good that she came home, and all is well then, right?" Jerry asks as he leans back in his chair, scanning the room as other students come in to find their seats for the meeting.

"Yeah, I guess," I reply with a shrug of my shoulders and hesitancy in my voice. I'm not sure why I want to, but I start to share some of my feelings with him about the situation.

"I get the impression that my mom is not being entirely truthful to David and me. I find it puzzling that she would get all dressed up like that to go out with just a friend. I can't even think of one person that she could call a friend anymore. With everything that goes on at our house, as you know, it doesn't leave Mom much time to have friends or go out, let alone when it comes to having money to be able to do things like that. So it just seems strange to me."

I slowly move my eyes to look up at him as his eyes meet mine, and he offers a soft smile. I'm not sure why I have never noticed that Jerry has a calming presence about him. When around him, I can be myself and am at ease.

"Yeah, I get what you're saying, Lisa. I'm sure your mom is not deceiving you like you think she might be. She really does deserve to make some time for her to meet friends with everything she's gone and is going through. I'm sure you know that more than anyone, though."

"Yeah, you're probably right." I shift my gaze to the front of the library as the Key Club Director gathers our attention to start our meeting.

I take a deep breath to focus on the meeting we're about to have, but my mind wanders, thinking about how caring Jerry seems and genuinely has an interest in what's going on in my life. Why does he care so much about me seemingly out of the blue?

CHAPTER 29

Lisa

July 1975 Age: 14

After the Key Club meeting, as I begin to walk home, I am caught in thought over my conversation with Jerry. That was probably the most emotion I have seen out of him in my whole life in one single conversation with him.

He didn't leave my side during the meeting. I even noticed at one point, his toe tapped mine. When I looked down to move my foot away, he looked up at me and smirked, giving me the impression that perhaps it was intentional-his little game of footsie.

I gave a smirk back, but honestly, I'm confused as to where his feelings may be coming from with me. Is it just friendship? Or could he be pursuing something more with me?

After school as I'm leaving the front entrance, I hear a voice calling from a distance.

"Hey, wait up!"

As I turn to look to see who it is, I see Jerry in the distance, with his hand up in the air as he tries to slip his left arm into the other loop of his backpack, running to make it through the other students in a rush to catch me. I stand there as I move my arms out to the sides as if to physically question what he is doing.

He runs to catch up to me, and when he finally reaches me, he says, "Wow, you really bolted out of there quickly!"

"Bolted out of where?"

"The Key Club meeting...You left so fast," he says, as if it's silly that I am asking what he is talking about.

"Well, I didn't want to have to sign up for any more projects. I am already working on a fundraiser coming up."

He lets out a deep sigh. "Yeah, I know what you mean. Mrs. Burkin really seems to like getting more people on her fundraisers and projects."

"She sure does. I noticed that *you* haven't been on any yet this year." I look up at him as we start walking in the direction of our houses.

"Yeah, I'm not overly eager to show that I have much spare time. It seems that as soon as you let her see that side of you, you're in for it, and she's asking you to do more and more. My mom does that to me, I don't need anyone *else* in my life doing that."

"Well, I wish someone would've told me that when I joined the club!" I retort with a chuckle.

"Well, how about this, when is the fundraiser you're

on coming up? Care if I join you? It'll look good on my college applications," he exclaims.

I quickly reply, "Oh, I see how it is for you, Jerry. You only care about how this will look for you and what it will get you in your future!"

Grinning a devilish sneer, he says, "Isn't that what the Key Club is for? Doing a bunch of BS to be able to say you did it later and hope that it gets you something down the road?"

I begin to giggle, and this time, I really can't stop laughing! Tears fill my eyes, and an ache starts to form in the top portion of my stomach—the kind you only get when you're laughing a true belly laugh that you just can't stop.

I glance up at him. "Yeah, I suppose you're right. Although truthfully, I've never thought of it that way. I'm on the car wash fundraiser. It's Saturday at 2 o'clock downtown."

"Sounds good, I'll be there," he comments with a grin.

"Don't you have anywhere more important to be than hanging around me, especially for a Key Club fundraiser?" I question, trying to get out of him, what his *actual* intentions are here.

"Wow, way to sell yourself and make people want to spend time with you, Lisa."

Snickering, I reply, "Well, it's just... don't you have anything better to do?"

"Well, it's a beautiful day. I'm with a beautiful girl, talking about beautiful things that could greatly influence my future, including seeing her again. What's better than that?"

Okay... He is certainly hitting on me now. If I needed the confirmation of whether or not he was into me, I guess I've got it...

"May I continue to walk you home?"

"I don't see why not, we're already over half of the way there, right?" We both smile at each other as we continue toward our houses.

"Well, great."

As we continue walking, he sighs and then casually asks, "So, about that date I asked you out on when I saw you out with your brother, when can we make that happen? I've been meaning to ask you, but didn't want to take the risk of embarrassing you at school in front of anyone."

Without any control of my own, my back lights up with heat, and my cheeks blush as I search for what to say in response to him.

"Oh, we could probably do it any time, I suppose?" I tell him with a bit of uncertainty.

I wasn't sure if it was going to be an actual date or not. So I guess it *is* one?

Without missing a beat, he states, "That is unless you don't want it to be?"

"No, that's fine... I guess," I reply with a bit of hesitancy, which makes him laugh, and then I follow his lead, breaking the ice.

Here we are chuckling with each other throughout the awkwardness. I am unsure of myself and find that I don't know how to act. Is this what flirting feels like?

We finish the walk back home, and as we part ways,

Jerry grabs my hand. "Can't wait for Saturday, Lisa. We'll have a great time together...I'm sure of it!"

My heart rate starts to quicken with his touch, and I'm stunned. He is holding MY hand.

I've not held hands with someone other than my mother when I was a child.

There is a pounding in my chest, and I think my hands just might start sweating. I stand there, dead in my tracks and look back at him like a deer in headlights.

"Yeah, me too." I abruptly pull my hand away and turn to head toward home.

I am taken aback by this whole day—I just need to get home.

I can't believe I have a date set with Jerry for Saturday. He walked me home, AND he held my hand!

Although there is giddiness in my gut and a smile plastered across my face, I first need to determine if I like him the way that I think he may like me.

I suppose if I wasn't intrigued by him, I wouldn't be looking forward to spending more time with him, right? He is good-looking, but do we have much in common?

I guess I'll find out on Saturday.

CHAPTER 30
Sandy

July 1975 Age: 35

When we come home from the rehab facility, it is quiet between myself and the kids. No one speaks a word—we all know what has happened, and we are all reminded of who Johnny is and what he is capable of, and I can see that David is struggling with coming to terms with the situation.

I am not sure if he actually wanted to kill his father when the fight took place after he found me beaten or if he thought perhaps the fight would change him and he would become someone new.

Maybe David hoped that Johnny would become a nicer version of himself, someone who would see life as something worth being treasured. Something to be grateful for. Perhaps he thought Johnny could be someone who would treat his family like his greatest prized possession.

THE END IS THE BEGINNING   175

I know that that is what I had hoped would happen to him while undergoing this life-changing event. I thought that this change in him could happen, albeit a small chance, since not everyone gets another chance at life. But none of us could be that lucky, unfortunately.

I'm only left with the reminder of this depressing life I've shared with this man.

What am I to do? How can I escape this? Not only for myself but for my children and my soon-to-be new baby.

When it is finally night, I call Bill, and he agrees to come over for a sneaky visit on the front porch for us to talk about what has gone on since our date and my shifts working at Meats and Beets.

Simply hearing his voice on the phone triggers a sense of peace and calm to wash over me, knowing that everything will somehow be okay. I know he will be here for me in whatever capacity I let him. I tell him to come over at 10 pm so that the kids are asleep and we can be together privately.

As I watch the clock getting closer to that time, the butterflies start fluttering in my stomach.

He arrives with a small tap on my front door, and my heart leaps as I rush to sneak out the door, being careful not to let the screen door slam shut behind me.

He greets me with a bouquet of red roses and the most delicious milk chocolates I've ever had. I recognize the box from when he brought it to me before.

The smell of his cologne makes these butterflies flip and flitter even faster in my stomach. I take a small step toward him and wrap my arms around his freshly shaven neck as I pull him close.

We share the longest, most sensual, yet softest kiss. It feels like we've been apart for a year when it's really only been a few days.

His arms wrap around my waist, which has continued to grow a bit more lately and makes me feel like a bloated beached whale, but with Bill, I feel so beautiful.

He runs his fingers through my hair as he caresses my back softly while his tongue is pressing against my lips. A small request for entry, and how can I possibly deny him this?

After what I have witnessed today, I want nothing more than to feel his tongue and anything else he'll let me...

He pulls away and whispers in my ear, "Do you prefer we just talk?" He asks so politely, but I can feel him against my stomach, knowing he's feeling exactly what I am.

Oh God, what am I to do? How can I possibly say no? The temptation is rising so strong.

Before responding, I kiss him gently trying to slow down the moment while I try to decide what I should do. I momentarily worry about someone seeing us, but it is dark out, only small hints of moonlight peeking down. Surely everyone is fast asleep by now... As long as we keep quiet, we should be safe to do what we please.

Taking both hands, I caress his neck and inhale the deep scent he wears—a mixture of sandalwood with crisp ocean freshness and hints of musk and pepper. I don't know what this stuff is, but God, it gets me every time. It has got to be an aphrodisiac.

Without any warning and surprising myself, I let out

a small moan. He reciprocates with a small squeeze of my ass as he grows firmer against me. It's almost reaching a point where I can't fight this overwhelming urge any longer.

"Can we do what we want and then talk?" I ask teasingly in between quickening kisses between us.

"Where would you be most comfortable doing this?" he asks as I try to look around my yard over his shoulder while he trails kisses down from my left ear to my shoulder along my neck and the skin raises with goosebumps.

These interactions with him are so overwhelmingly sensual that I honestly can't fight it. It could be the pregnancy hormones making me extraordinarily sexually aroused, but I don't recall ever feeling this way with... Johnny.

Ugh, why did he have to just pop into my mind? Pushing the thought of him out of my mind, I squeeze Bill from under his arms while I feel his back muscles tense against my hands.

He takes my hand and guides me toward his car, this is where this happens for us more times than not. I really don't know how this will go this time now that I have grown a bit of a belly though. It really does seem that the farther along I become in this pregnancy, the more I want... need sex.

It doesn't take much to arouse me, nor does it take long to satisfy me. Perhaps it's God's way of giving this to me now since once this baby comes, He knows I won't get much of it then.

As we arrive at his car, we can hear the crickets

through the warmth of the night. He guides me to the opposite side of his car where we couldn't be seen from the house or hopefully anyone.

As soon as we get to his car, he unleashes his truest lustful self, and with every moment passing, every inch of me he caresses, I am lost. I am entirely his—whatever he wishes to do with me, I'll do it.

There is no returning from this. I love this feeling; I love the anticipation. Most of all, I love being wanted. I feel the sexiest I have ever felt despite having this ever-growing pregnant pooch.

Most of the time, I feel self-conscious with this bump of a stomach protruding off the front of me, but not in his presence. With him, I feel like a model. Albeit, a growing pregnant one at that.

He uses his hands as he pushes himself away from me to get a look at me. I am breathing so hard I can hardly stand it. I NEED this right now. I can't wait another moment.

He takes his hands and he pulls my top down so that my breasts are exposed to the humid night air, and he looks at them with such love. I can see it in his eyes. He loves me, all of me. Imperfections and all.

It makes my heart leap, and I truly think I am either going to have a heart attack or orgasm right here just from him looking at me and me looking at him.

He takes my skirt and drops it down around my ankles and kisses my belly as he makes his way down to his knees.

He grabs my right leg running his fingers on top of my thigh as he lifts it to rest upon his shoulder. He takes his

THE END IS THE BEGINNING   179

other hand and slowly caresses my calf that is holding my body weight, and as if he can't wait any longer either, he kisses a trail from my hip bone downward.

The goosebumps form again, and I can't wait for him to read my mind... like he seems to do. He knows exactly what I need and where. He begins gently kissing and suckling, and I can't stand it.

I've gone from 0-60 in a matter of seconds.

I grab his head as I run my fingers through his hair and hold his head in place. He knows what I need, and with the last kiss, I am a goner.

It feels as if a bomb detonated inside of me, and I am sliding down the side of a mountain. He grabs my leg to help stabilize me as I experience the most exhilarating orgasm of my life. If I thought the last time we did this was good, I had no idea what was coming.

When he's sure I'm finished, he does small soft kisses and begins the trail back up and over my bloated belly as he makes his way to my breasts. He cups each in his hands and kisses them gently. He sucks each nipple with a soft yet roughness at the end of each kiss. I can't believe it, but it is as if I didn't fully come down from that orgasm, I am back on top of that mountain, ready to explode all over again.

He continues taking his time kissing and suckling, and I need him inside of me.

I reach my hands down to his pants, and I can feel they are tented so tightly from his erection that he is ready. I softly touch him and I can feel he can hardly stand waiting another minute either.

I was about to turn around to make room for him by

moving myself, but he grabs my stomach and directs me to him.

He steps back a moment and takes his shirt off over his head, and then drops his pants. Seeing him standing there in the moonlight, his muscles flexing and him yearning for me...Oh my God, I am so ready for this.

I know someone *could* theoretically see us, but it is dark out here. As soon as he moves toward me, a cloud seems to begin to cover the moonlight that darkens the night skies.

He bends down, taking my leg and lifting it. He leans me back against the car and looks at me to confirm I am okay with this. I give him a "let's do this, damnit" look and a slight nod while I slowly lick my lips.

He bends down and grabs my other leg, hoisting me up with his arms. Holy shit. If this isn't a sight. His shoulders and arms flexing while holding me up exactly how he wants me.

He inserts himself into me, and we both breathe air into each other's mouths. I attempt to help, holding my weight by resting my arms on his shoulders.

I'm glad that we have the car behind us for me to rest my back on while he does the majority of the movement.

He brings his head down and does small licks to my nipples, and I curl my legs around his back. Within a matter of seconds, we both orgasm with slow deep breaths as we try to keep quiet. I feel all of the blood in my body has left all my limbs and my brain and has gone entirely to my vagina.

He gently lifts me and sets me back onto the ground.

He bends down to get me my clothes and hands them

to me before getting his own. He leans into me and kisses me on the cheek while my breasts brush against the hair on his chest, and it feels like electricity is between us.

I can't believe how attracted I am to this man. Good God. It's like he could read my mind and felt the pull between us too. Before he hands me my clothes, he does swirling kisses to my nipples.

My head rolls back, and I lift my right foot off the ground, and he can feel it against his leg. Before I set it down, he grabs ahold of my knee and raises it to my side.

He reaches his hand down and begins rubbing swift motions side to side and in a circular fashion. How in the hell am I still able to be this aroused after 2 orgasms? This is turning into a marathon, and I can NOT say no.

He takes his fingers and reaches them farther back as he inserts two of them and then three of them, and I can't hold it in anymore. I start breathing heavily into his ear.

He wastes no time, wanting to make sure I am well cared for, he whispers in my ear, let me lay you down in my car so you can rest. I think I can 'go' just by hearing his voice and his offer to care for me.

Not responding verbally but by taking his mouth into mine and swirling his tongue with mine, he moves me to the right a step and opens his car door. He sets me inside and whispers in a gruff voice, "Just lay back and let me do all the rest. I love pleasuring you, my dear. You deserve to have it all... and then some."

I do as he says, my legs widening for him as if it were a command and my life depended on it. He enters the back of the car, breathing heavily, just as I am.

I take my hand and run it through his hair and we lock

lips and share a kiss that is so strong. We pull apart and are breathing even heavier now.

He heads down, pushing my thighs apart, and this time, at the same time as his tongue begins to swirl, he inserts a thumb just inside and applies a slight amount of pressure upward, and I know that I can't take it for long. I try to slow my breathing to make it last longer, to enjoy this moment.

But I can't wait any longer. This coupling sensation sends me over the edge, and I start to moan. I try to stifle it, but this is so all-consuming it's nearly impossible.

He continues the motions, getting harder and faster in rhythmic motion while I climax, and then he softens his touch as I come down from it, making it drawn out as long as it can last. I swear that was the longest and most intense sensation I have ever had.

How in the hell did I get so lucky to have this kind of love in my life? This kind of sex? It is unimaginable.

He runs his tongue up my stomach and swirls it around my belly button as he gives it a few small kisses, and he helps me up and offers me my clothes again.

Holy shit that took me by surprise. I was not ready for that, but boy, am I glad we did that.

We lock eyes, confirming that we're both ready to put them back on this time.

We smirk as we put our clothes on and make our way back up to the house, arms wrapped around each other's backs.

Bill clears his throat before he asks through a shit-eating grin, "So… should we pencil-in car sex for next week again? Same time, same place? It seems we have our best... ahem... 'experiences' when we're behaving like sneaky, scared-to-get-caught teenagers."

I place my hand over my mouth to stifle my laughter and keep it quiet as we approach the house with every step we take in tandem.

"Sounds like a plan to me! You sure know how to 'get me', Bill," I respond, my voice just above a whisper as I playfully squeeze his butt cheek before pulling away.

We sit on the rickety wooden front step of my porch and share some of the chocolates that he bought for me as I take a deep inhalation of the roses he bought.

These chocolates are delightful, especially coming off of the blissful, sweet, and sensual lovemaking we just shared.

"So... you wanted to talk?"

We both erupt in laughter as if we can just pick up where we left off before that wild, wonderful experience we shared.

But the funny thing is—we can do just that. That is the kind of love we share. The kind of love where we can have both—the mental and physical connection.

This must be what everyone is looking for in their quest for love in life.

How is it that I've found it while being married and pregnant with another man's baby?

CHAPTER 31

Lisa

July 1975 Age: 14

It's Saturday—the day of the Key Club Car Wash fundraiser. I never would have the jitters before a fundraiser like this usually but knowing that Jerry is coming to participate only for me and the fact that we have a date afterward, my very first ever date... this is a BIG deal.

The car wash doesn't begin until 2:00, but I'm getting ready, and it's not even noon. My hair has to be perfect. I have to have the best swimsuit top picked out to wear with my high-waisted blue jean cut-off shorts to show off my long legs.

I overheard the popular girls in Key Club talking about what they were going to wear, so I'm going to try to follow their lead with a revealing swimsuit top with cut-offs in hopes of fitting in or maybe even standing out with my own look.

THE END IS THE BEGINNING   185

Somehow, I have been blessed with being tall and lean, well-endowed, and having long silky brown hair with golden, light brown eyes and soft freckles that run across the bridge of my nose onto both cheeks.

The latter attribute though, I could go without.

I would love to have the kind of skin that is clear and uniform like many of the girls at school have, but I suppose we all have a thing or two we wish we could trade-in for something better.

If I could really trade something in, though, it would be my massively crooked teeth (mostly my upper teeth). But since we don't have much money, getting them straightened out just has never been in the cards for me.

Finally, it is 1:30, and with one last check in the mirror, I head out of the house to go downtown for the fundraiser. As I am walking out of my driveway I see a car backing out of Jerry's driveway. I try to act like I don't see him, trying to be nonchalant. Once I make it to the side-walk, he pulls up in his teal blue Plymouth Road Runner and rolls his window down.

"Hop in, hot stuff!" he shouts and then whistles, "Whoot whoo."

I can feel myself blushing already. Shit, why did I wear all of this? Didn't I want this kind of attention? With how I am feeling right now, I'd like to run back inside, change my clothes, and call this entire day off. Unfortunately, that is not an option for me today.

I get into his car, and immediately, he grabs my left leg, giving it a tight squeeze while winking his eye toward me.

"Hey!" I try to sound cheerful and hope it will hide my embarrassment.

"I'm sure glad I agreed to come to this fundraiser with you, Lisa. You ready to head over there?" he asks excitedly.

"Yeah, it'll be fun washing cars, let's go!" The sarcasm is evident in my voice.

He begins to accelerate and turns on the radio as we listen to "Go All the Way" by The Raspberries. This song was released a few years ago and has been popular ever since. But for some reason, the lyrics are starting to make more sense to me in this moment now than ever before when I've heard it.

I hear the lyrics mention going all the way and things feeling so right. As we listen further, the song continues with coming alive when she does things to him.

Hearing these words and noticing Jerry nodding his head to the beat, I start to feel slightly uncomfortable listening to it dressed the way I am, sitting next to him when we're about to have our first date.

I try adjusting my top to cover me up a little bit more and appear more conservative, but I don't really think it is working, and I am getting more nervous.

Breaking me out of my thoughts, Jerry starts to speak. "So, what did you want to do after the car wash for our date?"

"Uh, I don't know... hadn't given it much thought really." I try to hide my nervousness.

"You haven't given it much thought that we're going on a date? Well, I have. It's been nearly all I can think about. Never thought I'd look so forward to washing other people's cars!" He looks over at me, trying to gauge my reaction.

"Well, you can decide what it is you want to do after the car wash then." I flash a smile over at him trying to break the awkwardness that is in the air.

When we pull into the car wash we see there are stations set up for a team of 2-3 people at each station washing the cars.

We get out of his car and see Mrs. Birken directing other students where to go. When she spots Jerry walking up with me, she makes a surprised face with arms out to her sides, questioning what she is seeing. Oh great...

"Well, would you look at who decided to partake in a Key Club fundraiser... Would you look at that?" Mrs. Birken says.

"Yeah, I thought this would be a good one to do that would look good on my college resume," Jerry quickly comments without holding anything back.

Mrs. Birken's mouth opens a bit as she tries to mask her surprise at his blatant honesty.

"Well then... Whatever it takes, I guess," I say as if his reason wasn't enough of a 'reason'.

"I'll have you and Lisa over here at this station. The next car that comes will be directed to you both."

"Great!" Jerry says and walks right over to our station. He decides he'll test the hose out and sprays the ground a bit and then sprays it directed at me.

I scream as it is cold and shocking. Jerry starts to laugh uncontrollably.

"There, now maybe you'll loosen up a bit, and we can have some fun. Don't be nervous, Lisa. I'm not *that* cool to be around." He nudges me in the side just below my bikini top.

"I'm not nervous, Jerry! But now I'm freezing!" I cross my arms across my chest, trying to cover my breasts so that my nipples don't start to poke out in my navy blue swimsuit top.

Jerry looks cute with his dark brown hair combed over to the side while he is wearing a white wife-beater-style tank top with blue jean shorts. I never noticed until today that he has quite defined arm and back muscles. He must work out despite my knowledge of it. I never saw him as much of a sports kind of guy.

We begin washing our first vehicle at the car wash. And as I reach across the front window of the car to clean the windshield bugs off, I realize that my breasts are pressed into the glass. I only notice this because I feel the sensation of the water soaking through my swimsuit top as I step away from the vehicle to start washing the driver's side window.

Jerry is on the opposite side of the car looking through the window at me. He does that whistle again like he did earlier when he picked me up, and I look around to see if anyone heard him—I am immediately embarrassed. Luckily for me, the other stations have music playing so they can't hear us at ours.

"Lisa, don't worry, no one can hear me whistle at you. But even if they could, I'd do it anyway. This is the best car wash I've been to. Maybe you could wash my car next?"

"Yeah, sure, I could wash your car. You just have to pay up like everybody else! Except for you, you would be charged double the rate!" I shout as I begin making my way around the backside of the vehicle.

We finish washing that car and probably wash 10 others before our shift is up at the fundraiser. Jerry flashes a look at me as a smile spreads across his face, and he looks like he is up to no good.

"So... you ready to blow this popsicle stand and head on our date with me then, Lisa?" he asks so slyly as he leans up against the freshly washed and dried car.

"Yeah, I suppose I am..." I really don't know that I am actually ready, and my voice probably sounds hesitant, but I said I would, so I have to keep my word, right?

It's not that I don't necessarily want to go. It's more that I'm worried about how it will go and what to do and when.

"Alright, let's go get in my car. The day is still young!"

We head across the parking lot and get into his car. He peels out so fast I have hardly closed the door before he steps on the gas.

Where are we going, and what are we going to do? What if he tries to kiss me... I don't know how to kiss! I don't even know if I *want* to kiss him.

Swarmed by my thoughts, he drives us into town. Thankfully my swimsuit top is still a bit damp because otherwise, I'd be sweating from the adrenaline coursing through me.

CHAPTER 32

Sandy

July 1975 Age: 35

Bill is asking me how my last few days have been, and he interrupts himself to ask, "First and most important, how have you been feeling?"

He asks this as he slips his right arm around me and pulls me close while placing a small kiss on top of my head where my hairline meets my face.

"Well, it's been an interesting couple of days. The kids and I went to visit Johnny at the rehab facility for the first time in two weeks, and he said, without directly saying it, that he knows what is going on in his household, even when he is not there."

I shift my gaze down to look at the ground, to try to hide my shame and unease.

"He even accused the children of leading him on by acting as if they didn't know about... us. Needless to say, the visit didn't end on a good note, and we left in a hurry.

THE END IS THE BEGINNING   191

I am really not looking forward to him coming home. I honestly don't know what I will do on any level of my life. I don't know how to reintroduce him into our lives. So much has changed since the accident. My pregnancy, my new job, and... you and I, of course."

"Sandy... I'm so sorry you are facing all of these overwhelming and conflicting emotions. You know that I am here for you. How about I give you some money to have as an emergency fund and also a little extra to get some groceries and things before he comes home so that you can feel more prepared? And for when he comes home, if you're comfortable with it, I could be nearby and keep a watch out and only come inside if needed?"

"I am quite touched by your offers, Bill. But I honestly would not feel right taking any of your money." Before I can finish my sentence he interjects.

"You wouldn't be taking it. I am offering it. Think of it as a gift. Isn't that what you would do if you saw someone who needed something and they were in a desperate situation? Someone that you... Deeply care for? Maybe even someone that you would say you... love?"

I look at him quickly to try to read his expression and see that perhaps he didn't just say what I think he just said. When my eyes meet his, I can see it is truly and genuinely him. What he just said *is* how he feels... about me.

My breath has been completely taken away. Not like in the surprised kind of way, but as if I just had the wind knocked out of me. I cannot believe that he just said he... loves me. How can he know that already?

I impulsively want to say it back of course, but I'm

terrified of what that could actually mean... what would my life look like if I admitted this?

Of course I've thought of this before myself. Then there's the love we have made... clearly that shows how strong of a physical connection we have. There is no doubt about that.

I also feel we connect on a mental and emotional level. We have talked about future goals and hardships in life. Unfortunately, he knows more about mine than I feel I know about his.

We have shared our belief around religion and that we believe there is a God looking out for us in this life.

I really can't think of a topic that we haven't covered. As I'm running through all of these thoughts, he is just sitting there staring back at me, seemingly, awaiting my response. This kind of pressure feels so heavy—so important for our future.

"Bill... I think you already know that I... I care very deeply for you. I just..."

Bill interjects again. "Listen, Sandy, you don't have to say anything back. I don't want you to feel any pressure, and you are certainly under no obligation. But it's true, I absolutely do love you. I do know this, and each day going forward, my love will only continue to grow stronger and deeper for you. I have visions of our life together. And I would love to share some of them with you if you would allow me to?"

"I would love nothing more. But before I allow you to speak on that, you should know that my feelings for you have by far surpassed any expectations I had. Unfortunately though, I am still in a marriage and have a lot left yet to sort out. So I don't think I can put into words my emotions just yet."

"I completely understand, Sandy. I will always love you and be here for you. Now, let me share with you some of my visions for us—for this life you so desperately deserve to have. A wonderful and fulfilling life with... me."

I smile and squeeze him a little tighter around the waist as I rest my head on his shoulder and just listen.

True euphoric glee overwhelms me, and listening to him, I am in awe of this man and what our life could be. Is it only a dream? I can't seem to wrap my mind around how this could ever become reality for us.

But listening to him talk about it, it's all I ever want to have.

CHAPTER 33

Lisa

July 1975 Age: 14

Jerry pulls into the parking lot of The Dairy Drop, the nearest ice cream shop located in Edwardstown. As we pull up, I can hear 60's music playing, and there are many umbrella-covered tables and chairs for all of the ice cream go-ers to sit at.

As I reach for the door handle to open the door of the car, a warm breeze flows through the car and blows my hair back behind my shoulders.

I begin to open the door as I notice Jerry running around from his side of the car to open my door for me.

"My lady." Jerry nods as he opens the door with a bow.

I laugh and gently hit him on the arm. "You goof, I'm not your lady!"

Jerry chuckles. "Not yet, that is... but I plan to change that."

THE END IS THE BEGINNING 195

I want to play it off cool, but my cheeks are flushing, and my heart rate is quickening from embarrassment and nerves. What am I doing here?

Before I can think much about my anxiety, Jerry grabs my hand and guides me inside The Dairy Drop.

"Look over the menu. Anything your heart desires, you can have. Or, we could be romantic and share a sundae such as a banana split." He uses his own version of a French accent, clearly trying to impress me.

I smile at him with a nudge trying to make up my mind as the girl behind the counter is waiting for me to place my order.

"How about we do the banana split sundae? I'm not terribly hungry."

"Oh, the lady is trying to be romantic, can't you see?" he says, with a gesture of his hand toward me, engaging the girl behind the counter, whose name appears to be Janice, taking our order at The Dairy Drop.

"Okay, so I have one banana split for you to share. Can I get you guys anything else?" Janice asks with a wide smile across her face.

Jerry looks at me for reassurance before answering her. "No, that should be all. It's our first time here, but I'm sure we will be back again soon."

Jerry turns to me and winks as he takes the spoons and napkins from her.

It is a warm 80-degree summer evening, and we decide to sit out at one of the umbrella-covered picnic tables.

As we reach our seats, I notice right away that perhaps my shorts are too short, because the benches are made of stones that are not all flat. I can feel the stones digging into my bottom and the uppermost portion of my thighs. I try balancing my weight and leaning to one side while crossing one leg over the other in the hope that by doing this, it will give the leg that is crossed on top a break. Hopefully, this won't occupy my mind all night.

"Ladies first." He gestures toward the sundae for me to have the first bite.

I smile and take my spoon for a bite. The ice cream is so delicious, sweet and creamy. I can't believe how good it is. I have never been here before so to me, this is a real special treat.

Using the fact that I'm eating as an opportunity to speak, Jerry begins asking some questions.

"So that night, I saw you out with your brother looking for your mom. Did you find out who she was with? And also, how's your dad? Is he coming back home soon?"

"No, we didn't find out for sure who she was with. However, David and I don't believe it was a female friend. We know that Mom has been struggling, as we all have, I suppose, living with our father, and how he treats all of us. I would have no doubt that my mom, being beautiful as she is, would attract male attention. Maybe she just met a friend, but I'm beginning to wonder if she has been seeing someone while dad has been recovering since the accident. It hurts me to think of my mom not being faithful to my dad, but I can't say that I blame her, considering how he has treated her."

Having divulged so much information, I am reminded of who I am with and begin to feel uncomfortable at the thought of possibly having overshared. I take my spoon and go for another bite of the delicious banana split sundae.

"I don't blame you for questioning who your mom was with and if she may be seeing a man, but like you said, you can't blame her for all that she has been through. It also may come as a surprise to you, but you are beautiful and take after a lot of the traits of your mother, Lisa."

Upon hearing that, I take my spoon for another bite. Thank God this ice cream is here for me to stifle my embarrassment and avoid talking. I smile back at him, trying to express a "thank you" by taking a bite.

"So, how's things with your dad? Will he be coming home soon?" Jerry asks, trying to get to know the family dynamic.

"It will all depend on his progress, I think, and if my mom ends up accepting him into our house again."

"What do you mean? Why wouldn't she accept him?" he asks as he crosses his arms across his chest leaning on the table.

"After everything he has put her and us through, I don't know how much she will want to be around him, especially considering that she will be having a new baby for our family to care for soon. And not to mention, if she is, in fact, seeing someone, I'm sure that could heavily influence her decision of taking him back or not."

I love Jerry's demeanor right now. It clearly demonstrates how closely and attentively he is listening to me speak as he is leaning into the table and his eyes are locked on mine. Part of me realizes that I don't think anyone has ever listened closely to what I have to say, so it feels wonderful that someone would care enough to listen to me talk, but it also is a bit surprising that he would care as much as he is acting like he does right now. Maybe he is simply waiting to take his next bite of ice cream, and that is why he is listening and waiting so intently.

"I see… I suppose that does make sense. Although, for my family, it seems like my mom will always take my dad back no matter how bad it is." He leans away from the table and breaks eye contact.

I can tell that this has struck a chord with him, and he is trying to open up emotionally with me, but it is painful for him to share such vulnerable details.

I try to respond with something comforting to his small attempt at opening up to me.

"I completely understand that. Unfortunately, with you living close to our house, you've seen more of what goes on in our household than I would care for anyone to know about. However, I haven't seen as much go on with your house. Have you shared some similar experiences?"

I can tell that he is unsure of how much and what he wants to share with me. He takes in a deep breath, and then blows it out slowly.

Looking at his eyes, it seems like he is reviewing a multitude of events and determining which he wants to divulge unto me.

"Yes. Unfortunately, I have shared a similar lifestyle growing up as you. My dad has not been a good man to my mother, but it makes me wonder, are any men decent to their wives? My dad is someone who is outwardly racist and has expected me and my siblings to work and provide income for our household from a very young age. He has made that abundantly clear, and it doesn't matter how much we do around the house or outside of the house to contribute; it is never enough in his eyes, he is always expecting more out of us. Even with having a job, it never pleases him. He is constantly disappointed in us and my mom as well. He lets us know this on a daily basis —his disappointment and unhappiness. He chooses to communicate this to us, not only through his rage-filled four-letter word choices that he calls us, but also, with his...hands."

He shrugs his shoulders as if that would shake away what he just said and clears his throat like he is also clearing the air between us of this darkness he has just exposed to me.

I sit for a moment, taking in the warm night air, trying to offer an easy and open atmosphere to give him an opportunity to share more if he wants to.

After a brief moment, I reach my hand across the table and gently caress his arm. I am doing this instinctually before I even realize that I'm doing it.

When I do realize, I look down and jump a little, pulling my hand away from him. But with that, Jerry lifts his eyes and takes his hand to reach mine.

We are overlooking the parking lot as we sit at our table with our empty ice cream sundae glass holding hands. Feeling his hand against mine, my heart rate starts to beat rapidly, but as his thumb starts rubbing the back of my hand in a side-to-side motion, it immediately calms me, and I begin to relax.

The night continues with us sharing stories and relating over our troubled home lives. Eventually, we transition the topic of discussion onto school, and before I know it, the sun is beginning to set, and it seems we have left no conversation piece undiscussed.

When we walk to the car, Jerry runs around again to grab the door for me, but before he does, he pulls me in for a tight hug.

I am taken so off guard that I tense up but quickly become at ease again at the touch of his hands wrapping around my neck and the weight of his arms resting upon my shoulders.

As we back away from one another, I look up at him, and he looks down at me. I see his eyes glance from mine down to my lips and back up again.

Oh my God, is he going to kiss me? Is this going to be my first kiss of my entire life right here in the parking lot of The Dairy Drop?

Before I know it... his lips are on mine, and it is actually happening! His lips are soft and sensual, also gentle and as smooth as silk.

It is so good to be kissed and cared for by someone. Before my brain registers it, I am caught up in the moment and am squeezing his lower back, bringing him closer to me.

When we pull away, he smiles at me, and I reciprocate by looking up at him. All of the nervousness that I had amped up in me for this day simply washes away as the breeze blows my hair off of my shoulders as it lands on my back.

We get into his car, and he drives me home. He

reaches his hand over and rests it on my left thigh and this time, I reach my hand down and rest it on the back of his hand.

We don't talk much on the drive home. We are both caught up—mentally reminiscing about our evening together.

Soon, we are pulling into my driveway, and it seems as though it has only been a two-minute commute.

"Thank you for such a fun day and a really nice first date, Jerry." I swing open the door before I step my right foot out and get out of the car.

Jerry leans over and places a tender kiss on my left cheek as he squeezes my hand gently three times.

"Have a good night, my Lisa. I was going to get the door for you, but you are just one step ahead of me!" He winks with a smirk.

Did he just put a 'my' in front of my name? Does this mean that he is *claiming* me as his own?

My stomach flips and it flops. Here come the butterflies all over again circling in me.

"Good night, Jerry," I softly say, in a voice just louder than a whisper as I get out of the car and close the door.

I walk into my house with an extra pep in my step, and the remnants of my first kiss on my lips.

CHAPTER 34
Sandy

February 1976 Age: 36

Time has elapsed and life has seemed to only become more confusing for me in this love triangle I have inevitably created for myself. Even though Bill and I have experienced more than a couple rendezvouses and 'visits' on the front porch, I wake up today with a sense of confidence in what I know I need to do.

The life between Johnny and I can no longer exist.

As confident as I am in this, I am completely unsure of how I will deliver this message to him and how it will be received. A horrifying thought crosses my mind should Johnny not receive this news well... Will me and my unborn baby make it out alive?

I decide that I am going to visit Johnny one more time in the rehab facility to perhaps 'get on a better level' with him before he is set to come home. He has been showing improvement recently but has had quite a few setbacks. So much so, we thought he wouldn't ever make it out to come back home.

After the fight broke out last summer, Johnny was initially hospitalized to recover. Similarly to me, he had suffered several broken facial bones, including a severe skull fracture that led to a brain bleed which caused him to experience an altered mental status where he became increasingly more agitated and angry. I thought this was impossible...

I probably should have visited him more or called to check in, but seeing his anger and wrath—I have unfortunately known all too well over the years—unleashed onto the nursing staff, it was simply too much for me to bear.

Whether it was from the fight with David or when he was moved into the ambulance by the emergency personnel, Johnny had an upper cervical spine fracture that caused paralysis. It was initially believed to be permanent, but with his lengthy stay and recovery while wearing a halo, he learned to regain some strength to stand and take a few steps. He lost so much muscle mass in his lower body from recuperating from his injuries that he needed much therapy to regain his strength and to work on recovering his mental status too.

I mentioned my wanting to visit him to Lisa and David, but they both seemed very uninterested and expressed that they were not looking forward to him coming home this week. I don't want to force them to come with me and visit him if they really do not want to, but I was hoping to have some potential backup or witness with me. It will just have to be what it will be, I guess.

As I walk into the rehab facility, I am greeted by the same nurse that we saw last time when we visited. I greet her with a warm hello and smile and watch her as I say a silent prayer that she will be around his room in case Johnny raises his voice or, God forbid, tries to lay a hand on me during this visit.

As I pass the nurses' station making my way to his room, I hear a familiar tune from the radio they are playing. It is "Stand By Your Man", by Tammy Wynette.

The lyrics serve as such a stark reminder of what my role should be as Johnny's wife. The song mentions loving your man and being proud of him because everything else aside, he *is* just a man... So, stand by your man and give him your warm embrace to come home to, especially when times are lonely, show everyone around you that you love him and you will always be there for him as his wife.

The timing of this song playing seems to be impeccable. Is it meant to make me second-guess my plan coming here? Because it sure is working.

I walk past the station faster than I started walking into this facility wanting to stop hearing that song and shake off the worry over the decision that lies ahead and how I will go about all of this.

As I enter his room, I take a deep breath trying to clear my mind as I place a small, tap tap tap knock on the doorway, announcing my entry. He turns, and when he notices it's me, he doesn't acknowledge me.

I know that he saw me, though, so I walk ahead with

confidence. I pull a chair out to sit down, but instead, I don't sit. I remain standing because I know I should not be here long.

"Hey, how are you doing today?" I ask, trying to sound cordial and genuinely curious.

He does not look up at me even for a second.

He doesn't respond and after a few moments, I contemplate leaving. I suppose I could ask him what is wrong, but I'm fairly confident we both already know.

My stomach is growing larger by the day, which is just a glaring reminder of the life I am about to bring into a world where there is a lot of turbulence in the home environment that this new child will have. I wish more than anything that it wasn't Johnny's baby.

Why does it have to be?

With each second that passes that he does not respond, I become angrier. How dare he treat me with a cold shoulder. What does he expect? He has not treated me well for our entire lives. I would be lying if I ever said that I didn't wonder what would've happened if David had just taken him once and for all during their fight. David was, after all, fighting him in an effort to stand up for me and defend me as his mother, which no child should ever have to do to their father.

I want to spout off to him, all of my frustration and anger, and a sort of rationale as to why I have had the affair on him, but it takes everything in me to hold my tongue and not say what is on my mind.

"I think it's time we talk about our future... I'm not sure how you envision it looking, but for me, I don't see it as us being together. When you are released from here, you can go stay with your parents. I am happy to make a call to them for you to arrange it."

Saying this definitely gets his attention. He quickly snaps his head to lock his eyes with mine while I am standing, looking down at him with my arms crossed at my chest.

I will myself to be strong and persevere—to dig my heels in on discussing this topic with him, however painful it may be.

Although we have an extensive history of many, MANY bad memories, there are also a few good ones, and as I look him in the eyes, I see a flash reminiscing about them... perhaps not wanting to let this go due to our past.

I am reminded of the time when David took his first steps. We were in the kitchen, and I was holding him with his fingers while he was stepping with a wobble from side to side. I gradually let go of his hand and then eventually his fingers too and he walked three steps straight into Johnny's arms! We both were so excited and hugged each other with David smooshed in between us. That was such a joyous moment.

But unfortunately, I am also reminded of how quickly that joy faded when, that very night, Johnny became enraged over a conversation he had with some friends at the bar earlier in the night.

He felt that in comparison to the other men's wives, they did more for them than I did for him. After all, I was the only woman in the group at that time that had a child.

I was struggling to learn my new role as a mother and a wife. Of course, Johnny would be no help to me, especially not during the night and expected me to carry-on as

THE END IS THE BEGINNING   207

if I had not just grown a child the size of a watermelon inside of me—David was a large 9lb baby, that I managed to labor and push out without hemorrhaging or any large complications, and then, according to him, I was supposed to just bounce back as if it hadn't ever happened all the while being sleepless and hormonally off-balance?

I will never forget the resentment and rage that I felt toward him at that time in our marriage, but especially, that night.

As I reminisce, I was crying myself to sleep that night, while holding our son, David, praying to God to protect the both of us as we ventured ahead in this life. I felt so angry at myself that I would've married someone who had proven to be a monster and then on top of it all, had a child with him after being treated so awfully.

What kind of mother did that make me?

Johnny clears his throat, and I can tell he is contemplating his thoughts back to me, which snaps me back into this moment. I am partially surprised that he hasn't responded yet, but perhaps with all of the thoughts flooding my mind, not as much time has passed as I am imagining.

"So, you're telling me that you don't want to be with me anymore? After all I have suffered and gone through, you have chosen to shack up with somebody else? You do not deserve to be with someone other than me. I have worked my ass off here recovering and healing to come back home and be with you and raise our growing family together. It is blasphemous that you would go behind my back and deceive me."

He says this as he swiftly glances down, moving his eyes between my stomach and my eyes, reminding me of this unborn life that is just as much his as it is mine.

Ugh, the thought of hearing him say that he wants to "raise our growing family together" makes me want to puke and strangle him all at once. How can he possibly act like the raising of our children was ANYTHING that we did together?

I have done everything from start to finish from the day both of our children were born. It is sickening the false reality that he is living in—thinking that he had any part in their upbringing other than scaring them half to death with his violent acts and giving them the 'gift' of being traumatized for their lifetime.

Before I can respond to him, he stands up so quickly I hardly have a moment to react.

He grabs both of my hands and pulls me toward him. Initially, it feels like he is going to try to be intimate with me as I sense his breathing slowing.

I did not even realize that he could stand up since considering the times I have been here to see him, he has only been seated. I am shocked by his abrupt movement and I am hesitating in my attempts to back away.

It seems as though he has thought about this moment...

He directs me away from the eyesight of the door, where the thought crosses my mind: *what is he going to do to me that no passerby could see now that he has moved us?*

His grip is getting tighter around my hands as he moves up toward my wrists. It is all I can do but shake my head as I try telling him that I do not want to do what he is about to try to do.

He holds my arms tightly to my thighs and brings his mouth to my ear as he whispers, "There is no way you can do this to me. We have built this whole life together. You owe it to me to uphold the vows we took 17 years ago."

It surprises me that he can name the years that we have been together.

Sweat begins to form on my upper lip out of anxiousness and feeling his touch. He pulls away and looks me in the eye as he says, "You are no better today than you were the day I met you. You're just a stupid sleeping-around whore, that doesn't deserve the good life you have already had. Haven't you figured out I am the best you will ever get? You will regret anything that you do that's not with me. You will never get away with it. I will make sure of that, Sandy... Mark. My. Words."

As Johnny's words sink in, fear grips me tightly. His hold on my wrists is painful, and his sudden aggression catches me off guard. I struggle to break free, my heart pounding in my chest. Panic washes over me as I realize the severity of this situation.

I desperately scan the room, hoping for someone to come into his room and intervene, but it seems like no one is around.

Summoning every ounce of courage within me, I gather my strength and manage to pull one hand free from Johnny's grasp. With adrenaline coursing through my veins, I swing my freed arm, aiming for his face. But Johnny is quick to react, deflecting my blow and forcefully pushing me backward.

I stumble, nearly losing my balance, but manage to regain my footing just in time.

The room feels suffocating, and my mind races, searching for an escape plan. I can't let Johnny overpower me—I need to protect myself and this baby.

Suddenly, my eyes catch a glimmer of hope—a small what appears to be a stainless steel leftover food tray on a nearby table. Without hesitation, I grab it and hold it up as a makeshift shield, creating a barrier between Johnny and me.

Johnny's eyes widen, a mix of surprise and anger spreading across his face. He lunges toward me, aiming to knock the tray from my hands. We engage in a desperate struggle, the tray clattering against his fists as he tries to wrestle it away from me.

In the midst of the chaos, I spot a nurse rushing into the room. Relief floods through me, knowing that help is finally here.

But before the nurse can intervene, Johnny manages to wrench the tray from my grasp, sending it crashing to the floor.

Time seems to slow as we both pause, gasping for breath.

The nurse's arrival interrupts the tension, her voice authoritative as she commands Johnny to "Back away, NOW!"

He hesitates for a moment, his eyes locked on mine, filled with a mix of fury and defeat.

The nurse swiftly steps between us, creating a physical barrier. Her presence offers me a brief respite from the violent confrontation. I take the opportunity to back away, putting some distance between Johnny and me as I try to catch my breath and ease my nerves.

As the nurse tends to Johnny, checking his vitals and assessing the situation, I take a moment to collect myself.

The nurse should be checking *my* vitals—I am the one who was almost just attacked. *I am the one* who is very pregnant. What if all of this stress puts me into labor? Am I ready to have this baby?

The thought of having the baby without my situation with Johnny being more settled is terrifying. The danger might not be over yet, and I must find a way to ensure my safety and that of my sweet and innocent new baby, Lisa and David.

I quietly slip out of the room, grateful for the nurse's intervention but aware that the threat still looms. I am determined and know that I must act fast and decisively.

The time has come—to lean on the support of David, Lisa, and definitely Bill. I am going home to seek protection and with God on my side, break free from this man and this cycle of violence that has consumed my life for far, far too long.

CHAPTER 35

Lisa

July 1975 Age: 14

As I step into the house, a rush of emotions flood my mind. The taste of Jerry's kiss lingers on my lips, and I can't help but smile to myself. I've experienced a roller coaster of emotions tonight, from the discomfort of sharing our family struggles to the comfort of finding solace in each other's stories. It's as if our hearts have found a connection amidst the chaos.

Walking through the hallway, I hear my brother David's voice coming from the living room. I enter to find him watching TV, engrossed in a show.

He looks up as I enter, his eyes widening when he sees my flushed cheeks and probably a hint of sparkle in my eyes.

"Hey, Lisa. You look... happy. How was your date with Jerry?" David asks, a mischievous grin slowly forming on his lips.

THE END IS THE BEGINNING   213

I can't help but blush even more at the mention of Jerry's name.

"It was... uh... good. We went to The Dairy Drop, had a banana split sundae, and talked for hours. It was like we've known each other forever."

David raises an eyebrow, a smidgeon of comedy crossing his face.

"Lisa, you *have* known Jerry for nearly ever. He and his family have lived kitty-corner from us for as long as I can remember. But speaking of remembering things, do you remember that time a while back now when we were riding our bikes, and Jerry talked about wanting to be the butcher at Meats and Beets? I remember you seeming put-off by that comment that day. Did you see that side of him again? I only mention it..." His voice trails off.

"I mention it because I don't want you to get hurt, Lisa."

His words bring me back to that moment when Jerry 'flipped' his personality, and the scene flashed before my eyes. I remember how I felt that day and the reaction of the others that were with us. But I am surprised that after all this time, David even remembers what happened, and even more, he remembers how *I felt* about it.

Even though he is my brother, he can be rather charming when he wants to be. Witnessing Jerry behave that way was a glimpse into a side of him I hadn't seen before. But despite that happening way back when, my feelings for him are growing stronger, and I find myself attracted to him in ways I can't fully comprehend.

"I don't know, David. I'm surprised you even remember that day. Maybe since that instance, he's changed and matured. I mean, look at you, are you the same as you were 6 or, say, 12 months ago? Probably not, but it is confusing... I would be lying if I said that part of me isn't slightly bothered by remembering that, but another part feels this strange pull toward him. I can't explain it," I admit, my voice tinged with uncertainty.

David leans back on the couch, contemplating my words. "Look, Lisa, if anything doesn't feel right with him, you have to trust your instincts. You deserve someone who treats you with kindness and respect. Don't fall for anyone like Mom did with our winner-of-a-father."

His concern is touching, and I appreciate his protective nature. David has never been one to show too much of his emotions, so I have always wondered if he would have my back when we grew up and started having more friends and eventually boyfriends, etc, but now I know he does. It's comforting to know that he cares about my well-being and looks out for me.

"I understand, David. And I promise I'll be careful. I won't ignore any red flags. But I do think that I would have seen that in him by now if that was going to happen. I also think others would have seen that side of him since then too. I'm sure he has outgrown that phase. We were and still are so young, biking around town with nothing better to do than crack jokes to one another about weird things," I assure him, hoping to alleviate his worries.

He nods, a small smile forming on his face.

"That's all I ask, Sis. Just remember that you're worth more than any mistreatment. Don't settle for less."

THE END IS THE BEGINNING   215

With his words echoing in my mind, I head upstairs to my room, closing the door behind me. I find myself standing in front of the mirror, gazing at my reflection. The image staring back at me is filled with a mixture of excitement and apprehension.

I think about Jerry's touch, his warm embrace, and the way his kiss made me feel... like I've never felt before.

But I can't shake off the memories of his behavior on that bike ride with all of us—thanks to David reminding me. There could be a potential darkness that lurks beneath the surface with Jerry.

What does David know now about Jerry? He hasn't spent much time with him since we were kids doing the pyramids on the front lawn, waiting for a car to drive by so we could all wave and crash down in a pile of laughter on one another.

There's a small battle within me—torn between the attraction I have toward him and the need to protect myself.

As I lie in bed, my mind drifts between thoughts of Jerry and the uncertainty of where our connection will lead. Will something happen and the other shoe will drop? Will our feelings escalate and we could officially become boyfriend and girlfriend?

I begin to imagine what the kids at school would have to say about that. I can't deny the chemistry we share, but I must also listen if there are any warning signs. Love should never come at the cost of my well-being. I've witnessed this first-handedly with Mom, and I never want it to be repeated, not with me.

With a deep breath, I close my eyes and let sleep take over. Tomorrow is a new day, hopefully, a new day to see Jerry again and where or if this thing we've got going will go anywhere. There's a big part of me that would really like to see it go somewhere.

His kiss felt too right to be wrong.

CHAPTER 36
Sandy

February 1976 Age: 36

As I leave the rehab facility, my mind is racing with fear and uncertainty. The encounter with Johnny has left me shaken and desperate for a way out.

I know that I can't do this alone, and I need to focus on my health for the protection of this baby and my kids at home and to preserve the future life that I so desperately am yearning for. A future life for Bill and I to enjoy— to build our *own* happy family together. That is... if Johnny can accept it, and that is a big 'if'.

With trembling hands, I rush to the pay phone just outside the facility, and after inserting my 10¢, I dial Bill's number. He answers after a few rings, and I can hear the worry in his voice as he asks if everything is alright. He knew that I was coming here so it doesn't surprise him that I'm calling in a frenzy.

"Bill, I need you. Can you come and pick me up from the rehab facility? It's urgent," I plead, trying to keep my voice steady.

"Of course, Sandy. I'm on my way. Just stay put," he reassures me.

As I wait for him, I find a quiet corner outside the facility and take a few deep breaths, trying to steady my nerves. The gravity of the situation sinks in, and I know that I can no longer ignore this danger that I'm in.

Moments later, Bill's car pulls up, and he jumps out, looking concerned as he rushes toward me.

"What happened? Are you okay?"

I can hardly speak as I notice a sharp pang in my lower back, and it takes me quite by surprise. I stand there looking at him but hunching forward, trying to catch my breath. Once the back pain subsides, I quickly fill him in on the violent encounter with Johnny, leaving out no details.

Bill's face turns pale, his anger simmering just beneath the surface. He clenches his fists, visibly struggling to contain his emotions.

"First of all, are you okay? Secondly, I've had enough of this, Sandy. I won't let him hurt you or the baby," he declares with determination.

We drive back home in silence, my mind consumed with worry over the thoughts of how to break free from this vicious and violent man. I also am quiet because it seems these back pains keep coming every so often.

As we arrive, I see David standing on the porch, his expression concerned.

"What happened?" David asks, his eyes locking with

THE END IS THE BEGINNING 219

mine and then glancing at Bill as if to ask who he is and why he is here.

I take a deep breath, knowing that it's time to share the truth with him as well. The truth on more than one topic.

"David, honey... this is Bill." I raise my hand, gesturing to him standing beside me. "He is someone I met while working my shifts at Meats and Beets, and I have formed a very deep and meaningful connection with him. I hope that you will accept and welcome him into our lives as a dear friend of mine." Shifting my eyes to meet David's, I glance back and forth between his eyes, trying to gauge his reaction.

"He picked me up from the rehab facility when I called him in a state of panic after your father tried to attack me... again. He's becoming more dangerous, and I don't know how much longer I can stay with him. I don't know how to let him come back into our home and not live in complete fear. This time that he's been away, David, has been the best time of my life. Not having to constantly worry about how I can work at not upsetting him and fearing for my life."

David's face hardens, and I can see that his protective instincts are kicking in. "He can't come back here. I won't allow him to hurt you or anyone else in this house, Mom. I stepped in last time, and I'll do it again, should I need to."

He clears his throat and extends his right hand toward Bill. "Nice to meet you, Bill. I'm glad my mother has found someone to be there for her during this time."

Tears well up in my eyes as I feel a sense of relief knowing that my first son, my dear son David, is on my side in supporting me with Bill and protecting me from his father. It's the first time in years that I've felt protected and supported in this way. I know that I can rely on him and Bill too, to keep me safe.

As we enter the house, the sharpest pain sets into my lower back, and this time—it is not just in my back but also wraps around to my stomach, and I realize what this is.

This isn't random pain from pregnancy or from being shaken up today. These are contraction pains! Shit...

That bastard of a man. He rustled me up to the point of putting me into labor. There's no way that I can reverse this being this far along. I am lucky to have made it this far, being 38.5 weeks along. I can't believe this is all starting right now... when all of this is happening, and Johnny is supposed to be coming back home.

Lisa rushes to my side. The genuine worry, just like I used to see when she was so little, is once again evident in her eyes.

"Are you okay, Mom?"

As I look into the big brown eyes of my now seemingly teenager, teetering-upon-adulthood-Lisa, she has grown so tall. I remember when she was not much taller than my hip. But now, she is nearly as tall as I am, standing 5'5".

She has grown to be well-endowed, with a thin waistline, long slender legs, and silky smooth amber-brown hair that hits just between her shoulder blades. Her eyes seem to perfectly match her hair color as if they were chosen from the same paint swatch up in heaven when God created her. They sparkle flecks of gold with each blink of her eye which is clearly seen behind her thick eyelashes. There is no doubt about it, she is a beautiful young lady, and I can easily spot the features she received from her father and which are from me too.

My darling little girl, who used to run around the corner with little pitter-patter steps to check on me and see how she could help after a fight had broken out between Johnny and me, has grown so much physically but is standing here just as she did when she was so little asking how I am doing. Shouldn't I be the one asking her how *she* is doing?

The sight of her and David is a deep reminder of how much time has elapsed in their lives when they have had to witness the scenes of bloodshed and screaming matches between their father and me. The guilt cripples me when I am reminded of the past life I have led and inevitably made them walk beside me through.

"I will be, sweetheart. But we need to talk." I motion for her and David to join Bill and me in the living room. I keep the phrase short and sweet as another wave of pain takes over my entire midsection, but I try to stifle it with deep breaths and calming thoughts of reminders of what my future life will be.

I recount the events of the day in a concise manner knowing that within the next 8-10 minutes, I'll have another contraction, so I hold nothing back. Upon hearing me tell her who Bill is and what his role has been in my life, her expression softens as the corners of her mouth begin to curl. As I continue, her face contorts with anger and fear as she hears about Johnny's violent outburst. David's hands clench into fists, his jaw set in a determined line. I can tell that it won't be good when

Johnny arrives, and I begin to question if I should not have told them all that I have.

"I won't let him hurt any of you again. We have to protect ourselves." Bill's voice is full of resolve as he is sitting beside me, rubbing circles on my back to help the pain that he can tell that I am in.

"Bill's right, Mom. We can't let him back into this house. It's not safe for any of us," David adds, his gaze unwavering.

"I know, but what do we do? What if he comes after us?" I ask, my voice trembling. I know the stress that I have been under during this pregnancy hasn't been good for me or the baby, so I am trying to keep it together here, but damn, it is getting hard to do that.

"We'll figure it out together. We can change the locks, I can stay here around the clock if that would make you all feel safer. We'll take all necessary precautions to ensure everyone's safety," Bill suggests.

Hearing Bill's thoughtfulness and knowing that he is taking all of this on with me and my kids out of his love for me, only makes me love him more. I flash an adoring and gentle half-smile to him, letting him know my sincere gratitude.

Lisa nods in agreement, her eyes filled with determination. "We can't let fear control us. We have to stand up to him and protect ourselves and our new sibling we will soon have. And Mom, I'm happy you have met Bill. It seems like he has come into your life at a time when you need a true friend and confidant the most."

The weight of their support and determination lifts a heavy burden from my shoulders.

THE END IS THE BEGINNING   223

For the first time in a long while, I feel like I have a real chance at breaking out from this mess of a life I've created and inadvertently drug my innocent kids through. I can't make that same mistake on my third go-around at being a mother, which I have a feeling, will be sooner than I am ready for unless, for some odd reason, these contractions are only Braxton Hicks.

I rise from the couch with help from Bill, and I take two steps toward the kitchen, and it happens...

There is a crash heard as if a water balloon was thrown from across the room and met the floor with a wet splat.

I look down as a much stronger contraction now takes over my body to see that my water has, in fact, broken all over the living room floor.

Bill handles this so calmly and controlled that it truly amazes me. It is as if he is the one who has done this— labor-a-baby-thing two times before, not me.

He comes to my side, continuing the back rub and helping guide me to the door. I hear him ask me if I want to be taken to the hospital by him or for him to call an ambulance for me. It takes everything in me just to remind myself to breathe through the contractions and ride the wave as it increases in intensity and pain escalates.

I simply point to him to tell him that I want him to drive me since I can't get the words out, but then the thought crosses my mind—with David, I delivered relatively quickly, within eight hours. Then, with Lisa, I delivered even faster, in only five hours from contractions starting. What if the labor progresses too quickly, and we don't make it to the hospital in time?

That thought is absolutely terrifying.

He guides me out of the house and into his car as beads of sweat start to trickle down the sides of my temples running downward to my neck, but I can't bring myself to wipe them away or even care at this point.

I had forgotten how intense labor pains are—this fucking sucks.

My hips feel like they are widening with each contraction, and all I can do is lean back onto the seat of Bill's car and do short breaths out of my mouth while taking in long inhalations through my nose like I used to hear the women talk about having learned from their Lamaze classes. At this point, the pain is so intense I'll do anything to get past this.

Bill is speeding through town to make it to the nearest emergency room in Edwardstown. The sad reality, though, is that from Lemard to Edwardstown on a good day, it takes around 20 minutes to travel. When the contraction finally ceases, I take note of the clock and it is 2:44 pm.

I try to take a few deep breaths and steady myself in the seat even though it feels like I have to pee so badly, no matter what position I get into, the pressure seems to only become worse.

"Sandy, are you hanging in there? You're doing great. This is all going to be okay, I'll be with you every step of the way, my dear." Bill grabs my hand for a tight, reassuring squeeze, and then he proceeds to brush the hair out of my eyes.

THE END IS THE BEGINNING   225

It is now 2:47 pm, and another contraction comes on stronger than the last one, and it seems to last even longer. The amount of back pain and pressure I have in my pelvis is surreal. I honestly don't know how much more I can take of this pain. It is excruciating.

I am screaming and moaning as I attempt to ride these waves of contractions as the nausea is beginning to set in. I turn my head to the side as I think I could vomit out of his car window. Can he make it there any sooner?

Bill gently pulls a bag out from the center console of his car and hands it to me as if he knew I was going to become sick.

My natural instinct would be to feel embarrassed in a moment like this, but in the presence of Bill, I know that he has a deep and genuine love for me that will not waver around an instance such as this.

Thankfully, we are pulling into the emergency room parking lot and he runs out of the car to get someone to help me. All he can scream is, "The baby is coming, the baby is coming!"

They get me into a room on a stretcher, and I hear the nurse scream, calling for the doctor.

"We need somebody in here, this woman is having this baby right now! It's crowning!"

The contractions seem to be nonstop, and it feels like it is hard for me to breathe with all of the pain. I don't even have a moment to ask for any pain medicine or relief.

They tell me to try not to push because I know that they don't have anyone readily available to deliver the baby.

I look at the young nurse, who appears to be probably

in her early 20s without much life experience behind her, and surely, she has never delivered a baby before.

I yell to her, "This baby is coming whether I want it to right now or not. So get ready!"

I try my best to stifle the contractions from furthering my labor and delivery of this baby, but within a matter of minutes, a physician walks in with dark, jet-black curly hair, and he no sooner gets his gloves on as I make one push of the baby, and he is caught in his arms.

He shouts, "It's a boy!"

I feel so faint. It's hard to form a smile in a moment when I should be full of joy. They pass the baby up to me, and it feels wonderful having him here with Bill by my side.

I smile as tears form in my eyes. I am overwhelmed with feelings of gratitude to the Lord for giving me this beautiful child and having the wonderful support of this man by my side who truly loves me and, I know, also loves this child as if it were his own.

This feels like the life I always wanted to have, even dreamt of, but never thought I would ever get.

I hear the nurse, "Do you have a name in mind for this new little boy?"

"Patrick. Patrick William. That will be his name."

I smile down at him, and just like that, he stops crying and looks up at me.

I had to name him with Bill's name as his middle name...I just had to. I honestly believe that if it wasn't for him, I wouldn't be here and neither would Patrick. And for that, we owe it all to Bill for saving us from the destiny we might have faced otherwise.

This is all meant to be. We are all meant to be here, together.

Although this isn't Bill's baby, I know that without a shadow of a doubt, this child will have the best upbringing he could ever have.

Bill hugs me and Patrick together as he places a tender kiss on my head.

"You did it, Sandy. I'm so proud of you. I am so thankful to be here with you on such a joyous and special occasion. We're getting *that* much closer to living the life we've dreamt of. Together, raising Patrick, David, and Lisa too. I love you so much."

I can't find the words. I'm afraid there are no words for this moment. He has just said them all for me and much more eloquently than I could even phrase them.

I smile up at him—he is so right. We *are* getting closer to living the life we've dreamt of and I. Can't. Wait.

Even though I may have just realized it while being with Bill and falling in love with him, with this...with him... it is all I have ever wanted.

"I love you, Bill. I love you too."

Tears fill my eyes as I swallow down the large lump that has formed in my throat. I plant my first kiss on the forehead of my beautiful baby boy and whisper, "I love you, Patrick. I'll protect you and give you the life we both deserve."

CHAPTER 37
Sandy

March 1976 Age: 36

It is Friday morning—the day of Johnny's release. When I last saw him, he tried attacking me in his room until the nurse came to my rescue. Thank God for her coming. The thoughts crossed my mind of what could have been during that encounter.

As the anxiety and fear rise up in me, I am reminded of the newfound sense of empowerment that is replacing more and more of my worries.

I'm no longer willing to be the victim of Johnny's rage. I have my two grown children behind me along with a very new little life to protect and a wonderful man beside me supporting me.

This gives me the deepest confidence to face Johnny head-on and move forward with my life in a way I never thought I'd have nor did I believe I deserved.

The tension in the house is palpable as we await Johnny's arrival. I try to focus on keeping myself calm for the sake of Patrick, but my heart races with nerves and anticipation. Bill, David, and Lisa are all home with me as we prepare to stand together as a united front which gives me a sense of strength and reassurance.

We hear the gravel stones turn upon themselves and give one another a glance filled with worry and anticipation, knowing who it is in that car. I rush to the window just beyond the dinner table to look out as if I need confirmation of who is arriving.

Passing the dark wooden table with four chairs, I am reminded of all of the meals we've shared at this table, and with that visualization, the thought passes my mind – perhaps all of those days are in the past, never to be recreated again.

A sense of nostalgia washes over me and doubt begins to seep into my mind.

Am I making the right choice? Should I try to keep our family together for the sake of the kids? It *could* be better if we worked at it. Especially now that I've brought this new and beautiful life into this world and into our family —a broken family, that is.

It is as if Bill can read my mind and the hesitant thoughts. He comes to meet me at the window and wraps his left arm around my waist as he takes my right hand to remove it from covering my mouth. He wipes the tear from my cheek as he looks into my eyes with that direct, long-holding gaze like he does, and I know he is serious and he has got me.

All of my doubt fades away and is replaced with unwavering confidence. It's strange, but I'm taken back to when I first met Bill. As the flashbacks course through my mind of how our relationship has unfolded and how he has made me feel in a much shorter time frame compared to the amount of years I have spent with Johnny—a man who never respected or appreciated me, I know that I am making the absolute best decision for myself at this moment.

The time has come, and with the sound of the brakes stopping the tires from turning the gravel, shivers run down my spine amidst the nervousness coursing through my veins, and I break into a sweat.

Johnny is here.

I can hear the sound of the car door opening and slamming shut, and footsteps approaching the two steps to get to the porch and four steps to the front door.

Time seems to move in slow motion as I brace myself for the inevitable confrontation.

The door swings open, and there stands Johnny, looking different from when I last saw him.

His eyes are bloodshot, his face gaunt, and he seems agitated. He glares at me, his anger evident and palpable.

"Well, well, look who decided to show up," he sneers while looking at all of us but holding his gaze on Bill.

Bill steps forward, positioning himself between Johnny and me.

"You're not welcome here, Johnny. This is Sandy's house, and you have no place in it. You will not hurt her any longer and subject your children to the abuse either."

Johnny's gaze flickers to David, who stands tall and ready beside Bill. The realization that he can no longer intimidate us dawns on him. His eyes narrow, and he clenches his fists. He steps forward and gets in Bill's face.

"You think you can keep me out of my own home? You think you can steal my wife and get away with it? I'm not going anywhere. This is my house, and you're all trespassing," Johnny growls as he points his finger at each of us.

"It's not your home anymore, Johnny. You lost that privilege when you chose to abuse Mom and put our family in danger," David speaks up, his voice firm.

I notice he calls him by his name instead of 'Dad'. He's clearly taking this confrontation quite seriously.

Lisa chimes in, her voice unwavering.

"We won't let you hurt us again. We're done with you and the violence."

Johnny's face contorts with rage, and he lunges at me, trying to push past Bill and David. I step back, fear coursing through me, but Bill stands strong, blocking Johnny's path.

"Leave, Johnny. It's over. We're done with you!" Bill demands firmly.

Johnny's face distorts with fury, and he launches himself at Bill, throwing punches with wild abandon. David rushes in to help Bill, and with that, the chaos erupts.

The kitchen becomes a battleground as the three of them exchange blows, each one fighting for their own reasons.

Lisa is screaming, her fear and anger pouring out as she watches the brawl unfold.

I can't bear to see my children in such danger, but I know that I must stay out of it for the sake of the baby and needing to care for him. Instead, I find myself hollering from across the room, trying to keep my distance between myself and them, but it is killing me seeing Bill and David being beaten by him.

There is blood dripping from David's nose, and I can see Bill has a deep gash wound above his eye.

I can't take it anymore. I turn around, looking for something to break this all up. I grab my cast iron skillet off of the stovetop and rush over to the scene.

When I see David and Bill trying to team up on him, but with Johnny's big build and strength, they aren't making much headway, I reach my left hand to grab Johnny's hair at the nape of his neck. As I pull his neck back, I use all of my might and slam the black skillet into the top of his head, making contact with his face too.

Within a moment, as Johnny realizes what has just happened, he turns to face me, and as he lunges toward me, I step back, holding the pan up again, threatening to hit him again should he make another move. His eyes glaze over, and he collapses onto the floor at my feet.

I let out a quick breath of air—not realizing I had been holding it.

I look up at Bill and David, seeing them crouch over to catch their breath while their blood makes droplets onto the floor in front of them. This floor has seen more blood than any kitchen floor should ever see.

Lisa is standing behind the two of them with her hand covering her mouth, holding a stunned look on her face. It isn't until her eyes look up to meet mine that the realization hits me.

Is he simply knocked out, or... did something more serious just happen here?

"Bill, oh my God. What do we do? I didn't mean to hurt him. I was trying to protect you and David and put an end to this madness. I... I..."

My voice trailing off and sounding unsteady, I set the skillet down on the countertop with a thud. My hand covers my mouth, and my eyes are glued to Johnny.

I don't see him move.

Or flinch.

Not even an inch.

"Sandy, it will all be okay. Do not worry about this. We will call the authorities and tell them exactly what happened. Honesty is always the best policy. We were all fighting in self-defense." Bill's voice sounds empathetic as he stands up and wipes the blood from dripping down his cheek.

He comes to my side and offers me a warm embrace. I turn into him and sob into his chest uncontrollably, not knowing what the hell has just happened and what we are going to do about all of it now.

Patrick begins to wail from his bassinet in the living room, which causes my anxiety to spike as it courses through my veins. Lisa rushes in to get him and quiet him down, and once his cries soften, I can feel my nerves calm slightly, and I am hoping I can now get some clarity to this situation.

CHAPTER 38

Sandy

March 1976 Age: 36

After a few moments pass, (which feels like hours after what has just happened—all within a matter of 30 minutes or less since Johnny came home), I frantically run to the phone and dial the police.

How many times have I had to call the police or have had them show up for another fight of Johnny and I's? Too many to count. I never thought this day would come where I would be calling them but instead of out of protection for me, it would be for... him?

A low, masculine voice answers, "Lemard Police Department, what is your emergency?"

"Hi, this is Sandy calling to report an emergency at our residence, 1435 Main Street!" I exclaim trying to calm my voice with each word I speak.

"Hi, Sandy, is it your husband again? Has he gone and hurt you or one of your children?"

"No, sir," I hesitate. "I'm afraid it's the other way around this time. He was trying to pick a fight, and I tried to protect myself and my children, but now he isn't moving, and he's on the floor. So... I need help right away, please, sir," I tell him, speaking as fast as an auctioneer. My voice sounds more and more fragile as I listen to myself.

"Alrighty, Ms. Sandy. I'll send a crew right over and I'll also alert the ambulance team to come as well if needed. You just sit there and try to see if he'll be alright until we get to you."

I hang the phone up, not wanting to hear anymore. I think I should go to check his pulse but I am too scared to turn him over and see his face head-on.

What if it wakes him out of his unconsciousness? What if he attacks me and gets me once and for all?

As much as I don't want it to happen to me, I certainly don't want to be a witness as I watch it happen to David, Lisa, or Bill either. Thankfully, Patrick is now sleeping soundly, as new babies do during the daytime instead of at night, in the living room.

Lisa is still standing far back from the scene and I can easily see that she is worked up and anxious over this. She does this thing where she exchanges her weight from side to side, crosses her arms at her chest and rubs them as if it is cold out and she is trying to warm herself up.

David and Bill are standing near the kitchen counter looking down at Johnny as they are trying to discern what they should do next too.

I can't even find the words to say so I walk to the front of the kitchen to look out the front door and see if the police are coming up the driveway. I am terrified that they are going to tell me that he is… gone and that I am at fault.

Finally, the sound of sirens fill the air, and the flashing lights illuminate the evidence of the chaotic brawl that occurred inside the house.

As the men rush up the porch steps and in through the front screen door, my heart is pounding through my chest and my palms are beginning to become clammy.

Johnny hasn't moved since I hit him over the head with the skillet pan and even though deep down inside I think I know that he isn't here anymore, not that he *has* been 'here' for a long time, I worry over what may loom in our future.

Just behind the police are the paramedics. They rush in with even more urgency toward the scene, and I look over, and we are all lined up—Lisa and David, Bill and I. We are standing again like the united front we were when Johnny came home—he never stood a chance, one burly fired up and angry man to us four, all filled with pent-up anger from years in the making.

It's a strange feeling… Sadness takes me over while I am in thoughts over our life… Our life that we will never have again as we have known it, with us together as a family. Although it would probably be better than it was with him, I am concerned about what our future may hold without him in it.

I should probably be elated and jumping with joy now since I am finally getting what I wanted, shouldn't I? No more of the life where I have to live in fear, wondering

THE END IS THE BEGINNING **237**

how I will make it out alive and how the unending violence and trauma will affect my children, especially now that I have baby Patrick.

As the paramedics rush to be at Johnny's side, I see them exchange a look, and I know.

They try to turn him over, and as they do, his body appears limp and lifeless. His eyes are left open, staring straight ahead, and I know that he is probably not looking at me even though it feels as though his eyes are fixed directly on me.

The expression on his face tells it all. He looks shocked, surprised, angered, and also lost. It hits me – the realization of what this whole situation must've been like for him.

His anger takes him over and causes a fight between us, and after he beats me up, his son intervenes and badly injures his head. After an initial hospitalization, he is put into a facility to recuperate. Meanwhile, his wife has moved on with another man and has found the happiness that she has been in search of her entire life.

Even though he probably knew deep down inside that he could not give me what I needed, it still had to be a painful realization for him.

The guilt takes me over, and I fall to the floor in a heap of sobs. Bill comes to my side and sits beside me, holding me as I rest my head on his shoulder while the tears fall.

I hear a voice gently whisper in my direction, "I am so sorry ma'am, he is no longer with us. I am sorry for your loss."

Hearing those words, although I somewhat antici-pated it, I did not think that I would've actually killed my own husband. Even though I have thought of this day thousands of times, I never thought that I would feel such mixed emotions when and if it ever happened.

"Would you like us to give you a few moments with him before we take him?" a young 20-something-year-old paramedic asks me.

All I can do is look at David and Lisa and I know that we don't need any more time with him than what we have had. Their entire lives have been with him, which has given them nothing but horrible memories, and even moments of having to fight for their lives, or if not for their own life, for the sake of mine.

I can't bring myself to respond verbally, so I shake my head, telling them that they can take him.

As they lift his body and put it onto the stretcher, I am in shock.

Is this actually happening?

I glance at David and Lisa. David is strong—standing with his arm around Lisa, comforting her as the tears flood down her cheeks.

As we watch them take Johnny's pale and beaten corpse out of our home, seeing my children safe and knowing that we are, for the first time in their lives, finally free from him, the feelings of guilt and remorse wash away. They are replaced with a deep, comforting peace, knowing we no longer have to walk on eggshells worrying about what we may say or do that could royally upset Johnny and lead to another bloodshed, fighting-for-your-life fight fest.

I don't have to live in fear for when he may come home drunk from the bar and take it out on me. I no longer have to hide my bruises. I no longer have to hide my story.

I am free to love Bill without guilt and shame. I finally have hope for the future that I know I deserve to have.

Perhaps the end of Johnny's life marks the beginning of ours.

CHAPTER 39
Lisa

March 1976 Age: 15

It's Saturday morning and I'm waking up groggy with a massive headache since I wasn't able to get much sleep from the events that went on yesterday. All that has seemed to set in so far is shock and even though I was exhausted last night when I went to sleep, I kept waking up—having nightmares reliving the scene.

I dreamt that Dad tried attacking me, and I grabbed a kitchen knife and stabbed him in the chest as blood sprayed out of his chest cavity onto me, making me a self-defense murderer, potentially like what Mom could be considered?

Oh my God.

While attempting to wake myself by rubbing my eyes, I hear a tap, tap, tap sound coming from my window. I sit up and have to squint to keep from being blinded by the sunlight that is sneakily peering in

THE END IS THE BEGINNING   241

through the curtains on the window. I get up and feel my head pounding with the headache even stronger now. Surely, this is caused by a mix of crying last night and very little sleep.

I sweep my hair out of my eyes as I make my way over to the window and pull the drapes back to look out. I squint my eyes, barely able to open them as I peer out to see where that sound is coming from.

Maybe it was a bird tapping on my window?

As I scan the yard, I don't see anything, but as I turn my attention to the left, just near a tree, low and behold, it is Jerry.

He is standing halfway hiding behind a tree with his right pointer finger over his lips, making the *"shh"* sign while his left hand is in front of his chest, waving for me to come out to see him.

I rub my eyes one more time, confirming that it's actually him that I see. It sure looks like him.

I try to lift the window up so that I can talk with him through the window, but it is rickety, and it makes a loud creaking noise as I try to open it. Jerry covers his lips once more to tell me to keep it quiet and waves me to come out.

I respond nonverbally while holding up my pointer finger in the air, telling him to give me a moment. I pull the drapes back and turn to my dresser to throw some clothes on that aren't my pajamas. How embarrassing! Jerry just saw what I look like with my hair a mess and no makeup on, all while wearing pajamas!

Rummaging through my drawers, I pull out an old t-shirt and some cut-off blue jean shorts and run out the door of my room. I try to quietly tiptoe down the hallway to decrease the sound of the wooden floor from creaking and sneak out the front door.

I am uncomfortable walking through the kitchen with the memories on my mind of yesterday's events. Crossing my arms over my chest as I open the door, I realize I did not put a bra on. I cannot believe I forgot a clothing staple —my bra!

Oh well, I can't turn back now. I've already opened the door and closed it shut behind me softly. I walk around the house to the side where my room is and once again scan the yard for Jerry.

Finally I see him standing there waving at me with a sneaky smile resting on his face. I walk over with my hands held out to my sides and whisper, "What the hell are you doing here? It's not even 6 am."

"I just really wanted to see you, my Lisa. How are you? I was worried because I heard some sirens over here last night. Are you alright?"

He asks with a concerned facial expression as he places his hands on my upper arms and begins to rub my arms as if I was cold and he is trying to warm me up while also massaging my shoulders too.

I take a deep breath and hesitate before responding. Did he just call me 'his Lisa' again? Why does he keep doing that? I don't know if I should admit it, but I kind of like it. Regarding last night though, I don't know what to tell him or if I even want to.

"Uh... thanks for asking and checking in on me. There was so much that happened, Jerry. I'm still processing it since I haven't gotten much sleep," I reply with a sigh as I

THE END IS THE BEGINNING   243

look down at my feet. "Yesterday was really bad. For now, I would prefer to not talk about it."

"Do you want to go somewhere and we can do something to take your mind off of everything that has happened? Or we can get together later if you want to sleep some more? Or I could take you with me now, and we can watch the deer wander through the trees and enjoy the scenery at the Lemard Forest Preserve? I happen to know the perfect spot." He moves his hands to my shoulders while he looks down at me with eyes that are begging me to say yes, I can just feel it.

"Sure, that sounds nice actually. I don't think I could manage to go back to sleep even if I tried." Holding a half-smile, I look back up at him.

With that, we turn and walk toward the driveway.

"Wait, where is your car, Jerry? I didn't see it in the driveway."

"I actually took my dad's truck and parked it down the road so that I wouldn't make noise as I drove up your drive. I didn't want to risk waking anyone else or causing any trouble." He takes my hand and guides me through the yard and down the road.

"That was smart." While I hold his hand the butterflies start to form in my stomach. I'm wishing I had worn a bra now more than ever since we will be going for a drive in his truck. I am sure we will hit bumps that will cause me to... bounce more than I'd like with a boy I am starting to like. I don't need to draw more attention to myself than there already seems to be from Jerry. I'm already nervous just knowing he is interested in me.

As we get into his truck and start driving down the

road, he puts his right hand on my thigh again and gives it a slight squeeze as he looks over at me and winks.

Immediately, I start to notice my cheeks flush, and oddly enough, it feels like all of the blood that was circulating in my body starts to move... elsewhere.

This is strange, what is this sensation I am having? My heart rate is starting to quicken. I flash a small smile back at him, but I am worried that I am going to start sweating, and it is not even warm out.

"Lis, you look so damn cute this morning. Thanks for agreeing to come with me. This will be a good way to take your mind off of things at home." As he says this, he takes his hand and starts rubbing up and down my thigh.

What the hell is he doing? I feel like I should not want him to do that, and I should ask him to stop or move his hand, but there is something inside of me that really *really* likes this sort of feeling and attention.

It is like he knows that taking me here and moving his hand on my thigh like this will actually make me forget what has gone on, and as crazy as it sounds, it just might... At least for right now.

Without even realizing it, I am much more relaxed as I sit back into the seat and place my hand on the back of his. He looks over at me and smiles, and I don't look back at him—it's too awkward for me.

Instead, I softly smile as I gaze out the front of the truck and then turn my head to look out my window at the trees passing and hope that he doesn't notice me trying to catch my breath and regain my composure before we pull up to the forest preserve.

CHAPTER 40

Lisa

March 1976 Age: 15

When we arrive and get out of the car, I've never been more grateful for the cool morning breeze as it blows through my hair, and I slightly lift my arms to allow it to cool the sweat that has started to form there as well as strangely enough, other parts too.

I've been to the forest preserve before but never to where he is driving us. It seems that he actually does have a secret path that he is taking us down.

Once we arrive and he puts it in park, Jerry suggests that we sit in the bed of his truck. He gets a couple of camouflage blankets out from the cab of his truck and he lays one down for us to sit on while laying the other one across our lap for shared warmth. He also gives me a thick jacket to wear since I didn't grab one of my own before coming.

"I've come here before to hunt for deer. You see that stand over there in that tree? I've bow hunted deer from up there."

"Isn't hunting in a forest preserve illegal?" I question him. I thought I heard someone tell me that once before, but maybe I am mistaken. I have never been hunting in my life.

"Well, technically, yes, but if it is with a bow, no one can hear it, and no one ever comes back here. I've been back here enough times to know," he says confidently as he scans the area looking for deer. "Let's see if we can see any deer or other animals while we're back here. It sure is peaceful, isn't it, Lis?" He leans his weight back onto his hands that are situated behind him.

"Did you bring your bow with you today to hunt?" I ask, wondering if that is what he is going to want to do today. I am not sure how I feel about seeing any more bloodshed from anyone or anything after yesterday.

"Oh no, I don't want to hunt today. Today is about you and enjoying some time together. I've missed you and wanted to make sure you were alright." He places his arm around my back as he slides his hand around my waist and pulls me closer to him on the blanket. The blanket must be a little bit slippery because it feels like I slide over quickly... or maybe he is just that strong.

"That's nice, Jerry. I'm glad we could get away from the chaos of life and enjoy the views here. They are quite peaceful."

Feeling the warmth of his hand on my waist makes me start to get that warm feeling all over again like I did in the car. My back starts to get warm and I think I am going to start sweating again. I really should have worn that darn bra and also put some deodorant on!

I notice he starts rubbing my side up and down and since I am not wearing a bra, each time he slides his hand up under my arm, he is slightly touching the side of my breast.

I can't believe he is touching me this much and... there. At first, I am stunned and feel myself stiffen as I sit up taller, but the more we talk and enjoy the sereness of the view, I am once again at ease.

"Lis, are you okay with me touching you here and like this? I wanted to ask you something." He begins caressing the side of my breast but then moves his hand to my back and rubs between my shoulder blades as he pulls away to look at me in the face.

"What did you want to ask me, Jerry?" A half-smile forms on my face out of nervousness and excitement and avoiding answering his question around my comfortability with him touching me. It would be weird telling him no because I actually sort of like it. I have never been touched by a boy and he is my first kiss, so...

"Will you be my girlfriend, Lisa? I really enjoy spending time with you and we have a lot in common between our upbringings and shared similar situations. I'd like to see where this could go... that is, if you do too?"

He takes his left hand to squeeze my left hand, which is now resting on his thigh, to reciprocate the back rub that he is giving me.

"I've never been anyone's girlfriend before, are you sure you want me?" I am trying not to show my self-consciousness, but I am wanting to be honest with him.

"Lis, that is certainly part of my attraction to you. I love that you don't have much experience. I don't really either, honestly. I have only ever kissed one other girl. So, what's the answer, will you... be mine?" I can see that Jerry is now holding his breath, awaiting my response.

"Sure... yes, I will be." I try to quickly make my answer sound more confident and less hesitant.

We both beam a smile back to one another, and then Jerry takes his hand and tilts my chin up to him and our lips meet.

He is so gentle and soft with his touch, I find it so easy to follow his lead. It is like my mind is seeing pink hearts because something takes over me, and I am wrapping my arms around his neck, bringing him closer to me.

We both lean back into his truck bed and continue kissing.

I start to feel his tongue pressing on my lips as if he is gently asking for entry into my mouth.

Is this something people do? Maybe this is the French kiss I have heard the upperclassmen at school talk about in between classes when they are sharing the details of their weekends spent hanging out with their boyfriends.

Before I know it, we are exchanging tongue swirls and his hand is on my stomach. Not just on my stomach over the top of my t-shirt, but on my stomach like actually on my skin *under* my t-shirt. He is rubbing it up and down my stomach making way up in between my breasts.

Abruptly, he pulls away and asks, "Lisa, is it okay that we are doing this? If you are not comfortable with any of it, just let me know, okay?"

I nod a small nod, and as I look over at him, I notice

something... down there. His pants look like they are... hardening. Oh my God, does he have an erection? I am so surprised since I have never seen this before, I have only ever heard about this in health class.

When I look back at him, I can see his lips are wet from our kiss, and his arms are outstretched toward me. I begin to feel that sweaty and hot sensation take over my entire body, and although I don't recognize this feeling, I *really* am into it. I feel so wanted by him right now.

For a brief moment, I have a flashback to when we were younger and growing up and wonder if this is weird to be happening between us, but then I look at him right now, and no... nothing about this is weird.

This is perfect, and I love that I can do that to his body. I love that him kissing and touching me makes him feel *that* kind of way.

I lean back into his arms, and we are now kissing with forceful tongue swirls, and he reaches his hand back up my shirt and begins caressing my right breast and makes small circular motions around my nipples. I feel like my body may actually light on fire.

Is this what feeling *turned on* feels like? If so, I like it... I like it a lot.

While I have my right hand on his upper arm and feel his arm muscle tense, it is like a firework was set off inside of me. How are his arms this strong and toned? How have I never wanted to touch and squeeze them before now? I have been missing out, that is for sure.

He takes his hand now and slips it just underneath my shorts and undoes the button and zipper. My heart skips a beat with anticipation of what this could feel like. I have never been touched in my 'private girl parts' before. Where will he even touch? My mind starts to wander.

We take a break from kissing to catch our breath and he whispers into my ear, "Is it okay if I touch you here too? I'd love to feel... what you feel like. I've never done this before with anyone."

Before he can pull away, I whisper back, "Yes, please touch me there. I've never done this before either but I'd like to know what it is like." I squeeze the back of his arm and notice it's tense as he reaches his hand down farther and farther into my panties.

He gives soft rubs up and down with his fingers starting on the outside first and moving inward. I am shocked at how good this is. Who knew my body could feel this way? I sure didn't.

Something happens when he touches the middlemost spot. I tense and feel a strong pulsating sensation. It feels extra good when he touches there, and I involuntarily make a small whimper sound as I pull away from kissing him to breathe again.

We are both breathing so hard it is hard to focus on all that we are doing. As he presses himself against me, I take my hand and rub it along his pants.

I can tell he likes it because he starts breathing deeper. Instead of asking like he did for me, because I am simply not confident enough to put into words what I would like to try next, I just slowly take my fingers and unzip his zipper.

It is as if he was asking for me to do that because, without any effort, it just pops right out of his pants. His underwear is still covering him, but I start rubbing softly with my hand, and I find an opening on the side where I slip my thumb into and make skin contact.

We both stop what we're doing and make strong eye contact with each other confirming we are okay with it. I can tell that he is in just as much shock as I am.

"Only if you're okay with it, Lis," Jerry whispers, and the fact that he is so caring about my comfort level makes me want to do this even more. Even though I really don't know what it is that I am actually doing.

I am surprised by how soft and smooth it is as I run my hand down to the base and back up. I take my thumb and press on the end, and he lets out a deep breath, so I take that as a sign that he must like what I am doing.

Jerry takes his other hand and moves my shorts and panties down off of my hips to just above my knees while I continue moving them down my legs altogether. The feeling of the cool air feels so wonderful on my skin.

I am so hot... down there. We lay facing one another and continue moving our hands until I think I know what he is really wanting... sex.

"Jerry... do you want to...?" My voice trails off, not able to finish the sentence.

"Only if you want to, Lis. I've never done it before with anyone but I do have one condom in the glovebox of my truck. I can get it if you think you want to?" he asks through heavy breaths.

"I'll get it," I offer, sliding down the bed of the truck and off of the tailgate.

It feels strange but exhilarating prancing around his truck—pantless but I am excited to experience the 'first-time sensation' that I have heard small mentions of in the hallways at school.

When I get back to the truck bed, I hand the condom to him and he rips it open with his teeth. The sight of him doing that... SHIT, we HAVE to do this now!

I help him unbutton his pants and pull his pants and underwear down being careful not to hurt him.

He slightly sits up and grabs my hips as he directs me to sit on top of him. We sit like that while we rub ourselves toward one another and he reaches his hands up under my baggy shirt to fondle my breasts. I am SO glad I didn't wear a bra now. This feels so good as I move against him and he is caressing my breasts.

I can feel him slipping and wanting to enter... there. I take my hand and guide him into position. We make eye contact with each other in confirmation. When he pushes inside of me, the feeling is truly one-of-a-kind.

At first, it is really painful as I think my skin is stretching to fit him. It hurts and I squeeze my eyes tightly shut until the moment passes. But once he is in there...I am so full and the pain slowly begins to transform into pleasure. I only move small amounts, not confident of how to do this so that it feels good and not wanting to hurt either one of us.

It doesn't take long for us to figure out what feels right, and we are moving in sync, like when the band at school puts all the instruments together, and everyone is playing the same song in harmonious union, and it sounds beautiful.

He makes a strong push deeper inside of me, and it causes me to feel a head-to-toe all-encompassing body jolt. It takes everything in me as I rest my hands on his stomach while we both... finish.

This must be what the girls at school call, 'the big O'. I now can see why it's called *big*. I collapse on top of him and he kisses me on my forehead and whispers, "I'm so glad you're my girlfriend. You're beautiful, and I'm so happy to be with you."

I rest my head down on his chest and take in the moment as I listen to him breathe in and out, feeling his chest rise and fall.

"Thank you, Jerry. I'm happy to be your girlfriend too."

The breeze starts to pick up and it moves my hair off of my back as we are both trying to catch our breath from the surprise and adrenaline that is coursing through our veins over what has just happened.

What *has* just happened?

CHAPTER 41
Sandy

March 1976 Age: 36

In the days that follow Johnny's death, I am completely lost in the sleeplessness of having become a new mother and shock over what has actually happened to really notice his absence. Especially since he has been gone for some time—having been in the hospital and then the rehab facility, I have admittedly, moved on and reallocated my priorities as a woman and mother alike.

Bill begins staying at the house full-time to help with the care of Patrick as well as myself. He makes me meals, checks on me, and offers to take Patrick so that I can get some rest or things done around the house.

It's truly amazing what a difference having a good man in your life can make. I think it makes me adore and love him more because of my abusive history. I can easily see all of his strengths comparatively and it makes me appreciate him even more.

Our relationship has evolved into something that I never knew was possible. The love and support that he has shown to me while caring for me during such a vulnerable and transitional time in my life where I'm physically healing from delivering a baby, mentally coping with postpartum hormones and stressors all the while, grieving from losing my husband which brought a horrific and traumatizing time in my life, brings me great gratitude for Bill.

When I cannot get Patrick to sleep at night, I find myself becoming consumed with the guilt over being responsible for taking Johnny's life. Although he did so much wrong to me over many years, was it right—what I did to him?

Did I make the right decision in the heat of that moment? Although I knew I was always going to pick Bill over Johnny, I didn't think it would come to me choosing life for Bill while inadvertently choosing death for Johnny.

I have to remind myself that I reacted in an act of self-defense. Nothing more, nothing less.

Could the police come after me for being liable for killing him? Could I be put into jail? How do I explain what happened if I am called upon? Will simply telling them, "it was all in self-defense," actually work to save me?

The answers to these questions... I don't know. The fact that I don't know the answers though, may be even more terrifying than the questions themselves.

I decide that I should call my parents to tell them

what has happened. In their true style, my mother reveals an empathetic attitude toward the situation and offers to come to the house to help knowing I have a newborn at home as well as I am dealing with all of these recent events.

Meanwhile, my father provides his unsolicited opinion and advice. "Sandy, you better make sure you've got your ducks in a row here. I know you never liked him too well and he was dangerous from the start... which is exactly why your mother and I tried to steer you away from him. But back then, *you* knew more than we did, of course... You never know what the law may think of this nor how his parents could react and request further investigation of his death."

How am I supposed to hear this and not be spun into further panic mode? I despise the timing of all of this.

Any woman who has ever gone through having a child, multiple children at that, while dealing with the death of a spouse on top of it, the timing of all of this couldn't be worse.

Without having had Patrick, I would already be concerned over this situation of course but the mix of sleeplessness and postpartum stress, I can tell that I escalate to an elevated level of anxiety and frustration much faster than I would otherwise.

This, coupled with my lack of control over it, feels like I'm a spectator of my own life, and my reactions around everything that happens in it leave me feeling helpless and hopeless.

CHAPTER 42

Lisa

March 1976 Age: 15

So much has happened in the last few weeks, it has left my head spinning. I seem to have lost two things in my life that I will never get back. My horribly abusive father is gone one day and then the following day, I lose my virginity to Jerry in the bed of his truck at the Lemard Forest Preserve!

My entire life has become something that I hardly recognize anymore—my family dynamic has shifted between the addition of Patrick, the new permanent absence of my dad, and to top it all off, I did something with Jerry that I will never get back to experience with someone when I know that I am truly in love.

My mind is racing with the guilt over having made such an impulsive decision with him and hoping that it was the right one.

I know that I like Jerry but would I say that I 'love him' today? Probably not.

Would I feel better if I could say that I 'loved him' before having had sex with him? Possibly?

I guess I want to have peace over that decision but I may never actually get that.

Although my dad had physically been gone for some time due to the incident with David leading to his hospitalization and then rehab stay before his passing, I have had some realizations over what I envisioned our relationship would be like. I always hoped throughout my childhood that I would have a fatherly love sort of connection with him my entire life.

When I was little, I wanted there to be that kind of relationship where he takes me fishing or teaches me things just to spend the time with me. As I grew older, I wished for him to simply take the time to get to know me and we could form a bond over similarities in our personalities and it would bring him joy to spot those things in me—knowing they were traits from him.

It is probably an odd thing to be thinking of—instead of grieving the loss of him and what many people probably grieve is the knowing that the memories made cannot be re-lived or recreated. but for me, I am grieving the life I had been dreaming up since I was a much younger girl and was still hoping to see come true.

I am disheartened to know that there is no chance for me to sit him down and really get through to him... To make him see the verbal and physical abuse he inflicted on his family, to make him see the trauma he put us through, and to make him *feel* the guilt that we will never get to have those moments back. Those moments that he ruined through the fear that he instilled into us while we witnessed his monstrous rage unleash during his drunken spells. I had a plan to at least *try* to make my point with him.

I never could believe that the reason he treated my mom so poorly and in turn, us kids poorly too, was purely out of a want to be a total and complete asshole. Who would actually do that? I mean, yes, maybe someone out there would, but I never wanted to believe that was him. There had to be something in him that my mother once saw and fell for. David and I turned out alright so far so he couldn't have been all *that* horrible his entire life, right?

So... I grieve over thoughts of 'what-if' and 'what could have been'. I was under the impression that once he came home, perhaps he would have a renewed perspective from having been away. While he was cooped up, I hoped that he would have gone through alcohol withdrawals and having spent time away from all of us too, it might have caused his mind to be clearer to listen to me upon returning home.

I guess we will never know what could have been with him. For me, I am not as much sad for myself as I am for Patrick knowing that he will never get to know who his true, blood father was. But I only feel that when I have the confidence that I would have been able to spend the time with my father and have made some progress toward getting him to see 'the light' toward kindness and generosity and proving that myself and my siblings along with my mother too, are all worthy of receiving those things amongst many other better forms of treatment from him than we ever received.

It is now Sunday morning, and since I have been having trouble sleeping lately and I'm already up in such a deep train of thought, I decide that I will get dressed and sneak out of the house to attend my first-ever service at the Lemard Congregational Church, just a few blocks down the street. I'm not sure what it is that I am hoping to receive by attending this service, but feeling as low as I am right now, maybe it will somehow cause me to feel slightly better—even if it is only for while I am there.

I figure that I have nothing to lose by going, and if anything, it will get me out of the house so that I don't have to listen to Patrick scream and cry like it seems he does nonstop around here.

I search my closet and find a cloth A-line dress with pleats from the waistline downward. I slip it on and run my fingers through my hair attempting to appear more presentable.

I decide to not head to the bathroom and brush my teeth since I don't want to make much noise and want to slip out without anyone seeing or questioning where I am going wearing a dress on a Sunday morning at 8:30 am.

As I walk into the church, it smells of coffee, and I can hear many people talking about things happening in their lives and others offering to pray for them during their time of struggle or need. I can't quite figure out why, but simply being in this building and hearing the people talk where it sounds like they are being supportive makes me believe that I am safe and free to be here. It's comfortable.

I head up the stairs and turn to go into where I hear

the music being played on an organ coming from, assuming that is where the service must be held. As I walk in, I hear a woman say, "Good morning there, sweet darlin'. Welcome to Lemard Congregational Church. We are so pleased to have you here with us this morning."

I am standing with my hands clasped together in front of myself and sense that I may be out of place here. I look up to see who has just spoken to me and cannot believe my eyes.

It is Marianne. Marianne... Clark. My stomach drops as if it has just fallen out of my body like how it does on a steep drop on a roller coaster ride.

I swallow and stand, stunned, staring back at her. How can a woman who was behaving as an innocent yet slutty swinger be here acting like she is a goodie-goodie, church-going woman?

The moment this thought crosses my mind, I realize, is that not what I am trying to do?

I feel guilty over having had sex with Jerry and am upset over the future chance I thought I would have had with my father to better him and create a more healthy relationship.

Am I a picture of perfection? No, that is why I am here.

Perhaps that is the same situation for Marianne. Maybe she has changed and is here searching for a token of forgiveness and a chance at proving she can be better and she can do better.

CHAPTER 43
Sandy

March 1976 Age: 36

We have had sweet little Patrick in our lives for almost a month now, and I am reminded of all of the joy that comes with having a new baby, but more than anything right now, I am reminded of how much work goes into raising a little human.

Since David and Lisa are so much older now, it seems like a century ago that I was raising them as babies. With the lapse of time since then, you really forget how much goes into keeping a baby alive in the first stage of their life.

Patrick still has his nights and days mixed up and is doing a lot more sleeping during the day than he is at night, which makes it very challenging for me, but I'm sure it is also quite a shock for Bill, considering he has never undergone anything like this before.

THE END IS THE BEGINNING   263

I can tell now that it has been a few weeks of us both being sleepless and off of our normal routine and schedules, it is starting to hit him. He has offered to take Patrick in the night so that I can get some sleep after I have nursed him.

Most women use formula for their babies so when I told them at the hospital after delivery that I was going to try to breastfeed him, although the nurses didn't say much, I could certainly sense their surprise and judgment. I even overheard a few of them talking at the nurses' station just outside my room about my choice and how "it is not the norm."

I overheard one nurse comment, "I think it's nice she is trying to breastfeed her baby. That seems like the most natural thing to do." Her comment made me smile, but I noticed not a single nurse responded to her, and the conversation fell flat.

It seems most women have the financial means to afford formula for their new babies, but for me, especially when Lisa and David were babies, we hardly had money to provide a meal for myself and Johnny let alone for the children as well, so I had no other choice but to try to drink as much water as I could and eat what we could afford in order to provide milk for them.

On one hand, I have thought about giving Patrick formula since Bill has been kind enough to offer some money and financial assistance to me to buy it. But since this is all I have ever done, I feel I should continue my trend with Patrick as well.

Now that it has been a few weeks, we are settling into even more nursing sessions it seems. The demand of a near constant need for feeding is becoming exhausting. For the first time yesterday, I had to ask Bill to watch Patrick in the afternoon while he was sleeping so that I could get some rest and be prepared for the nighttime shift again.

But other than the feeding needs of Patrick and constantly changing his diaper, which inevitably, makes more laundry for me, using the same cloth diapers I had kept in a bin in the basement from when it was David and Lisa's time, he is overall a good baby.

I can't remember how long it took with the kids until they got onto a schedule of their own and had only one maybe two at the most, night wakings. I'm wishing more than ever now that I had kept a notebook that I could've been reading to remind myself of when the light at the end of this tunnel will come. When you're in it, it feels so dreadfully permanent even though you know it certainly cannot be.

I'll never say I regret having any of my children, but wow, what a true statement it is that the older you become, the more you forget, and the more tired you are.

I am somewhat grateful for the timing of having Patrick, though, because it has served as such a grand distraction for me from the loss of Johnny.

Of course, I think of him every day, but my thoughts are not grieving ones.

He pops into my mind, and I think, "Oh yeah, I probably should be sad because I am now technically considered a widow." But it really feels like a weight off—having him gone.

What is really strange, though, is that I have not heard

anything from Johnny's parents since his passing. It's almost as if he was already dead to them...as well?

Wow, I know that that sounds really horrible to think of someone actually being dead while they are still living, just simply not with you, and in your home. But with the life that Johnny gave to us, maybe his parents knew more than I ever let on, and they are relieved for me and the kids as well?

Perhaps I'll never know.

On the other hand, though, I find it strange that I haven't heard from them to check on how we are all doing and to ask about Patrick. However, I can't say that I am yearning to maintain a relationship with them, considering I have Bill, and we are slowly but surely building our own life and new family dynamic with the addition of him and now Patrick as well.

Coming into the kitchen this morning, Lisa's already up singing, bright-eyed and bushy-tailed, but I could be perceiving her that way simply because I am merely moving like a zombie. My body is moving as it should, but my mind is hardly functional.

I look over at her and try to form a smile to appear pleasant and approachable, as a mother should be.

She smiles and says, "Good morning, Mom. How are you today?"

I am taken a bit by surprise, seeing her be so pleasant to me, but before trying to think about it too much deeper, I am simply grateful for her mood this morning, and I'm sure once Patrick starts to cry soon, she will be nice enough to take him for me while I get a few things organized and breakfast started.

"Good morning, honey. How are you doing today?" I say as I clear my throat and try to make my voice sound more awake instead of raspy and gruff.

"I'm doing fine, Mom. I wanted to talk to you about what our plans were for Dad's funeral."

Without really registering what she has said, just hearing her say 'Dad' makes me look at her quickly out of surprise. I'm not sure how this time has gone by where I have not given much thought to the need to schedule and plan a formal funeral for Johnny.

This is truly a sign of how being immersed into 'new motherhood' again affects us and how time continues to pass while I am only half alive trying to function each day from my sleep deprivation and the spike in hormones postpartum.

"Okay, honey. What did you want to talk about?" I reply, trying to sound pleasant.

I am unable to ask many more questions around it, because I am overwhelmed with guilt that I have practically forgotten that after someone dies, you plan a funeral service for them.

What kind of wife was I?

Although Johnny was very rarely good to me, the least I could do is to have remembered the traditional American culture following death, and have planned some of this by now.

"Well, I recently attended a service at the Lemard Congregational Church, and I was thinking that maybe we could have the reverend there do a graveside service for Dad?"

"Why would you want to have a reverend at a service

THE END IS THE BEGINNING   267

for your dad? He was the most opposite from God-like in man form of anyone I have ever met!" I blurt out rather quickly without giving much thought to my words.

The look on Lisa's face adequately represents the emotion that is playing through my mind as I have just spit that out to her. Of course, we all had our negative feelings toward Johnny, but that was probably crossing the line as far as judgment goes with him.

"Mom, don't you realize by now that funeral services are not so much about the dead as they are for the living? Do you ever think about anyone other than yourself?" Lisa says snarkily trying to pass guilt.

"Of course I do, Lisa!" I shout back to her, each word louder than the last as the rage rises in me.

A loud screech of a cry comes from the living room, signaling that Patrick is up and probably needs a diaper change. This *would* all happen at the same time.

"Just because you didn't think of planning for your own husband's funeral and I *did* and had a good idea, doesn't mean you have to treat me poorly, making me feel bad for suggesting something that is actually really good, Mom! For someone who now has three children, you really seem to never think about other people as much as you think about yourself!" Lisa shouts back as she walks away from me out of the room to go get Patrick.

Man, she can really be such a little bitch sometimes. Whoa, that is out of character for me to think of anyone, let alone my daughter, but damn, she is getting on my LAST nerve this morning.

I take a deep breath and turn my attention to figuring

out what I can make for breakfast while she calms him and changes his diaper.

After I get a few plates out and begin to open the refrigerator door, Lisa passes me in a hurry with Patrick in her arms, a small bag filled for him and rushes out the door of the house.

I run after her, shouting, "Where in the hell do you think you are going with my baby?"

"I don't know why I thought that you would even care, Mom. You seem to be so self-centered over your life and your relationship with Bill that you couldn't care less about your children or your dead husband!" Lisa furiously screams as she gets in the car and hurriedly slams the door shut.

I rush to the passenger side of my car, pulling at the door handle, screaming and hitting the window.

"You get your ass out of that car right now! You are not driving off as an underaged driver with my baby in the car when you are letting your temper get the best of you!"

Surprisingly, when I look back and see Patrick, he seems quiet and settled in the backseat, but it is probably out of shock from all of the shouting going on around him.

Why did I not go get him myself when I heard him cry? Shit!

Lisa drives off and the gravel dust is all I can see. Dammit. Where in the hell could she be going?

Of course I am worried about her, but more than that, I am fearful for what Patrick may be in need of that she cannot provide him. Lisa is a great help to him, but unfortunately, she does not have the breasts to feed him nor does she have the motherly experience to know what his cries are in need of, and how to appropriately calm him.

I turn and run back into the house to see Bill stepping out onto the front porch, rubbing his eyes while looking at me quizzically.

"What was that all about?" He lets out a drawn-out yawn and reaches his arms up to stretch his back.

"Lisa just took off in the car with Patrick after she and I got into a fight over her wanting the reverend at Lemard Congregational Church to officiate a graveside funeral service for Johnny. I have no idea where she went or when she will be back AND she has Patrick with her while she is in a fit of anger. This cannot be happening, Bill. This cannot be happening right now! I cannot take ONE MORE THING!" I fall into a heap onto the wooden floor of the porch surrendering to my tears.

CHAPTER 44

Lisa

March 1976 Age: 15

Why did my mom have to be such a bitch when I am trying to help discuss a plan for my father's funeral?

She should be the one thinking about the plans and have already made some of them by now—since it has been nearly a month since he has died.

She should be thankful that *I* have given it some thought and the fact that *I* actually have some good ideas for what we could do for his service.

As I drive off in the car, tears stream down my cheeks out of frustration and anger. My own mother doesn't seem to listen to me, why does she have to patronize me?

I look into the rearview mirror and see Patrick who seems to be content, although he is grimacing. I hope he will continue to be comfortable, and not scream while I am driving. I have so many thoughts rushing through my mind that I just need him to be cooperative right now.

Not to mention the fact that I'm technically not of legal driving age—so I really need to concentrate.

As we make our way toward the highway to cross it, I can feel the tears filling my eyes as I continue to contemplate everything that has just occurred. I blink quickly to rid my eyes of the tears and briefly look in both directions to pull out into the traffic and get onto the highway. As I'm making a sharp left turn and step on the gas to catch up with the flow of cars, there is a sharp jolt to the car.

Seemingly out of nowhere, we are moving in a circle as if we were on a carnival ride that has malfunctioned and is spinning out of control with no end in sight.

I just want this over. Can this just be over?

I grab the steering wheel white-knuckled, attempting to stop the sensation and regain control of this situation.

At this point, we have spun out two, if not three times. The car screeches and then comes to a halting crash into the ditch as I am holding my breath and attempting to be as still as possible and prevent injury. When my head slams back into my headrest, I realize this crazy ride is finally over. Thank God.

I inhale and notice the smell of smoke coming from the engine of the car. As I begin to open my eyes to catch my bearings and take in my surroundings, I quickly look in the rearview mirror to make sure we aren't going to be hit again.

Fortunately, it seems that we're in the clear.

I look to see Patrick sitting there as quiet as a church mouse but he is holding an expression equally as wide-eyed as I am. I frantically rush to get my seatbelt off to run to the back of the car and check on him.

What the hell is wrong with me? Why did I think it was a good idea to rush out of the house with him after what had happened between Mom and me? If anything happens to Patrick, I will never, EVER be able to forgive myself and I know Mom will not be able to either.

I put my trembling hand on Patrick's forehead, and as he looks at me, I see only fear in his eyes, and I'm sure he is—wondering where his mother is.

As I continue looking down at his little, small, and innocent body, I notice his leg on the side nearest the door that was hit is swollen and forming a bruise quickly.

I take my hand to wipe my hair out of my eyes to get a better look at him and I notice someone getting out of their banged-up car and coming our way.

Well, at least this man is doing okay. I notice that he is walking with a limp as he makes his way closer to us.

"Hi there, everybody doing alright today? That was some stunt you tried there—pulling out directly in front of me. Damn-near could've killed you. You really need to look twice before pulling out onto oncoming traffic like that, young lady."

Hearing him say this makes me realize that this accident is entirely my fault. I look down at the man and back at Patrick as the lump in my throat grows larger and the water in my eyes multiplies. Today has been a plain, shitty day.

Patrick begins to make a scowl expression, and I know that his big wail of a cry is soon to follow.

Shit, what am I going to do? I left the house and have

THE END IS THE BEGINNING   273

no food or way to feed him and now he is clearly injured. Of course, he is going to do nothing but cry... all because of me.

I could cry too.

As I look back up to the man, I notice a woman standing behind him now. He and her exchange looks, but I can tell that they do not know one another.

"Everything all right over here? I heard a crash and came out of my house. I see you have a little baby in the back there. Is he doing alright, dear?" the woman asks, her voice sounding concerned.

"No. I think we need to call an ambulance for him. The crash happened on his side, and he has a bruise forming quickly on his leg now, and he clearly isn't too happy about it," I say with a short tone to the woman as Patrick's lungs open up and he unleashes his high-pitched blood-curdling cry.

"Alright, dear. I will head back into the house and make the call. Shall I call anyone else for you?"

I can tell she is getting a closer look at me and now Patrick too, and is probably realizing that I am too young to have a child this age. I do want my mother to know, but I am fearful of what will happen when she finds out about all of this. I guess she is going to find out eventually anyway, so what is the difference?

"Will you also call this number? 237-8037? Tell my mother, Sandy, what has happened, where we are at, and if she can meet us at the hospital. Thank you, ma'am."

The woman nods and smiles as she walks back up toward her house. I can't help but feel embarrassed over this happening. I am hardly five minutes away from home and this horrible accident occurs.

I can't decide if I should try to get Patrick out from the backseat, or if that would risk furthering the injury to his leg. I continue to rub his head and shush him in hopes of comforting him, but it doesn't seem to be working. His cries only become louder and sound more and more like screams.

Has it been an hour? It sure seems as though hours have passed by the time that the ambulance arrives. They quickly take Patrick with them and offer me to ride along too.

As we pull into the emergency room parking lot at Edwardstown Community Hospital, I immediately spot Bill's car. Mom rushes out and heads to the ambulance to stand and wait to meet me.

As soon as the door opens, I read the expression on her face; it says, "I'm so sorry about all of this."

We hug, and just like that—tears pour down my face as I land in my mother's warm and welcoming embrace.

There's nothing quite like a mother's hug and love.

CHAPTER 45
Sandy

March 1976 Age: 36

The blonde hair, blue-eyed doctor comes in and assesses Patrick while I am breastfeeding him. I can tell that it is uncomfortable for the doctor to be assessing him while Patrick is suckling on my breast, but considering how much screaming I heard when the ambulance pulled up coming from him, probably from pain and also hunger, he should really be thankful since he is keeping quiet while he is eating. I really hope that this is helping to lessen some of his pain as well.

Poor little Patrick... Being driven off in a car by an angry, hormonal, and underaged teenager... How could I have let this happen to him?

After looking him over, the doctor suggests they take him for an x-ray of his leg. I nod in agreement for him to be given the x-ray and I shift my eyes to look down at his little body as I frown. I find it hard to look at anything other than him.

It's easy to tell that Lisa is so worried about him and I can hardly take seeing this sight. Why did we have to fight over what happened with Johnny? He's dead anyway—what a waste of a fight.

The medical staff come get Patrick and Bill and I scurry along as they take us to a small room where they lay him on a table and shine a bright light with a black 'X' over his upper leg. They ask me to hold him still, and we hear a high-pitched beep sound and the technologist tells us it will take a little bit for the images to be processed in their dark room before we know the results. She takes us back to our room in the emergency department while we wait.

As we return to the room, Patrick is still whimpering from being startled and having to be held still for the x-ray. He is much happier in my arms, and to keep him that way, I offer to breastfeed him more as a source of comfort and to make up for him not having eaten this morning.

I'm holding and shushing him, trying to call him, and as I look over at Lisa, she is sitting down, holding her head in her hands, weeping.

"Lisa, what's going on, my dear?"

Lisa is crying with such force. I don't think she even heard me ask her the question. I walk over and shake her shoulder to get her attention. As she looks up at me, she squeezes her eyes shut as if the sight of me holding Patrick makes her more upset, and serves as a stark reminder of what has happened today.

"Do you want to talk about what has gone on here?

THE END IS THE BEGINNING   277

Now is probably as good a time as any," I say, trying to get the inevitable over with and offer her a chance to get this off of her chest.

I look over at Bill, and he shifts his gaze to the door, asking me if he should leave so that she and I can have a moment. I nod, and he gets up to leave.

I love that about him—he is so respectful and in-tune with the dynamics between my children and me, it makes me adore him more. I know that he has no child-rearing experience other than the past month that he has done alongside me, but he acts as if he has done this all many times before since he picks up on the cues without prompting.

I sit down on the stretcher in the room to get more on Lisa's level. When she finally looks up at me, her eyes are bloodshot and her cheeks are red and puffy. I can't believe that this has happened today and of course, I wish more than anything I could erase the day and we could just start everything over from this morning.

I wait for Lisa to speak, not wanting to pressure her into conversation. She wipes tears from her face and looks up at me briefly before looking out of the corner of her eye away from me as if she is hesitating. She clears her throat and begins to speak in a soft tone.

"I just wanted to talk to you about the plans for Dad. It wasn't meant to get you so upset like it did and cause for me to leave in such a fury of anger over pent-up emotions from all of the years and recent happenings. I never thought that by leaving that it would..." She inhales deeply, trying to get the rest of the sentence out as her bottom lip rapidly quivers and the tears well up in her eyes once again. "It would result in Patrick being in his first ever car accident and...being injured. I can't believe that this is all my fault."

She sinks forward. Her shoulders are trembling as she is attempting to stifle her cry to not allow it to become louder than a whimper. I reach out to her, placing my hand on her shoulder to get her attention and calm her.

"Lisa, honey, first of all, I want you to know—I am just so thankful that neither you nor your brother are hurt more seriously. This is actually not your fault. It's *my* fault. I should have been more prepared and open to the discussion that you were trying to have with me. Since having had your brother, I have undergone a flood of emotions, hormone changes, and sleep deprivation, which caused me to forget how much it takes out of you when raising a new little one. It is not an excuse. I simply haven't had the energy or the time to put forth much thought about the funeral for your father. Unfortunately, I hate to admit this, but since he has been gone from the house for so long, when he officially passed with the timing of everything, my mind was more focused on keeping our family together and keeping going and since I had the relief of our newfound safety with Johnny actually being gone, I hadn't thought about his burial. So when you brought it up this morning, I had been short on sleep, and was not prepared for that discussion. I'm very sorry for my reaction and everything that it caused today. Please do not carry this burden. It is mine, and mine alone to carry, my dear."

As I say this, the relief washes over Lisa as she begins

THE END IS THE BEGINNING   279

to sit up a little bit taller, and she looks at me with a look of seriousness.

"Okay... Thank you, but the truth of the matter is, it is still my fault. I really think that with everything that has happened to us all lately, it might be a good idea to have a little more God in our lives. That is why I suggested the reverend officiating the graveside service."

Hearing the words "have a little more God in our lives" cross my young, beautiful daughter's lips is like a symphony of music to my ears.

All of my life I have believed in God. There have been different trials and moments that have brought me closer to Him but also instances that have pushed me away and made me question everything I once believed.

I dreamt of taking my kids to church, but Johnny never wanted that, and I was too scared of his wrath to ever push it by trying to take them.

I am so happy to know that my daughter wants to pursue a path following The Lord and wants to honor her father, who deserved literally nothing from her for the final event of his life.

"Oh Lisa, I love that you want us to have a little more God in our lives. You are absolutely right. I think that we should definitely talk about that option in more detail and maybe after things settle down a little bit more, we can go and talk with the reverend at the church. I am so appreciative to have a daughter like you who, even after you have been treated so poorly by your father and have witnessed so much, is willing to give him a respectful burial service to mark the conclusion of his life."

Our eyes meet one another's—both tear-filled—one

blink away from them falling onto our cheeks as the doctor pulls the curtain back and enters the room. As he steps into the room, we look at him trying to gauge his facial expression to read the news that he is about to share.

"Well, I'm afraid to say that your son has a femur fracture. At this age, we call them "greenstick fractures", meaning it didn't go all the way through the bone. We call them that because infants' bones are like a green piece of wood—they are so soft and pliable at this age, they bend before they break, unlike a dry piece of wood, which would crack and break much easier under the same pressure. Hence, these are not uncommon fractures to see. Little Patrick will need a lot of rest and comfort for the pain. Otherwise, he should be just fine."

My baby has a broken leg? My tiny baby has already broken a bone?

How did I nearly raise my two other children to not have any lasting problems or broken bones but I can't seem to keep my sweet, barely-even-one-month-old out of harm's way? I can hardly wrap my mind around this.

If this isn't a wakeup call to be more aware with my children and to make time for each of them individually when I can with Bill's help of course, I don't know what is.

If I had just made a few moments of time for Lisa and had allowed her to bring to me her ideas and would have been willing and able to listen to her, how much differently could this day have gone?

I know I can't change the past, but right now, more than anything, I *really* wish that I could.

CHAPTER 46

Lisa

March 1976 Age: 15

Rising up from the chair to leave the hospital with Patrick, Mom, and Bill, I'm unable to fully stand and straighten my legs so I lean back to grab a hold of the back of the chair and steady myself. I seem to be a bit unsteady at the moment...Or perhaps I am dizzy?

When was the last time I ate today? Maybe I am hungry, and I should get myself a sandwich. The sandwich I most enjoy is ham and Swiss cheese on Rye bread. Typically, the thought alone of eating that sandwich makes me crave it even more, especially when it has some mayonnaise on it, but right now, the mere thought of it makes my stomach churn.

I seem to be forming more and more saliva in my mouth so I take a couple of extra swallows. The strange thing, though, isn't only that I'm forming all of this extra saliva, which would typically be due to craving the sandwich, but rather I am being nauseated by it. What the hell?

Everyone has started exiting the room and Mom looks back to see if I am following along. When her eyes meet mine, the demeanor on her expression tells me that I must be wearing a look of repulsion quite blatantly on my face.

"Lisa, is everything alright, dear?" Breaking eye contact, Mom looks around making sure that she hasn't left anything in the room while she simultaneously does a slight bounce of her arms to keep Patrick happy and comfortable.

I can see that she is trying her hardest to maintain her patience and she is concentrating on the speed at which she is speaking to me so that I don't feel rushed or that by her standing here while I am holding her up from leaving the hospital is actually problematic.

I try to stand up taller in hopes of appearing like I am more 'with it', but as I do stand taller, it feels like my shoulders are heavy and my arms are weak. It is the kind of feeling you get when you are coming down with a cold where your shoulders ache and your arms become fatigued.

Is this a late onset from the accident? Is there something more seriously wrong with me?

I clear my throat and shake my head, moving my hair out of my face.

"Yeah, I'm good." I force myself to smile a reassuring kind of smile.

"I was just wondering... You look a little... sheepish. As

THE END IS THE BEGINNING   283

if all of the blood had rushed from your face when you stood up. If you feel 'off' at all from the accident, now is the time to say so, before we leave here," she says matter of factly.

I thought that I felt fine. I haven't felt this way all day.

Do I agree to stay here and be checked out? Or should I brush it off so that we can get headed back home?

"I think I'm fine, Mom. I don't know what happened. It's probably just a mix of things going on since we have had an unexpectedly chaotic day and I haven't eaten much."

Mom nods her head as if trusting me, but I know that it is against her will because she holds her gaze with mine for a few seconds longer than usual as if she is waiting for me to just come out and tell her something to save us all some time but I honestly, have nothing to tell.

I use my right arm to motion her toward the door and nod as if telling her I will be right behind her. I take a couple of deep breaths before following her, attempting to shake this off.

As I take a few steps to leave the room, my vision starts to get bright in my periphery. I see Mom walking down the tan-walled hospital hallway, holding Patrick in her arms. Even though I know that she is worried about him, I can tell by watching her strides that she is much lighter and happier now that she has Patrick, David, and Bill and not having to worry about my dad.

Initially, it seems as though she is walking away quickly, but as the seconds tick by, things start moving in what seems to be slow motion. I reach to grab the doorway to get ahold of myself, but I am too late.

Within a moment, the room is spinning around me, a wave of nausea hits me, and then... everything goes black.

When I slowly open my eyes, everyone is still moving in slow motion like they were when I last was watching Mom walk down the hallway, but now, it seems that my vision has changed.

I can make out silhouettes of those around me, but I don't seem to recognize anyone.

Faintly, I hear people's voices talking about different tests that should be run and I soon realize... they are talking about me.

My body feels heavy and limp as if I am paralyzed. I try to move my legs or sit up, but it is like I am in a state of very deep sleep where my mind wants so badly to wake up but my body cannot physically do it.

A nurse applies a sharp prick to my arm to draw blood for labs and on the other arm, someone is pressing on my wrist to get my pulse and blood pressure. I blink my eyes shut tightly hoping that when I open them, this vision will drastically change like it is all just a dream.

When I press open my eyes with might, I notice my eyelashes are matted down and wet.

Did I cry? Or am I sweating?

"Lisa," a nurse whispers as she pokes her head in the doorway, "We have drawn some blood samples and will be back soon to tell you the results, dear. You had a fainting spell and we are looking into what could have caused that."

"Thank you?" I say questioningly since I am still quite confused as to what happened and why I'm even here now as a patient.

THE END IS THE BEGINNING   285

I hear someone with a familiar, masculine voice call my name and as I look to the doorway to see who it is, I can't believe he is here.

It's Jerry.

I'm so relieved to see him since it has been about a week since we last were together. We were most recently talking about plans for my dad and he was supporting me in getting the reverend in contact with us for his funeral.

He rushes over, taking both hands on either side of my face to look me directly in the eyes, and just like that, I am fully awake and alert.

"Hey, Lis, I've been missing you. Are you doing alright, my dear?"

I smile up at him while he wipes the sweat from my brow.

"I thought I was doing just fine. Honestly, besides feeling so guilty over the accident with Patrick, I physically felt fine."

He clears his throat and takes hold of my hand.

"The nurses said you took quite a fall here, and they couldn't release you without further testing. They're worried something happened to you in the accident that you aren't saying. Your mom and everyone went home to take care of Patrick. I said that I'd give you a ride home once everything checked out for you."

The excess saliva begins to form again, and my arms are becoming heavier. I certainly hope that nothing actually happened to me in the accident.

As we sit and wait for the nurse to come in with my lab results, Jerry tries talking to me, asking how I have been this past week and when we can go on our next date together. I'm trying so hard to focus on the conversation he is attempting to have with me, but unfortunately, another wave of nausea begins and it is nearly impossible to talk with him right now.

I interrupt him mid-sentence as he is asking to make a plan for next week.

"I'm sorry Jerry, I'm really not feeling well all of a sudden. It's making it hard to have a conversation right now."

I worry that I may have said that a bit too harshly as I watch his facial expression go from excited to stunned, but he quickly recovers as he puts a hand on my shoulder.

"Absolutely. I'm so sorry I was talking about anything other than how you are doing right now. It's just so good to see you again. I thought talking about plans would help to take your mind off of everything that is happening here."

I look over and up at him. "Yes, of course, it's nice to distract my mind, so thank you for that."

We hear a tap on the doorframe outside of the room we are in, and the curtain is drawn back. The nurse who took my blood is standing in the doorway.

"Lisa? We have some lab results to notify you of. Is now a good time?" She clears her throat. "As you have your... guest here with you? Where is your parent or guardian?"

The nurse looks between my eyes and Jerry's, and I am surprised she is even asking. What would she have to tell me about that I wouldn't want him around for?

"Yeah? My mom left to take care of my baby brother. They were just here." I respond quizzically.

THE END IS THE BEGINNING   287

I see her hesitate as she enters the room holding her manila envelope as she pulls out the papers.

"All of your labs came back within normal limits except one of them... It revealed something to us that should explain all of your symptoms..."

Before she spits it out, she looks up from her papers and makes eye contact that shifts 2-3 times between Jerry and me again.

Why does she keep doing that? It's so strange. The results are not for Jerry. They are mine!

She clears her throat again.

"Lisa... It appears that you are pregnant... It is very early yet, but you are, in fact, pregnant."

She finally takes her eyes off of her paperwork to look up at us, and I don't think I have blinked or swallowed in 30 seconds.

"I'm sorry, I am what? Pregnant?" I finally blurt back.

Instead of responding verbally, she simply nods her head very slowly. The look on her face must be a mirror of the look on mine... sheer horror.

I try to swallow, but instead, the nausea that I have been feeling decides to kick in full force, and I vomit all over my lap.

I raise my head to look over to gauge Jerry's reaction, and as his eyes shift to meet mine, the look that I see in his green eyes is the first I have ever seen of it.

I can't quite tell if I am looking into the eyes of my late-father, or my boyfriend. The eeriness of this sight sends a chill down my spine sitting in this stiff hospital bed.

Seeing this flash of anger ignite in his eyes terrifies

me. What is it that he is thinking of this news? Yes, I am shocked too, but not angry. What good would that cause?

Is he going to keep this secret between the two of us? How am I going to tell my mom? *That* is a scary thought in and of itself.

I have so many questions but with no answers to give.

The only thought I'm able to come to at this moment is, it seems there is in fact, a circle to this *thing* we call life.

It took losing my father for my mother to gain a new and freer life with Bill, David, myself, and now Patrick.

And I, too, unbeknownst to me, have also gained a new life, and while it may not be as freeing as my mother's life now is... perhaps the end *is* the beginning... the beginning of how it all is meant to be.

If you're interested in leaving a review, I'd greatly appreciate it! Below are the links where you can show your support. Thank you so much!

Goodreads | Bookbub

Acknowledgments

Completing this book has been a deeply rewarding journey, made possible by the steadfast support and love of my family and friends.

First and foremost, I am thankful for my Lord and Savior and His guidance in writing this novel. I truly believe we are called for certain things in life, and I am grateful for all I've been given, especially this opportunity to write my first novel!

To my caring husband, Robby: your unwavering belief and support sustained my determination, and for that, I owe immeasurable gratitude. Thank you for celebrating each small victory leading up to finally publishing. I'll never forget the memorable dinner you took me out on to celebrate completing my first draft after reaching that 70k word count! You made every victory feel like a big one, and *that* is love.

To my incredible mom, Tari: your constant encouragement fueled my passion. Thank you for patiently listening to all my ideas and supporting me through the highs and lows of this journey. You have always been and always will be my biggest cheerleader!

To my supportive and loving grandma, Sylvia: thank you for your deep and genuine interest and support in my book. From the moment I mentioned writing my first book, your confidence in my abilities surpassed even my own. I am incredibly grateful for that.

To my friend, Toni, who connected me with Victoria: thank you. Victoria, you quickly became my amazing mentor and friend. Your guidance and wisdom steered me through this creative process. Without you, I wouldn't have published my debut novel. Your selfless assistance remains one of the most profoundly generous acts I've witnessed. You've inspired me to pay forward your kindness to others seeking guidance and support.

I extend heartfelt appreciation to my dedicated beta reader team —Tammi, Kara, Allison, and Emily—alongside my meticulous editor, Virginia, extremely thorough proofreader, Michele, talented formatter, Nancy, and the visionary cover designer, Kate. Your contributions brought this book to life, and you all hold a special place in my heart!

A special thank you to my book promotional company, Give Me Books, and the incredible community of online book supporters. Your enthusiasm and encouragement kept me going towards publication.

With the most sincere appreciation, thank you all from the bottom of my heart. Your support has been invaluable, and I'm forever grateful for your love and encouragement.

Here's to stepping out and trying something new because that is what life is all about!

Jennifer

About the Author

Jennifer is embarking on her debut as an author with her novel "The End is the Beginning." She is married to Robby, a caring and loving man, and is the devoted mother of Norah, her very smart and sweet daughter, as well as a dedicated dog-mom to Mia, her Weimaraner.

Jennifer earned her bachelor's degree from Northern Illinois University and has worked as a Radiologic Technologist for a decade. For the past five years, she's specialized in the Cardiac Catheterization field, particularly in Electrophysiology (that's right, embracing the super-nerd status).

A lifelong Midwesterner, Jennifer finds joy in staying active outdoors, whether it's going for runs with Mia and Norah, enjoying family bike rides, or simply soaking in the sun. Her most productive writing hours are between 8 and 11 PM, when her daughter is fast asleep. During this time, she channels her creative energy into crafting dark romance stories.

Jennifer enjoys creating storylines that form deep emotional connections between readers and characters. She roots for the underdog and crafts narratives where true love wins!

Follow Jennifer on social media!
https://linktr.ee/jenniferlloydauthor
tiktok.com/@author_jennifernlloyd
instagram.com/authorjennifernlloyd

Made in the USA
Monee, IL
01 June 2024